THORNS IN THE CROWN

THORNS IN THE CROWN

Tanushree Podder

B L O O M S B U R Y
NEW DELHI • LONDON • OXFORD • NEW YORK • SYDNEY

BLOOMSBURY INDIA
Bloomsbury Publishing India Pvt. Ltd
Second Floor, LSC Building No. 4, DDA Complex, Pocket C – 6 & 7,
Vasant Kunj, New Delhi 110070

BLOOMSBURY, BLOOMSBURY INDIA and the Diana logo
are trademarks of Bloomsbury Publishing Plc

First published in India 2023
This edition published 2023

ISBN: 978-93-90358-20-5; e-ISBN: 978-93-90358-39-7
2 4 6 8 10 9 7 5 3 1

Typeset in Fournier MT Std by Manipal Technologies Limited
Printed and bound in India by Thomson Press India Ltd

To find out more about our authors and books visit www.bloomsbury.com and sign up for our newsletters

For the unsung heroes who sacrificed their lives for India's freedom

'The hour of departure has arrived, and we go our separate ways, I to die, and you to live. Which of these is better only God knows.'

—Socrates

PART ONE: 1924–35

Nineteen twenty-four was a leap year. It was also a year of many disturbing developments, both national and international. Political upheavals were underway throughout the world. Far away, in Russia, Vladimir Lenin was dead and Joseph Stalin became the de facto leader of the USSR. Adolf Hitler was sentenced to five years in jail for his participation in the Beer Hall Putsch. Fascists won the election in Italy. Fascism was on the rise and Kemal Ataturk had finally ended the Islamic caliphate of five hundred and sixty-two years, giving birth to the Republic of Turkey. Tremors of the global political mayhem were also felt in British-ruled India.

In Calcutta, Gopinath Saha, a Bengali freedom fighter, made an attempt on the life of Charles Tegart, the chief of the Detective Department of Police. Tegart escaped and a civilian named Ernest Day was killed in a tragic case of mistaken identity. Saha was promptly hanged for his crime and Tegart lived to tell the tale. This was the first of many attempts made on Tegart's life but each time he dodged his assassins. The conceited man used a defused bomb as a paperweight to remind himself of the attempts made on his life.

Tegart's was not an isolated case. Assassination attempts on British officers had reached unprecedented levels that year, as had cases of brutal torture and hanging of Indian freedom fighters. The cauldron of unrest in India bubbled with growing intensity but the British rulers remained unfazed.

I

Peter

Pathankot

In a missionary school for orphans run by Irish Jesuit Brothers at Pathankot, a boy stood waiting for the rector. From time to time, he stole a glance at the Englishman who had brought him to the orphanage.

That morning, the orphan had scrubbed the back of his ears, oiled and slicked back his unruly hair, and styled it with a neat side parting. He had trimmed his nails and polished his scruffy shoes. His frayed shirt had been washed and ironed. Although it had been an unpleasant task, supervised by the old khansama, he had gone through the motions of bathing himself with a jasmine-scented soap.

He looked around the room anxiously, like a trapped animal looking for an escape route. It would not end happily, he sensed. The child stole another glance at his benefactor who stood staring resolutely out of the window, hands behind his back.

Two thin lines of perspiration trickled down the child's temples. It wasn't often that he wore anything more than a vest and a pair of shorts. The faded blue shirt stuck to his back and his groin itched. The boy clenched his hands by his side and waited. The Englishman had promised to buy him sweets if he bathed and behaved well.

Minutes ticked by and the rector finally strode into the room, dwarfing everyone in it.

'Good morning, Brother,' greeted the Englishman, and nudged the boy. He had spent considerable time that morning issuing instructions to the boy.

'Good morning, Sir,' the boy parroted.

The rector returned the greeting and requested the Englishman to take a seat.

'This is the boy I mentioned, Brother,' said the Englishman, wiping his brow with a spotless white handkerchief. 'His mother was employed as a servant in my household. She died of influenza a month ago and now this poor boy has nowhere to go.'

The grim-faced Irish rector contemplated the boy and nodded. The clothes were frayed but clean and the boy seemed obedient.

'I would have kept him in the servants' quarters,' the Englishman said, coughing apologetically, 'but I have just received a transfer order to Madras and my future is uncertain at the moment. The boy is an orphan, so I thought you could teach him to be a good Christian.'

It was a clever line—one that the rector could not resist. The idea of teaching the boy to be a good Christian did not fail to charm him.

A streak of sunlight filtered through the green wooden slats of the window, making interesting patterns on the red cement floor. The wall clock chimed, and the boy crept closer to the gora sahib. He wanted to go home.

'How old are you, boy?' the rector asked.

There was no reply from the boy, who was now staring at the punkah overhead that was dispersing the muggy air in jerky movements. White men did not frighten him for he had grown up in the gora sahib's bungalow. It was the rector's penetrating eyes that bothered him.

The grief of losing his mother clung to him like an amorphous cloud, not yet frozen into a mass. More than sorrow, the fast-changing circumstances fazed the child.

'He is around nine years old, I presume,' replied the Englishman. 'There is no record of his birth.' As an afterthought, he added, 'But he has English blood and the mother was an honest woman.' He had no way of knowing that the big-built boy was only seven and a half years old.

'I don't think he has had any schooling,' mused the rector, studying the fair-complexioned boy. The child had inherited his build and grey-green eyes from his father. 'We will have to start from the very beginning.'

'I guess so, Brother. He is an intelligent boy and I am sure he will be quick to pick up the skills required of him.'

'What is your name?' the rector made yet another attempt to draw the child out.

The boy, who had been distracted by the antics of a lizard on the whitewashed wall, finally replied. 'Prakash.'

'Well, that won't do. Let us give you a new name and a new life. From today, you will be called Peter.'

The boy rolled the name around on his tongue, fascinated by the sound of it. It was unfamiliar and uninteresting. Prakash meant 'light', his mother had told him, but Peter? He had no clue what it meant. Perhaps they would change his name and let him go. He was desperate to leave the forbidding room.

'Take these, child,' said the Englishman, handing him the promised sweets. 'There are many boys like you in this school. These kind men of god will look after you. One day you will become an important person and make us proud.'

With a sigh of relief, the Englishman ruffled the child's hair, thanked the rector and hurried towards the door. Ever since he had learned of his transfer, the boy's future had weighed on his mind. The mother had been a loyal woman who had worked in his bungalow for three years and he felt duty-bound to settle the boy down.

Realising that he was being left behind with the frightening rector, the boy ran after the Englishman. Tugging at the sahib's shirt, he pleaded, 'Please take me back with you.'

'That is not possible, Prak . . . Peter. This is where you have to live now. I am going away to a far-off place and I can't take you with me.'

Stunned, the boy clung to the Englishman who had sheltered him since his mother's death. He was the only stable factor in his life. 'I will not bother you, Saab. I will do anything you say—sweeping, cleaning bathrooms, tending to the garden. Anything!' he cried. 'Take me back with you.'

The rector summoned a helper. 'Take him away,' he ordered.

The boy kicked and screamed, wrestling against a pair of powerful arms that took charge of him.

Helplessly, he watched the Englishman hurrying away without a backward glance. The last vestige of security had been rudely snatched from his life.

The boy darted an anxious look at the large courtyard abutting the principal's office and broke into loud sobs. Several boys gathered in the courtyard, stopping to stare at the newcomer. *This is not my home; it could never be my home.* Then the truth sank in. The Englishman had abandoned him. The bungalow and the familiar faces were gone. He liked neither his new name nor the faces milling around the large courtyard. All he wanted was to run back to the bungalow in the cantonment. That was not possible, he knew. The orphanage would now be his home.

That morning, Peter became yet another Eurasian in an orphanage crowded with fifty-two boys of mixed parentage and joined the ranks of the sizeable number of children born out of wedlock. Their white-skinned fathers absolved themselves of any responsibility and the mothers, driven by shame and societal compulsions, were often forced to abandon them. The hapless children found themselves at the mercy of the Jesuits who rejoiced in bringing up these children as good Christians.

Caught between the supercilious British on the one hand and the inflexible Indians on the other, these children grew up on the fringes of Indian society, their identities lost forever.

For the last few years, the boy had lived with his mother in the servants' quarters of the gora sahib's bungalow, surrounded by a brood of dirty children sired by the bearer, cook and gardener, playing under the neem trees on the compound. There had been no rules to follow. The only rule laid down for them was to keep out of the goras' sight.

Surrounded by oleander and bougainvillea shrubs tended to untiringly by an old gardener, the rambling bungalow stood in the centre of an enormous compound. The servants' quarters, screened off by trees, were tucked away at the rear, far from the eyes of the gora sahibs.

The boy's mother, Radha, an attractive young woman from the Himachal hills, worked as an ayah in the bungalow. Of his father, he knew nothing except that he was an Englishman named Flynn

Sahib. His life till now had been carefree, with enough food, some clothes and many playmates. But his world collapsed the day his mother died.

Now, he had a new name, a new religion, new playmates and a new home. Instinct told him his life would never be the same.

2

Olivia

Rawalpindi Cantonment

The beautiful town of Rawalpindi, nestled serenely against the backdrop of the scenic Margalla Hills, was an idyllic place. The cantonment was neat, compact and green, although the city was a different matter altogether. It was dusty, crowded and dirty. The city had two main roads. The Grand Trunk Road, which ran roughly from the southeast to the northwest, transformed itself into the Mall as it passed through the cantonment. The other road was the Murree Road that broke north off the Mall. Sadar Bazaar lay at one end of the cantonment. Arrayed with colourful stalls and shops that sold everything that one would need for a comfortable life, the bazaar was the nerve centre of the cantonment.

A six-year-old girl in a frilly chintz frock and red ribbons stood gaping at the confectionery displayed in the window of a bakery in Sadar Bazaar. She had slipped out of the shop where her mother was inspecting the newly arrived supply of printed silk. Attracted by the rhythmic beat of the *damru*, she joined the crowd gathered around a pair of monkeys prancing and looping to the orders of their master.

The firstborn of Captain Ralph Bradley, Olivia was an obedient child. It was only at the bazaar that she forgot her parents' rule of keeping away from the natives. A few minutes later, the worried mother located her daughter near a bangle shop.

Olivia's house was the last one at the end of a shaded avenue to the south of the cantonment, where the pavements were ablaze with the fiery flowers of gulmohar. Most bungalows were hidden behind the dense foliage of the trees that lined the driveway, giving them an air of mystery. During autumn, the quiet street was carpeted with fallen petals, and peacocks strutted around enticingly in the backyard.

Cocooned and isolated from the tremors of the world, the Bradleys lived a charmed life in the safety of the cantonment. It was a happy life for the girl, whose fate had been linked with that of India from the very day she was born. Neither Irene Bradley, Olivia's mother, nor any Indian would ever forget that day. In a hospital in Madras Cantonment, Irene went into labour at 4.30 p.m. on 13 April 1919, at the precise hour when Brigadier General Reginald Dyer opened fire on an unarmed gathering in Jallianwala Bagh.

The firing in Jallianwala Bagh went on for about twenty minutes. In the hospital, Irene continued to scream as her labour pains intensified, her body thrashing about on the bed. Olivia came into the world even as Dyer and his men marched away, unperturbed by the screams of the dying multitude.

'Today is my birthday,' Olivia declared to the old shopkeeper of the bangle shop.

'Happy birthday, child,' said the shopkeeper to the little girl, his eyes shrouded in pain. With a deep sigh, he handed her a dozen bright-red bangles. 'Birthday gift,' he explained.

'Your birthday will never be forgotten by Indians,' the shopkeeper added.

Olivia thanked him, a little surprised by the sadness on his face. Wasn't it normal to smile while conveying birthday wishes? The man's words stirred her curiosity.

It would take her a few years to learn why her birthday was an unforgettable day for the people of the country that she loved so dearly.

3

Indraneel

Brahmanbaria, East Bengal

At about the time the seven-and-a-half-year-old Anglo-Indian orphan walked down the corridor of the orphanage in Pathankot, far away in a village in East Bengal, a group of adolescent boys was perched on a tree on the bank of the village pond.

'Shh!' Lalu admonished the young lad dangling from a lower branch. 'Do you want to get us thrashed?'

'The branch is slippery,' protested the newcomer, the youngest in the group. They hauled him up to safety as a curtain of rain surrounded them, its large drops dancing flamboyantly on the water's surface. It plastered their hair, soaked their skin and ran down their backs in thin rivulets. Unmindful, the boys watched the women through the mist rising from the pond. There was something magical about the moment.

Hidden in the foliage, they waited for the women to emerge from the pond, their saris clinging to their bodies. Rain pelted the lads' faces as they gawked at the outline of the breasts and nipples visible through the women's wet garments.

'There she is. Look!' The sibilant whisper came from Noni, his attention riveted on a lissome lass swimming lazily in the pond. Most boys of the village were ready to give their right arm for a smile from the girl. Indraneel jostled his friend for a better view and received a push in return. The next moment, he slipped and fell into the pond.

An outpouring of curses followed his fall. The women waved their fists threateningly at the boys. 'Rascals, wait till we get our hands on you!'

In his scramble to get back on the tree, Indraneel scraped his elbows and knees.

'Scoundrel! How dare you ogle us?' A woman glared at him. 'Wait till your father hears of this.'

The threat was enough to send Indraneel, the third child of the government school teacher Manik Bose, sprinting towards the modest three-room brick house, his feet propelled by the fear of his father's cane.

Indraneel and his friends were an impish lot. They scaled walls, climbed trees and used catapults to steal fruits from orchards. Neel's back was perpetually black and blue from the caning he received from his teachers in school and his father at home.

Despite his mischievous ways, Neel was the darling of his grandmother, a woman with strong opinions. Widowed at seventeen, she spent most of her time in the small puja room, chanting Sanskrit verses and praying to her umpteen gods. For her grandchildren, she was a repository of stories about Hindu gods and demons.

Thakuma, as the children called her, kept innumerable fasts and ate two simple meals a day, which she cooked on a wood-burning stove in the little shanty that functioned as her private kitchen.

Neel's mother, Annapurna Devi, was a timid woman who rarely ventured out of the four walls of her house. The kitchen was her haven. She entered it at the crack of dawn and left late at night. If she was not cooking a meal, she was preparing pickles and papad. With not much money and never-ending chores to keep the home machinery running, life was tough for Annapurna Devi. But no one ever heard her complaining, or maybe no one wanted to.

Manik Bose was a strict disciplinarian with little time for silly stories or superstition. With seven mouths to feed and a limited income, he had no patience for frivolous matters.

The school was on the opposite bank of a minor tributary of the Titas and the boys had to cross the river to reach it. Some boys used the *bhella*, a simple raft fashioned out of six sturdy banana trunks tied together with rope, to save the few paise that it cost to travel by boat.

Indraneel's life was simple and enjoyable. With just two sets of clothes, a belly full of food and his dreams, he had not a worry in the world.

4

Peter

The Orphanage, Pathankot

The orphanage was a block of four stark, double-storeyed brick buildings. A high wall ran around the four flanks of the open quadrangle. The colour grey dominated the lives of the boys there. It was everywhere: the floor, the uniforms, the chapel next door; even the once-white walls of the orphanage had gone grey with the severe lashings of rain they received for four months every year. Mildewed and musty, the rooms the boys inhabited were no better than a beggar's, where a mass of limbs rested after a torturous day.

The central courtyard was the nucleus of the orphanage. The rector's office and classrooms occupied three sides of the courtyard while the fourth functioned as accommodation for the missionaries. It faced the east and was the best one in the complex. It was here that the first rays of the sun fell to announce the beginning of a new day. The upper floor was where the orphans lived. The dining room, punishment room and study were all housed on that floor. The cookhouse and stores were at the rear of the main building.

A small chapel, the fulcrum of their lives, abutted onto the eastern periphery wall. It stood contrasted against the orphanage building. Instead of white walls and red-tiled roofs, the chapel had grey walls and a black-tiled roof outlined with a white crenulated trim. A small gate connected the orphanage to the chapel.

Twice a day, the boys filed to the chapel to pray for deliverance before the tragic figure hanging from a cross. This was an unfamiliar god to Peter. For as long as she had lived, his mother had narrated stories of Hindu gods and their powers. In a little alcove in their home stood those gods with beatific smiles and multiple limbs. Those were the gods he knew. The god in the chapel was a stranger with two limbs and an unsmiling face.

The long dormitory where fifty-two orphans of varying ages and sizes slept was cold and uncomfortable in winter and unbearably hot in summer. During the long months of the monsoon, the roof leaked in places and the children huddled together in dry corners.

Winter brought misery to the orphans. The blankets were threadbare and the slippers thin. Cold seeped through the stone floor and the walls. The only things the orphans owned were two sets of clothes and their dreams.

Life in the orphanage was difficult. The day began at the crack of dawn with prayers and ended at 8 p.m. with another round of prayers. In between lay endless hours of studying, chores and more prayers. Breakfast was half-baked chapattis made from the cheapest flour available in the market, served with a watery potato curry and tea that was nothing but lukewarm milky water with a hint of sugar. Lunch was a repeat of the same fare, with the addition of a watery soup. Sometimes they were fortunate to be served rice instead of the inedible, rubbery chapattis. The boys were served mutton or chicken on festivals but the cooks reserved the best pieces for the Brothers. Easter was the only time the orphans tasted eggs.

The cooks pilfered whatever there was to pilfer. They stole bits of vegetables, lentils, rice, milk—everything that was worth stealing.

The food the orphans received was never enough, especially for robust and energetic boys like Peter. He was taller than the other boys in his class and looked at least two years older than his age. With his brown hair and grey-green eyes, Peter stood out. His sharp brain helped him top the class in every examination. The results brought him attention—some welcome, some not so much. While the teachers praised his performance, the bullies singled him out for punishment. Sometimes they vented their frustration by beating him up. At other times, they snatched whatever was worth snatching from his plate. Nature grants people the weapons to survive their circumstances. It gifted Peter with aggression.

The Irish Brothers who ran the orphanage were a stern lot who didn't shy away from inflicting severe punishment for minor infractions. The cane was their favourite weapon and, on an average day, at least ten boys suffered from sore bottoms. Being denied a meal or two was not uncommon for the boys, nor was a couple of days in isolation.

Grappling with his new name was easier than forgetting the prayers chanted by his mother every night. Peter struggled to convince himself that Christ was the supreme god and that the deities worshipped by his mother were nothing but silly clay toys.

The zealous keepers of faith taught him to live as Peter but their fanaticism worked adversely on the impressionable boy. Instead of becoming a devout Christian, he turned into an atheist.

Peter's cynicism grew in proportion to his height. And along with cynicism came hatred. He hated his mother for dying. He hated the unknown Englishman for spawning him. He hated god for all the injustices inflicted on him. Most of all, he hated the orphanage. Peter was determined to make a getaway.

Each night, he dreamed of escaping the four walls of the orphanage to make a life for himself—to eat whatever he wished, to sleep whenever he wished, to go wherever he wished.

5

Olivia

Rawalpindi to Agra

In Rawalpindi, the family lived in a large, shaded bungalow set back from the street and surrounded by gardens, facing a parade ground. The house had large, airy rooms and high ceilings. Its tiled roof flamed red against a rich green canopy of mango and neem trees.

Life in India was much more luxurious for Irene Bradley than it had been in the tiny English village from which she came. She ran an efficient household with the help of her staff. The ayah fed, bathed and dressed Olivia, told her stories of Hindu gods and demons, and crooned her to sleep each night. The cook, a wizard in the kitchen, could conjure up just about anything. His repertoire was inexhaustible, with all kinds of Indian dishes from fiery mutton curries and tangy Mulligatawny soups to deliciously flavoured chicken roasts, aromatic pulaos and biryanis. His flair for dishing out Western delicacies like steak and kidney pies, mince-filled potato rissoles and crepe pan rolls was equally commendable. But his desserts were legendary. From roly-poly pudding to semolina halwa, gulab jamuns, chocolate soufflés and cakes, he could prepare them all.

There was also the bearer, a tall Sikh with a ferocious-looking moustache and dense beard. Dressed in his white baggy trousers, a white starched coat and a *pagdi*, he was a brooding figure.

The gardener was a humble man. Brown like the very earth he worked on, he grew colourful flowers throughout the year. The searing heat did not faze the man, nor did the bitterly cold winter that drove everyone to the fireplace. Black-red, pink, yellow and vibrant sunset shades of rose planted along the length of the driveway grew under the gardener's loving hands. Even in the height of summer, he coaxed a few straggly marigolds and sunflowers into surviving. The jasmines blooming on the bush that stood by the veranda suffused the evenings with their sweet and cloying scent.

However, the idyllic life in Rawalpindi ended one cold and overcast morning when Captain Bradley received his transfer order to Agra. While the Captain geared up for his assignment, Irene greeted the news with reluctance. The onerous task of setting up a house in another place and adjusting to its demands distressed her. She had grown to love Rawalpindi and the exciting social life the town offered.

For Olivia, the excitement of travelling by train through mountains, rivers, green fields and deserts diminished the sadness of losing friends. The green leather upholstery embossed with the railways logo promised adventure. There was a sense of romance in the mirrors and lampshades etched with the symbol of the railways.

They travelled by first class as did all British army officers. The second class was meant for Europeans and the third class for Indians. The first class, with its cushioned seats, was a luxury compared to the third class, with its hard, bare wooden seats and common bathroom that seemed likely to run out of water within a couple of hours. No Indian, however rich, could travel by first class.

The Bradleys' bungalow in Agra was one of eight along the shaded lane that stood at a right angle to the main road leading to the headquarters.

The officers' club was within walking distance of the residences. A popular haunt of officers and their families, it was equipped with a swimming pool and badminton and tennis courts. There was also an enormous ballroom with a polished wooden floor. Next to the club was an open-air theatre where English movies were screened.

As soon as the Bradleys had settled down, Olivia was enrolled in the convent school and it was left to old Dinanath to ferry her to school in his tonga. Since most of the officers' children had been sent back to England for their education, there were very few British children in the school. The majority were Anglo-Indians and, though Olivia was happy to be their friend, Irene Bradley did not like her daughter rubbing shoulders with the 'half breeds' as she called them.

The house in Agra was not too dissimilar from the one in Rawalpindi, nor was there any difference in the fast-paced social life in the cantonment. Soon the Bradleys began to feel at home.

The approach to the residential area was through a large gate that was guarded day and night by fierce-looking soldiers with their guns ready for action. There were rumours that revolutionaries had attacked British officers in various parts of the country and a blanket of insecurity hung over the cantonment. Reports of undercurrents of trouble added to everyone's anxiety. The administration was especially worried about the revolutionary youth who believed in violent methods to attain freedom for their country. These troublesome young men shot British officers, judges and administrators whenever they found the opportunity.

Olivia had her first glimpse of the 'rabble-rousers', as her father called them, while returning from school one day. She spotted a young man surrounded by a dozen-odd people. He was speaking in Urdu or Hindi, so she could not understand everything he was saying. But Olivia understood he was appealing to people to protest against the British.

'What is he saying, Dinu?' Olivia asked the tonga wallah.

'Don't listen to these madmen, Baby. They bring nothing but trouble,' replied the wizened man, urging the horse to move faster. 'It will be better for us to get away before there is trouble.'

Curious, she looked back and witnessed a commotion. A posse of police had arrived. The tonga wallah cracked his whip with renewed urgency and the horse began trotting faster.

Olivia craned her neck to watch. 'What will the police do, Dinu?' she wanted to know.

'They will use their lathis to disperse the crowd and arrest a few people,' grumbled the old man.

'What will they do to the man who was making the speech?'

'If he has any sense, he will run away before they can lay their hands on him. Anyway, you should not bother about them and don't mention the incident to your father. He won't be pleased.'

Olivia knew her parents wouldn't be happy to learn that she had witnessed the incident. A few days ago, while at the club, she had stumbled upon a group of officers speaking in hushed voices about the natives trying to rise in revolt.

'They think it's child's play,' said an officer, taking a swig of whisky from his glass. 'They appear to have forgotten the aftermath of 1857.'

'I guess it is time to remind them of those days.'

'I say, just hang a few of them and things will fall back into place,' was her father's opinion.

Shuddering at his words, Olivia quietly slunk away to where her mother sat with the other ladies, enjoying a session of cards and gossip.

Untouched by the turbulence brewing in the country, the British officers continued to enjoy themselves. The parties, picnics and merrymaking continued as usual.

October heralded the end of the monsoon season and the weather became pleasant. It was also an exciting time for those waiting for the catalogues that would arrive from England. Captain Bradley and his wife spent long hours going through the items, trying to decide what to order for Christmas.

Christmas gave way to a brand new year and the days rolled by pleasantly. Both Irene and Olivia found new friends to keep them company while Captain Bradley was engaged in matters of military importance.

It was a memorable day on 14 July 1927 because Irene Bradley brought home a brother for Olivia, who was now eight. She instantly fell in love with the chubby, golden-haired Christopher, whom the family called Kit.

Soon Kit was crawling all over the house. He was nine months old and a very active baby. He made cooing sounds in acknowledgment of Olivia's gushing words. Those were happy days, perhaps the happiest of her life. The Bradley family basked in the warmth of togetherness and all was well with their world.

Good times, however, don't last forever.

6

Peter

The Escape

There was a bunch of uncontrollable adolescents in the orphanage that terrorised the juniors, broke all the rules, bunked classes and often escaped to the city at night. At thirteen, Peter became a part of the group. The boys were at that age when testosterone suddenly kicks into overdrive. Erotic dreams filled their nights. They fought over the cigarette butts they found near the boundary walls and smoked on the sly. They scaled the walls to escape the oppressive confines of the orphanage and belted out popular songs on deserted streets at night.

Locked in their rooms to enjoy a cup of wine, the Brothers seldom ventured to the dormitories after the lights were out and the boys had gone to bed.

After a while, Peter broke away from the group. It was more challenging to go out by himself than with the other boys. By now tall and muscular, with a shock of thick brown hair and piercing eyes, he looked grown up for his age. One evening, after a brawl with a bully, Peter scaled the wall and escaped for a stroll around the town.

While on his rounds of the dormitory, Brother O'Reilly spotted Peter's empty bed. The warden had long suspected the bullies of mischief but had no proof to substantiate his hunch. So on this night, he waited for the boy to return. Peter had barely jumped over the outer wall to get back to his bed when he ran into Brother O'Reilly. The inevitable followed. Caned till his bottom was sore, Peter was locked in the punishment room with orders that he should not be served any food for twenty-four hours. There was an unwritten code among the boys not to snitch on each other but promises made during good times are easy to break after a brawl. Peter suspected someone had alerted the warden.

The punishment room, with bars on its door, was like a prison cell. Boys were frequently locked in the cell, sometimes for a few hours and sometimes for a full day and night. Though Peter had spent innumerable hours in that cell, that night he was restless. Sitting in the cramped and damp cell, he thought of ways to escape the diabolical warden and the orphanage. Just after lights out, when the boys were in bed, there came a timid tap on the cell door. It was Massey. A few weeks ago, Peter had taken charge of the diminutive boy. Almost all the boys bullied the short, dark, skinny boy until Peter became his protector.

Massey stood outside the cell now. In his hand was a plate with a couple of dry chapattis and a glass with a little dal. He must have saved them from his dinner. Peter inched his way towards the bars and took the plate from under the door.

'Thank you, Massey,' he whispered, dunking a chapatti in the dal.

'It's all right,' the boy responded, darting fearful glances around the corridor. 'Now I must go. I will be caned if the warden finds out.'

'Massey, I want you to unlatch the door.'

The whites of the boy's eyes widened with fear at the order. 'I can't do that. Brother O'Reilly will kill me,' he whined.

'Nothing will happen to you. How will Brother know you unlatched the door? I will not tell him.'

Massey turned to go. Desperate, Peter threw a chapatti at him. That stopped the boy.

'I will bang my head against the wall till I die.' Peter began to hit his head on the wall to prove that he would carry out the threat.

The younger boy was torn between his fear of the warden and his loyalty towards the protective senior. Peter continued banging his forehead on the wall. Distraught, the horrified boy stared at the trickle of blood that had started flowing down his mentor's temple.

'No,' Massey whispered, trying to reach him through the bars. 'Please don't hurt yourself. I will open the door.'

The frightened boy unlatched the door and melted into the darkness before anyone could see him. There was no time to waste. Peter raced down the corridor, scaled the wall and jumped over it. He didn't stop running till he reached the tonga stand, five miles from the orphanage. Hearing footsteps behind him, he stopped and cocked his head to listen.

No one called out. No one ran after him. Sighing with relief, he halted to catch his breath. Then, he ambled down the street, undecided about his next move. He was free, with nowhere to go. Running away wasn't so difficult; finding a place to stay turned out to be far trickier.

His mind ran over the options. There seemed to be none. Unable to decide, he walked towards the railway station in the dead of the night. The only thing he knew for sure was that he would be hunted as soon as his absence was discovered.

At the railway station, as he sat on a bench wondering about his next step, Peter remembered his mother's stories about the small village in the northern hills. 'Our village is beautiful. It is called Kun,' Radha had told her son. 'It is not very far from Simla. You have a large family, with several uncles, aunts and cousins. One day, I'll take you there.' With nowhere else to go, Peter decided to knock on his uncle's door. *My mother's family will be happy to see me. I am their kin, after all.*

By picking pockets and begging, Peter was able to pay for his food and tickets, reaching his destination in a week. His misgivings dissolved at the sight of the small shacks standing amidst terraced mustard fields. The slate roofs and colourful doors and windows, contrasted against the green background, looked picturesque and welcoming. The houses rose in a straggly manner from the gurgling brooks that streamed among enormous boulders. It seemed a happy place, one where he could see himself content, living with his large brood of uncles, aunts and cousins.

It was late afternoon when a tired and dishevelled Peter peeped through the door of what had once been his mother's house. The door was wide open. It was several minutes before a young man noticed the strapping boy lingering near the door.

'Who are you?' he asked.

'Prakash,' replied the boy.

The man seemed to recognise the name though there was not an iota of warmth in his voice as he questioned, 'What do you want? Why have you come here?'

Surprised by the cold and hard expression on the man's face, the boy hesitated.

A flock of children arrived to stare curiously at Peter. Soon other members of the family gathered around. There were close to twenty of them, varying in age and size. Peter looked at them expectantly, wanting to belong.

The men went into a huddle, discussing the sudden arrival of a bastard nephew. There were arguments and heated exchanges. Listening in, the boy could make out that only one brother was championing his cause while the others were shouting him down. After a while, a woman brought him some food and water. The children, his cousins, continued to stare from a distance as he gobbled down the food. His last meal had been several hours back.

After almost an hour, the eldest of the brothers announced the family's decision. The boy could stay in the house that night, but he would have to leave as soon as the sun came up. The verdict didn't come as a surprise. Having heard the arguments between the brothers, Peter knew he was not welcome.

'We can't keep you here. Our sister sinned by giving birth to an Englishman's son,' said the eldest brother.

'We have nothing against you.' There was pity and regret in the younger brother's voice. He had championed the boy's case. 'But we are helpless. The villagers will ostracise the family if we allow you to live with us.'

There was no mercy on the faces around him.

Unsure of his next step, Peter walked away from the house. Suddenly, he heard someone calling out to him. News of his arrival had made its way around the village.

'You must be Radha's son. I heard you were here,' said a young woman from the door of a nearby house. 'Her brothers must have thrown you out of the house.'

Seeing the puzzled look on his face, she continued, 'I am Jamuna, your mother's friend. Her brothers are heartless. They had no scruples while taking Radha's money, and now they talk of her wrongdoings.' The woman's eyes blazed with anger.

'I have run away from the orphanage. Now I have nowhere to go.' Peter shook his head sadly.

She looked at his forlorn face and sighed. 'You may stay with me for a couple of days, and then you must return to the orphanage.' She added a warning, 'I can't afford to keep you for long. The villagers wouldn't spare me if I did.'

7
Indraneel

The Wave of Patriotism

The arrival of a *jatra dal* heralded the onset of the festive season and was always a cause for celebration. At the close of the monsoon, just before Durga Puja, a theatre troupe arrived in the village. Soon a camp was set up at the far end of the large maidan and a rickshaw went around the village announcing the title of the play. It was an event no one wanted to miss. Bigger and brighter than the annual mela, the jatra drew theatre lovers from adjacent villages. The troupe performed every evening during their stay in the village, with many from the audience watching the jatra repetitively.

Petromax lanterns hanging from bamboo poles lit up the stage known as the *asar*—a simple platform at the centre, with the audience seated all around. At dusk, dressed in their best clothes, the villagers made their way to watch the jatra. The asar was where magic unfolded for three or four long hours. For those few hours, the audience escaped into a world of dreams, forgetting the problems and the surrounding turmoil.

Although the ticket was half an anna, some of the young boys could not pull together the amount. Missing the jatra was unimaginable, so they clambered on the adjoining trees and watched the drama perched precariously on branches. Fascinated, they followed the story of the pining beloved of the valiant warrior who fought till his last breath.

They whistled and cheered as the hero fought the villain, sympathised with the snivelling heroine and lamented when the lovers were parted. Good always triumphed over evil and everyone went home happy with the outcome.

Manik Bose disapproved of jatra, but this was one objection that neither his wife nor his mother heeded. Their lips stained with paan, they made their way to the maidan to watch the magic of the jatra unfold. Neel never missed a jatra. He was there, astride the branch of his favourite tree every evening for as long as the jatra dal performed in the village.

The growing rumbles of the freedom movement had begun to touch the lives of many in the village, but they did not yet affect Neel and his spirited friends. The occasional rally of khadi-clad men and women was a welcome diversion for the adolescent boys who followed them down the lanes of the village shouting 'Vande Mataram'. They joined the march more for fun than patriotism.

These harmless bands of young people sang patriotic songs and shouted slogans of freedom, urging the villagers to join the freedom movement. They burned the Union Jack or unfurled the tricolour flag. The crowd vanished as soon as the police made an appearance. And when they were not quick to disappear, they were taken to the police station, beaten and released after a few days.

The teenager remained oblivious to the changing mood around him. More and more people joined the Non-Cooperation Movement announced by Gandhi. In the village, people discussed the impending conflict between the British and the Bengal revolutionaries. Mutinous men created bonfires of Western clothes and made rebellious speeches. They distributed subversive leaflets and pasted posters on the walls. Surprise midnight raids by the police became frequent. Even the smallest evidence could lead to arrest. Lured by the promise of reward, some villagers began helping the police identify the troublemakers. Indiscriminate arrests and torture took the villagers by surprise.

But the tide reversed swiftly and unexpectedly. The groups of khaki-clad young men and women increased in number. They no longer vanished upon seeing the police. Instead, they offered themselves for arrest. Old and young, everyone was caught in the freedom fervour.

At school, the boys discussed the *andolan* launched by the frail and harmless-looking Gandhi. They spoke of the atrocities committed by the British. Teachers drove home the point to their students in subtle ways. Patriotic songs replaced popular ones at all gatherings.

The spark of freedom had grown into an inferno and it was impossible to douse it. It spread through villages and towns as leaders exhorted people to defy the laws that restricted their freedom. In the wake of the protests came more arrests, torture and hangings.

It was impossible for Neel to remain impervious to the rising surge of nationalism and, like his friends, he too was now caught up in the zeal of patriotism.

8

Peter

The Truth

In the tiny shack, seated near the *chulha* with Jamuna's three children, Peter relished the frugal meal served by his mother's childhood friend. Food had never tasted so good. Perhaps it was the magic of the idyllic village or the affection with which Jamuna served the simple Pahari food.

That night, he tossed and turned on the lumpy mattress, his mind seized with conflicting thoughts. A while later, giving up the futile effort to fall asleep, he wandered out and sat on a boulder, watching the full moon that shone like a luminous pearl in the sky. The distant gurgle of a mountain stream sounded like music to his ears after the incessant chatter of the boys in the orphanage.

'You should sleep, son,' said Jamuna, sitting down next to him.

Peter remained silent.

'You have a long journey tomorrow,' she said after a while. 'It would be wise to catch some sleep.'

'I can't sleep. Please tell me about my mother.' He remembered the childlike face of his mother, her dark flashing eyes and cascading hair. The image seemed to fade with each passing year and he was desperate for the missing pieces of the puzzle to fit.

'She was a beautiful and innocent girl.' The woman pitied the boy who had been rejected by his kin.

'My uncles say she was an immoral woman. Is that true?'

'No.' Jamuna shook her head sadly. 'It is not true. She was as good as any girl from the village.'

'How did she give birth to a gora sahib's bastard if she was a virtuous woman?'

'It was a bad time for the village. It hadn't rained for two consecutive years. The fields dried up, as did the wells. Cattle died and people starved. Hunger forced many men and women to leave the village. They went to the nearby towns looking for jobs.'

Peter remembered his mother narrating the circumstances under which she had arrived in the city to work for Flynn Sahib.

'I was working in the cantonment during those years. I came to know the Flynns were looking for an ayah to take care of their children, so I took Radha to their bungalow. And your mother found employment in the officer's house,' Jamuna continued. 'The job provided Radha with a belly full of food and a regular salary.'

'Was she happy with her job?' Peter was keen to know. He remembered his mother's tuneful lullabies.

'Of course she was happy. Her employers were kind and generous. They gave her gifts; sometimes it was extra money, sometimes a bauble or new clothes.'

Jamuna paused and wiped her tears before continuing. 'It was a chilly December evening when the Flynns's younger daughter came down with pneumonia. The doctors admitted the child to hospital, and Flynn Memsahib along with her. She left her older daughter with Radha. "Don't leave her alone. Sleep in the nursery with her," she instructed while leaving for the hospital.'

Peter pulled his knees to the chest and wrapped his arms around them.

'That night, Flynn Sahib returned from the club, drunk to the gills. The cold northerly winds howled through the evening, driving needles of chills through the house. The town was freezing. No one stirred out of their home; not even mongrels wandered after sunset. It was an evening that would change her life forever.

'Radha was beautiful. Despite her shabby clothes, she attracted attention. Flynn Sahib was no different from the other men. His wife was away and he took advantage of the opportunity and raped Radha. Her protests and cries remained buried within the four walls of the room.'

'Why didn't she return to her family in the village?'

'Those were trying times and, like most people, Radha was doing her best to survive.

'Five months passed. It became impossible for Radha to conceal the child in her womb. What began as gossip amongst the servants soon reached the memsahib's ears. Flynn Memsahib was furious. She threw Radha out. Everyone blamed your mother and not the monster who had hurt her.' Jamuna sighed. 'Radha returned to the village but the villagers called her names and her brothers abused and thrashed her.'

Peter shivered. A heavy rock settled on his chest, immovable and weighty.

'By the time you were born, Flynn Sahib had been transferred to Lahore. Radha's father, her only ally, died soon after. The brothers threw Radha and her baby out of the house. "Go back to your gora sahib with your bastard," they mocked. The poor girl went back to the cantonment to work as an ayah for another sahib. Radha moved from one job to another, shunted out on the whims and fancies of the lecherous sahibs and ill-tempered memsahibs. Weighed down by a child, she slogged from dawn to dusk. Then she found a job with a kind English sahib. He must have been the one who took you to the orphanage.'

Peter felt his journey had been worth every blister on his feet. Hearing of the hardships faced by his mother, he was convinced his uncles were wrong.

Three days later, hungry and cold, he returned to the orphanage. This time, he was ready for Brother O'Reilly's cane. The caning was less painful than the rejection by his kin or the knowledge of the circumstances of his paternity.

9

Indraneel

Joining the Rebels

Neel was sixteen and preparing for matriculation when he stumbled upon evidence that his elder brother and sister were working for a well-known radical organisation.

A wave of nationalism was sweeping the country. Children as young as ten were taking part in protest marches. They mouthed slogans and sat on dharnas. Unrest was spreading all over the country. The word 'freedom' was on everyone's lips. In schools, students spent more time discussing violent versus non-violent methods of fighting for freedom than they did studying for their examinations. Some believed in the non-violent ways of Gandhi, while others swore by leaders like Subhas Chandra Bose who had given up a coveted job with the civil services and returned to India. The leader's revolutionary ideas had caught the imagination of young people.

The youth were keen to enrol in underground revolutionary groups, wanting to flex their muscles, but the elderly advocated non-violent methods. Anyone who could put pen to paper began composing patriotic songs. People sang about the grandeur of their land, extolling its virtues and rosy future. So potent was the wave of patriotic emotion that many of Neel's friends pledged to die for the nation. Despite all the enthusiasm and talk, the boys were like unguided missiles. Beyond shouting slogans or abusing the white-skinned fellows, they did not know how they could help the country attain independence.

One night, Neel awoke to frantic knocks on the rear door which opened towards the pond. Creeping closer, he saw his cousin, Haren, who lived in the adjoining village. Neel's father quickly pulled Haren into the house and bolted the door.

They spoke in hushed voices for some time and then made their way towards the kitchen.

Curious, Neel crept up to the kitchen door, where his parents were huddled around his cousin. Straining his ears, Neel tried to eavesdrop through a crack in the closed door but couldn't hear anything. He peeped through the crack to see what was going on. His cousin had just finished dinner and was washing his hands. Then, he took out a pistol from the folds of his dhoti and handed it to Neel's mother before slipping out of the house into the darkness outside.

A few days later, tipped off by an informer, the police raided a nearby godown and found a cache of weapons and crude bombs. Five young men, including Neel's cousin, were shot while trying to escape.

Neel was worried that his brother too might be shot by the police. 'Dada, I know you are involved in the underground movement. Aren't you afraid of being tortured or shot like Haren?' he asked his brother.

'Everyone has to die one day.' Bikash placed his arm on his younger brother's shoulder. 'I will consider myself lucky if I die for a worthy cause.' He laughed and tousled Neel's hair. 'Don't worry! I will not get caught.'

Neel ruminated over his words for a long time that night.

Their cousin's killing was just a precursor. Two more incidents in quick succession were to shape Neel's future. The English teacher at his school, a popular figure in the village, was reciting a poem by Rabindranath Tagore when a British school inspector arrived for a surprise visit.

Where the mind is without fear . . .

'But we live in fear. It is an existence fettered by fear,' explained the English teacher fervently. 'The day we unshackle ourselves from fear, we will be free. Free of all bondage.'

Just then, the inspector stepped into the classroom with the headmaster. He strode towards the ageing teacher and slapped him across the face.

'How dare you instigate the youth?' shouted the inspector. Stunned, the boys watched their teacher as he stared unflinchingly into the Englishman's eyes. He neither apologised nor offered any explanation.

'Vande Mataram!' The teacher's voice rang out loud and clear.

Fired up, the students chanted, 'Vande Mataram!'

Soon the chant was taken up by children in other classrooms. 'Vande Mataram!' A hundred voices rose in support. The headmaster raised his hands to silence the students but they were in no mood to listen. Fully charged up, the boys continued to chant. Frustrated, the inspector slapped the teacher again and again until he collapsed and fell to the floor in a heap. The chanting grew louder with each slap until the furious Englishman stomped out of the classroom, vowing to teach a lesson to the entire village.

The next morning, the teacher was taken into custody on charges of sedition. The headmaster was taken to task and some senior students were also picked up by the police. They returned home with lacerated backs and wounded souls.

Most of the young boys of the village wanted to join the Anushilan Samiti but few were successful. The samiti had become one of the most disciplined and popular revolutionary associations, especially in East Bengal, where they had several branches that carried out major offences against the British. Its members pledged their lives to the cause of freedom. Many of the members had been hanged, tortured and deported to the Cellular Jail in the Andaman Islands. But no amount of intimidation or torture could douse the patriotic fervour of the young members of the samiti.

Neel decided that the time had come for him to join the freedom struggle.

The family had just finished dinner. Manik Bose was reading a book when he noticed his son hovering near the door.

'Do you want to say something?' asked the father. Pushing his glasses down his nose, he stared at his younger son.

'I want to join the Anushilan Samiti,' Neel announced.

This came as a surprise. No one expected Neel, the irresponsible and carefree boy, to join the crusade.

'Fighting for freedom is not like stealing fruits from trees or ogling at girls,' said Manik, going back to his book. He noticed the determined look on Neel's face and knew it would be difficult to stop his young son who was now sporting a moustache to declare his adulthood. Manik sighed and put his book down.

'You are much too young to understand the seriousness of such a commitment.'

'I am not much younger than Khudiram Bose. He began planting bombs at sixteen and died at eighteen.'

'All in good time,' replied the father. The incidents taking place in the village and nearby towns were a cause for concern for the man who already had two children working for a revolutionary party. And now the third wanted to join too.

The next evening, Neel was returning from a meeting called by the local leaders of the youth wing when dark clouds began to gather in the sky. He hastened home, his mind on the agenda of the meeting.

Suddenly, a young man rushing out of a narrow lane collided with him, throwing him off balance. The two of them fell to the ground. Cursing, Neel got up and brushed himself down. It was then that he noticed that the man could not get up. A bright-red stain spreading rapidly on the stranger's kurta caught his attention. Blood oozed and dripped down his right arm and onto the ground. 'You are bleeding!' Neel exclaimed, trying to help the man to his feet. 'Your wound needs attention. Come with me to my house. It is not far.'

They were standing near the thick bamboo cluster opposite the pond.

'It is too late. I have been shot . . . I am dying . . .' the man mumbled, his face contorting with pain as he tried to stand on unsteady feet. His breath was coming in quick gasps. A minute later, his knees buckled and he collapsed on the ground.

Neel stared helplessly at the dying man. 'Let me get you some water,' he offered.

With trembling hands, the man extricated a revolver from the folds of his clothes and handed it to Neel.

'Keep this with you. Kill the bastards! Kill as many as possible.' The effort of speaking was too much for him. Tears of frustration flowed down his cheeks and he struggled for breath even as life flowed out of him.

Alarmed by the man's condition, Neel dragged him behind a thicket, his path marked by a trail of blood. The clouds let loose their burden and heavy drops of rain began pelting the ground.

I have to take him home. Baba will know what to do.

Suddenly, the shrill sound of a whistle drowned the pitter-patter of the rain. It was followed by the sound of heavy footsteps. Neel looked helplessly at the young man. *How can I carry him to my house without being seen by the police?* His distress must have conveyed itself to the stranger, for he opened his eyes. With his face blanched and eyes glassy, the man whispered, 'Run, go.'

'But you are wounded,' Neel protested. 'I cannot leave you.'

'Don't . . .' Each word was an enormous struggle but the urgency in the stranger's voice prodded Neel to obey. 'Go! Don't let them find you. Run!' The stranger lost consciousness.

Tucking the revolver into his clothes, Neel began running. Slowly at first, glancing back frequently, then speeding up as he heard heavy boots draw nearer. Without a backward glance, he continued to run. At last, exhausted, he sat down heavily at the base of a tree. A few minutes later, a gunshot rang out and Neel knew the hunters had found their prey.

Leaning against the tree trunk, he closed his eyes and tried to control his trembling limbs. His heart thumped as the after-effects of the shock set in.

I shouldn't linger. I'm too close to the scene.

Alerted by the sounds, he peeped from behind the tree and witnessed a horrific scene. The police were dragging the stranger's body by the legs over the uneven ground. A trail of blood appeared, only to be washed away by the rain. The scene was to remain imprinted in his memory for a long time.

The encounter had a disturbing effect on Neel. 'Kill the bastards!' The dying man's words continued to ring in his ears.

Neel spent many hours pondering his future. The young revolutionary's death strengthened his resolve to join the freedom struggle. After several days of deliberation, Neel approached his elder brother and narrated the episode. To substantiate the story, he brought out the pistol given to him by the dying man. The sight of the pistol in his brother's hands upset Bikash. Snatching the weapon, he warned his younger brother against speaking about the incident to anyone. 'You must not get involved. Isn't it enough that Charu and I are contributing to the movement? Someone has to look after our parents. All of us can't die for the country. Just imagine our parents' condition if all of us were imprisoned or hanged.'

'Let Bishnu look after them,' Neel declared stubbornly, referring to their youngest sibling. 'God has chosen me for a purpose. Why else would I run into the young man? Why would he give me the gun? It is a sign. I want to join the Anushilan Samiti.'

'Father will not allow you to join. Besides, it is not yet time for you to join the movement.' The brother was determined to prevent Neel's enrolment.

Bikash's arguments failed to convince Neel and he issued an ultimatum. 'If you don't help, I will find some other way. Nothing you say will change my decision.'

A few nights later, Manik Bose summoned Neel to discuss the matter.

'What is this I hear about your ultimatum to Bikash? I respect your patriotic feelings but not everyone can become a revolutionary. Some of us are required to work in the background. You must study and become a lawyer so that you can defend people against the unfair judgments doled out by the white judges.'

None of the children ever argued with their father. He was the undisputed king of their little world. This time, however, Neel protested.

'Baba . . .'

'Enough! Not a word more on the subject,' thundered Neel's father. 'Concentrate on your studies instead of wasting time on silly arguments. Let us not have any more discussions on the subject.'

Help came from an unexpected quarter. Seated in a corner of the room, running her prayer beads through her fingers, Neel's grandmother had been listening to the exchange between her son and grandson. The old lady cackled. 'There is no law against anyone joining the revolution, nor is there any age bar. God knows we need as many hands as possible to fight the oppressors. I think you should not deter him,' she said.

Her outburst took Manik by surprise. She had always supported his decisions.

'Ma . . .' he began.

'Don't you try to use your schoolteacher tone with me,' the old lady cut him off before he could finish. 'What if Khudiram Bose's father had thought his son was too young to fight the

British? What if all the parents didn't let their children join the fight for freedom? Let the boy do what he has set his heart on.'

Neel's mother was sobbing softly in the background. No one asked for her opinion on the matter.

Manik Bose had never questioned or disobeyed his mother.

'As you wish, Mother,' he responded unhappily.

Neel's path was clear.

10

Olivia

Struck by Tragedy

In the servants' quarters, the gardener's child came down with smallpox. He was told to vacate the premises immediately.

'Have mercy, Saab. Where will I go with a sick child?' he cried.

When his pleas failed to move Captain Bradley, he appealed to Irene Bradley. 'Memsahib, I have served you faithfully for many years. Please give us time till my child recovers.'

His tears, however, did not affect the lady or the captain. A couple of hours later, the gardener, his wife and the wailing child departed with bundles on their heads. From a window, Olivia watched them go.

No one knew if it was the curse of the gardener or the fallout of an epidemic. But first Kit and then Olivia contracted the pox. Medicines failed to help the little one. His fever raged for a couple of days and then his body went cold.

The girl survived but her face was scarred for life. Olivia never forgot the horror on her mother's face after the scabs fell off and the scars stood out on her face.

The Bradleys were devastated. Kit's death was a severe blow to the family. While Irene immersed herself in religion, the captain turned into a workaholic. Wrapped in their misery, the couple forgot about their heartbroken daughter. Olivia hated the pitiful looks and curious questions that came her way. Gradually, she isolated herself from the other children who called her 'Pocky'.

The women, who earlier pinched her cheeks and declared her a pretty child, now avoided meeting her eye. 'Poor child,' she heard them mutter under their breath.

Irene's obsession with religion soon became a point of conflict between the couple. The captain had never been a religious man and couldn't understand his wife's dependence on it. Things went from bad to worse when she took to seeking solace in occult practices. Ouija boards, planchettes, voodoo, séances, ash-smeared sadhus—nothing brought her peace.

Captain Bradley's objections to the séances made Irene secretive. Often, when the captain was at work, she stole out of the house to attend a séance. Sometimes, Olivia returned from school to find her mother's room locked, with strange sounds coming from behind the closed door.

Irene cared for neither her husband nor her child. The servants now had a free hand in running the household. They stole and pilfered freely.

The Bradley family threads were unravelling fast. Captain Bradley worked till late at night, after which he went to the club and drank until he could no longer stand on his feet. The daughter locked herself in her room and wept for all that was lost.

A year rolled by and the arguments and rows between the couple became a daily affair. Slowly but surely, the family was falling apart. A mute spectator to the growing discord between her parents, Olivia continued to suffer from her insecurities.

Tragedy had not ended for the Bradley family. One morning, while on her way to a séance, Irene met with an accident. For three days, the woman remained in a coma. That was the only time the captain stopped drinking. He sat by her bed, holding her hand, begging her to open her eyes. Flooded with guilt and remorse, he promised to reform himself.

'You will survive, Irene,' he told her at least a dozen times a day. 'We will begin afresh. Don't worry. Everything will be all right.' Bradley was sure his wife wouldn't die.

'Your mom will come home. Don't you worry, Olivia. I'll bring her back,' he promised.

Irene Bradley didn't come out of the coma. A few days later, she died in the hospital.

Captain Bradley didn't forgive himself for the death of his son and wife. During the day, he worked like an ox, only to drown himself in alcohol in the evening. His foul temper kept everyone away. The servants avoided the captain and his daughter dreaded her father's moods.

Am I invisible? Olivia wondered, staring at her reflection in the mirror.

She wandered around the house like a waif, trying to keep out of her father's way.

Bradley's hard work brought him prominence, a promotion, accolades and medals, but it didn't bring him peace. Now a major, he didn't want any encumbrances. He requested his sister in England to take charge of Olivia. The sister, a sickly woman burdened with five children, had no desire to add to her brood. Bradley met with a similar response from his brother. No one wanted additional responsibilities. Even his promise to pay handsomely to compensate for the expenses had little effect. The Great Depression had robbed most people of their wealth and almost everyone found it difficult to maintain any semblance of comfortable living.

Their refusal to house Olivia came as a relief to the girl who had no wish to leave India for an unfamiliar place. Instead, she escaped into the world of books. For a girl her age, Olivia was well informed about the events taking place outside the confines of her home.

That summer, she was eleven years old. It was also the year Gandhi went on his Salt March. Gandhi, along with seventy-eight faithful *satyagrahi*s, marched to the western coast of India to protest against the British Salt Tax which made it illegal for Indians to sell or produce salt. After offering prayers at the site, the diminutive leader picked up a tiny lump of salt, signifying the violation of the law.

The British officers in the club called him a foolish man. No one could achieve freedom through nonsensical acts, they scoffed. But Olivia was fascinated by his courage.

II

Indraneel

Fleeing to Calcutta

'I want to join the party.' Neel had been begging his brother for several weeks, unable to make any headway. When everything else failed, Neel resorted to Gandhian methods. 'I will eat nothing till Bikash agrees to take me to Master Da.'

Undeterred by his father's angry reaction and his mother's pleas, Neel was determined to prove his point. On the third day of the hunger strike, Bikash relented.

'I will try,' was all he said.

The words promised nothing but Neel felt he was one step closer to his goal.

Surya Sen, known as Master Da by his followers, fought for freedom in his own way. Slippery as an eel, cunning as a fox, he confounded the British. His band of boys used homemade bombs and crude pistols to fight the white rulers with his brilliant strategy. Such was his charisma that young boys all over Bengal wanted to join Master Da's revolutionary group.

Since he was always on the radar of the British, knowledge of Master Da's movements was restricted to a few trusted lieutenants. He moved like a panther, swiftly and stealthily.

This was necessitated by the police's intensified efforts to catch young revolutionaries. The shadow of death reached out to grasp more and more young men in its arms. Bikash, the eldest Bose child, was missing. He had left on a covert mission a week ago and there had been no news since. Everyone feared the worst.

Neel would peer through a gap in the bedroom door to watch his father pace all night. The sound of a racking cough, which his father tried to stifle, did not escape his ears.

One evening, ten days after Bikash had left home, the family was at dinner when there was a sudden knock on the door. Fearing it was the police, Manik walked with heavy steps and opened the door. Dishevelled and drooping with fatigue, Bikash stood on the threshold. His father pulled him inside quickly, shutting the door behind him. Dinner was forgotten and everyone rushed towards the young man. Questions rained on him.

'I haven't eaten for the last forty-eight hours,' said Bikash, letting his body drop to the kitchen floor.

'Stop snivelling and give him food,' Manik said to his wife. 'Leave the boy alone till he has eaten and rested.'

Wiping her tears, Annapurna placed a plate before her exhausted son. She served him the best pieces of fish that were usually reserved for her husband.

It was only after Bikash had eaten and moved to the small bedroom adjoining the kitchen that Manik began questioning him.

On the other side of the door, Neel tried to listen in but could barely hear the conversation as the howling wind carried the words away from his eager ears.

The next morning, rested after his ordeal, Bikash emerged from the room. Expecting to learn about the events that had prevented him from returning home, Neel lingered around his elder brother.

'Come with me,' said Bikash, leading him towards the large jackfruit tree at the far end of the courtyard. 'Neel,' he said, stroking his brother's head affectionately, 'you have always wanted to do something for the organisation. Haven't you?'

'Yes, Dada,' he replied, thrilled at the idea of being offered an opportunity.

'I am under police observation, so I have to lie low for a while. I think they suspect that I am connected with the organisation. You will have to act as a conduit for communication. Will you be able to do it?'

His eyes lit up with excitement. 'Yes, Dada, I will do whatever you say. I am ready to lay down my life for the country.'

Bikash continued to stroke his younger brother's head. 'Silly boy! You must live to serve the country.'

'I will be very careful,' Neel promised.

'Don't underestimate your role in the movement. It is crucial for us to use a person who is not under suspicion. At the merest suspicion of being watched or followed, just swallow the pieces of paper. Never get caught with them in your possession,' he warned. 'That would mean death for you as well as other members. And we cannot allow that to happen.'

Neel's heart thudded wildly as the implication of Dada's words sank in. There were a hundred questions in his mind. He wanted to know where and why his brother had been missing. But he knew Bikash would answer none of his questions. He was confident his brother would tell him everything one day. All he had to do was carry out the tasks given to him.

For the next two weeks, Neel ferried innocuous-looking chits of paper to Bikash's comrades. Sometimes they were hidden between the pages of his notebook and passed on to a member while travelling by boat. At other times, they nestled between Neel's thumping chest and a secret pocket in the thin vest he wore under his cotton kurta. Each assignment was different. The meeting places were as natural as possible and the circumstances prearranged. It required a lot of ingenuity to bring about an exchange of notes without attracting attention and Neel soon became proficient at delivering messages.

He was a minor cog in the wheel of revolution that was spinning with zeal.

Things changed abruptly. In April 1930, Surya Sen's Indian Republican Army (IRA) attacked the Chittagong armoury. Emboldened by the victory, Master Da launched a full-fledged attack on British troops in Chittagong and succeeded in beating them back. It was a daring step that motivated freedom fighters all over the country. The next step was to declare a provisional revolutionary-democratic government. There was jubilation in the rebel camps. Unfortunately, the triumph didn't last too long. Chittagong remained in their control for exactly three days.

After licking their wounds, the British called in reinforcements and attacked the IRA in Jalalabad. This time, the IRA faced heavy losses as dozens of revolutionaries lost their lives. Master Da was shrewd enough to realise that an all-out war against the British was impossible, so he resorted to guerrilla warfare.

The British declared a reward of ten thousand rupees on Surya Sen's head. The small fortune was meant to tempt people into betraying the master. Master Da went into hiding. Faced with a leadership crisis, the revolutionaries broke up into small groups and the British captured many of them.

To ward off police suspicion, Manik suggested Bikash take up a job in the nearby town and lie low for a while.

It was the month of June. The weather was unbearably hot and stifling. Everyone was at home since schools and colleges had closed for the summer vacations. A district magistrate had been killed in the neighbouring town. His killing caused a furore and the police let loose a reign of terror. There were umpteen stories of arrests and atrocities. Almost all the able-bodied young men from nearby villages were rounded up and interrogated. Police informers went into overdrive as they reported on suspected rebels.

Bikash and Manik were also taken to the police station. Although the father was released the next day, the police did not release Bikash. Manik and Neel ran from pillar to post trying to bring Bikash home but they ran into a stone wall. There were rumours that Bikash and a few others had been taken to Calcutta to be put on trial. The family did not know whether to grieve or pray for their son, joining countless other families who did not know whether their sons were dead or alive.

The family's troubles didn't end with Bikash's disappearance. Ever since the police discovered his connection with the revolutionaries, they spared no opportunity to harass the family. Neel was frequently taken in for interrogation, which always ended in a beating. The police were intent on breaking bones and killing spirits.

One evening, Neel limped home after an interrogation, his body covered in injuries and lacerations. The sight of her son's swollen face moved Annapurna to tears. She dressed his wounds and gave him a cup of hot milk laced with turmeric. 'I can't bear to look at your injuries,' she wailed. 'You must escape to Calcutta. You shouldn't suffer this torture any more.'

With shaky fingers, she wrote an address on a piece of paper and gave it to Neel. 'This is my cousin's address in Calcutta. He will house you for as long as you want. You must join college and complete your education.'

'I won't leave the village.' Neel balked at the thought of deserting his helpless family. 'Let them kill me if they want. Running away will convince them of my guilt and they will make all of you pay.'

'Neel, listen to your mother,' his father appealed. 'Save yourself. As long as I am alive, your mother and sister will be safe. And then, there is Bishnu.'

'I think you should go,' Neel's sister begged. 'You cannot help us by staying here. Bikash is gone and we don't know what awaits you tomorrow.'

In the end, Neel yielded to their pleas.

It was a long journey to Calcutta. Anyone trying to escape the village was taken into custody, so he could not risk travelling by train or bus. Neel's best bet was to take a circuitous route through Agartala and gradually work his way towards his destination.

Keeping close to the wooded area, he walked for miles in the darkness, his feet sore and scarred. Sometimes he was lucky enough to get a ride on a farmer's bullock cart. Hidden in the mounds of grains and vegetables, he journeyed along the rutted lanes. Through Srirampur and Akhaura he travelled by bus disguised as a Muslim mendicant. It was a journey fraught with danger that had him constantly looking over his shoulder. The habit gained over those weeks would remain with him forever.

Weeks later, he reached the outskirts of Calcutta. His hair was long and his clothes filthy. With his gaunt body and calloused feet, Neel looked like a beggar. Calcutta was dotted with beggars and no one paid any attention to yet another, but Neel didn't take any chances. After spending a couple of days near a slum, he approached the house to which his mother had directed him. For a few minutes he stood across the street, studying the neighbourhood.

It was a bustling middle-class locality of the city and the house was a fairly large one. Looking around surreptitiously, Neel rapped the heavy brass knocker. The door was opened by a servant who looked disapprovingly at the unkempt man outside.

'Wait,' he instructed. The neatly dressed, stocky servant crinkled his nose with disgust as he disappeared into the house. 'Young and able-bodied and asking for alms. Lazy beggars!' Neel heard him mutter.

The servant returned with some food and offered it to Neel.

'I am not a beggar,' said Neel, with an exhausted smile. 'I am here to meet Subir Roy.'

The servant threw a suspicious look at the dishevelled man standing on the threshold. 'He is a busy man,' he said.

'Please tell him Annapurna's son is here,' Neel pleaded, showing him the letter written by his mother. 'Give him this letter.'

Leaving Neel to wait at the door, the man vanished inside the sprawling house. A few minutes later, a young man rushed out and hugged Neel. Then, holding him at an arm's length, he exclaimed, 'So, you are Annapurna's son? Don't stand at the door like a stranger. You are a member of the family.'

Neel was surprised by the warmth of the young man. He could no longer control his tears. His sorrow, pain and frustration welled, and he sobbed without restraint.

Subir, the anglicised young man in his mid-twenties, worked for an English newspaper. He took Neel under his wing.

Neel began living in the triple-storeyed house with a brood of uncles, aunts and cousins. The house was a beehive of tireless activity all day long until it heaved a sigh of relief late in the night. It echoed with the sounds of laughter and chatter. Those who arrived for help were never turned away, no matter how remote their connection with the family. Relatives and friends flocked to the house throughout the year, so Neel's arrival caused no flutter. For the first time in many weeks, Neel felt safe enough to sleep through the night.

A week later, rested and healed, he set out to familiarise himself with the city. He wandered through the ever-changing flow and ebb of humanity on the busy streets, absorbing the sounds and the colours that surrounded him. It was a fascinating world, very different from the one back home.

Subir was doing well in his job, which required him to be on friendly terms with many British officers and Indian politicians. Neel and he spent many hours discussing the prevailing situation in the country. They argued about the methods employed by

Gandhi but Neel had little respect for the non-violent ways of the man.

'Freedom can't be gained by going on a fast or offering oneself up for arrest. It has to be fought for,' Neel raged on one occasion. The two of them were sitting on the terrace parapet watching the setting sun.

'Easy, young man! Such talk will get you into trouble,' Subir cautioned. 'I am not a revolutionary but my sympathies lie with them.'

'Mere sympathy will help no one.'

'I am a British stooge,' Subir joked. 'They pay me and I write what they want me to write. My bread and butter come from the British, so I won't go on a warpath. However, I won't allow them to control my thoughts. Like every young man, I too dream of freedom.'

'Dreams without action are a waste of time,' retorted Neel. 'Freedom calls for struggle.'

'Well, let me warn you, Neel, that if you are thinking of joining a revolutionary group, you will have to leave this house. I will not allow you to endanger the lives of the people living in this house. Also, don't expect any help if the police catch you. I will provide food and shelter for the sake of your mother but will not condone any nationalistic activity under this roof.'

Neel had no wish to abuse the hospitality of the generous family. 'I will do nothing to endanger anyone's life,' he promised.

'Power comes through education,' Subir continued in a calm voice. 'Without education, you cannot bring change. I feel you must complete your graduation before you think of revolution.' He lit an expensive cigarette, inhaled deeply and let out a ring of smoke.

'I will use my connections to secure your admission.' Subir patted Neel's arm. 'Your parents have sent you to Calcutta so you are safe, and I would advise you to follow their wishes.'

Although Neel joined a college in Calcutta, his heart was not in his studies. The unjustified excesses of the police in his village continued to haunt him. His blood boiled whenever he remembered the humiliation of his father and the disappearance of his elder brother. Those memories continued to feed his anger against the British.

Letters from home were infrequent and he worried about his family. A couple of months after he arrived in Calcutta, his sister wrote to inform him that the police had taken their father and Bishnu in for interrogation. Neel's disappearance had convinced the police of his involvement in revolutionary activities. Manik Bose was a broken man. On his return home he fell on his bed, never to rise. The schoolteacher passed away a few days later.

The tragedy faced by the family and the repeated summons by the police took a toll on heartbroken Bishnu. Six months later, the fourteen-year-old boy took his own life. Unable to bear the tragic loss of their loved ones, the women of the family slipped away to an undisclosed destination one night. News from the neighbours included rumours of them journeying to Kashi.

A distressed Neel wanted to return to the village. 'I have to go back to settle scores with the police,' he informed Subir, packing his few belongings.

'Are you crazy?' Subir scolded the impulsive young man. 'What can you achieve by going back? Your father is dead; your brothers too are dead. You do not know whether your mother, sister and grandmother are alive.' Subir unpacked Neel's bag and walked him to a chair. 'The police will arrest you the moment you reach the village. Stay here, study law and defend the young men who are arrested for sedition. That is what your father wanted you to do.'

'That will take a long time,' Neel smashed his fist against the wall in impotent rage. 'I can't wait that long.'

'Anger is ruining your peace of mind and health. Let things take their natural course.'

'I have nothing to look forward to; no home, no family, nothing,' grieved Neel.

Three days later, Neel made up his mind. Walking up to Subir, he declared, 'I am joining the activists.'

'Finish your studies first. Once you have finished your graduation, I will not stop you from joining any organisation.'

For a while, Neel went back to his studies but he couldn't concentrate. Every time he opened a book, the faces of his father and brothers floated before his eyes. He would no longer listen to Subir's advice, he decided. Graduation could wait.

The next day, he joined a group of young rebels in the college. This time he didn't consult Subir.

12

Peter

Another Escape

Life at the orphanage had become unbearable for Peter. He hated the strict discipline and constant supervision. He wasn't the only one. Almost all boys of his age detested the confined environment of the orphanage and spent most of their time plotting a getaway.

A few weeks earlier, a new warden, Barry Collins, had arrived from Ireland. It didn't take him long to become a much-hated figure in the orphanage.

A corpulent man with a mottled complexion and thinning hair, Collins was sluggish in his movements. Although missionaries maintain an austere life, the new warden was a self-indulgent man. Overly fond of food and the bottle, he believed in living a comfortable life. Worse, the man was obsessed with cleanliness and discipline. He made surprise rounds of the hostel and the kitchen at odd hours of the day and night. The boys and the cooks were equally terrified of his temper.

A few weeks after his arrival, Collins had summoned a boy to his room just as everyone was getting ready for bed. An hour passed, and then another, but the boy didn't return till midnight. The next morning, everyone questioned him about the evening's goings-on but the boy was too dazed to say anything. After much prodding, he confessed that he had given a body massage to the warden and been rewarded with a piece of chocolate.

Since then, Collins summoned a boy for a massage at bedtime every night. The boys always appeared traumatised after the experience. Soon rumours that Collins had behaved indecently with the boys began floating in the corridors of the orphanage. The whispers grew in strength as days passed.

The boys dreaded being called to the warden's room though no one spoke openly of the reason.

Peter ignored the rumours until the warden summoned him one evening. Feeling brave, he knocked on the door and entered.

He let out a low whistle at the sight of the well-appointed suite. In the small outer room lay a comfortable couch flanked by an ornate wooden shelf stacked with books and curios. Framed pictures of Christ hung from the wall. A crystal decanter and a wine goblet stood on a side table near a rocking chair. There were expensive drapes on the windows and a bright rug covered most of the floor. Wondering where Collins had disappeared to, the boy stood in the outer room. *The sooner I get out of here the better.* He cleared his throat to remind the warden of his presence in the room.

'Shut the door behind you and come right in.' The warden's guttural voice floated out of the bedroom.

An uneasy feeling gripped Peter as he stepped into the warden's bedroom. The first thing he noticed was a beautiful silver candlestick placed on the mantelpiece over the fireplace. The room resounded with cheerful Irish music and Collins lay on the bed, crooning tunelessly to the music. Clad in his underpants, he looked like a dugong. He was drunk to the gills.

What the hell does he want? Peter stood near the door, rooted to the spot and unwilling to step closer to the half-naked man.

'Don't stand there like an idiot. Come here,' the cleric shouted over the music, and his lips curled into a smile. Peter shuffled closer to the bed, his mind replaying the stories he had heard.

'Massage my shoulders,' ordered Collins, pointing to a bottle of fragrant oil on a side table. 'Take that oil and get started, boy. Don't waste time.'

Drawing a deep breath, he began massaging the man's fleshy shoulders. Shoulders done, the warden instructed him to massage his back and legs.

'Put some strength into it,' the warden scolded. 'Don't you eat, boy?'

It was a repugnant task. Collins's lumpy body was pliant under Peter's kneading hands. Exhausted and sleepy, Peter continued massaging, hoping the man would fall asleep so he could steal out of the room. Suddenly, he felt the warden's hands creeping up his thighs. A lopsided smile playing on his face, Collins pinned Peter down on the bed. Shocked, the boy pushed the groping hands away and sprang up from the bed.

'You will like it, I promise,' the warden whispered, his voice hoarse with passion. 'No one will know . . . I will reward you.'

Peter inched back, horrified. *The rumours were true, after all.* Collins was muttering terms of endearment as he stretched his hands towards the boy. 'Don't be scared. I will not hurt you,' the man murmured, breathing heavily.

'What do you want?' Peter jumped away and looked around. His eyes settled on the silver candlestick.

Collins was losing patience now. 'Don't be insolent, boy. Come here! Immediately.' He sat up on the bed and snarled at Peter. 'I won't spare you.'

Grabbing the candlestick by the stem, Peter hit out blindly at the warden. There was a crunching sound as metal contacted bone. Like an axed tree, Collins fell back on the bed with a loud thud. Stunned, Peter stared at the man. The warden lay motionless. *Was he dead?*

Fear propelled Peter's feet. Grabbing Collins's wallet which lay beside the bed, he slipped out of the room. His heart was hammering wildly as he stood in the corridor, trying to gain control of his trembling limbs. The warden was dead. He had to make a getaway before the police arrived. He had to run far away from the orphanage.

Spurred by fear, he inched his way to the boundary wall and vaulted over it to fall with a thud on the other side. The next moment, he began to run like a frightened rabbit towards the railway station.

Not once did he look back as he made his way to the station. Just as he entered, a train chugged in and a multitude of passengers jostled each other, trying to clamber onto it. There was no time to figure out its route or destination. All Peter wanted was to get away before the police discovered the warden's body. He muscled his way into an overcrowded compartment, his ears perked for the police's whistle and the sound of running feet. There were none. He heaved a sigh of relief as the train began moving.

Peter joined a cluster of passengers huddled on the floor, his mind in a tizzy. Resigned to the dictates of destiny, he tried to make himself comfortable. It was a long time before the rhythmic motion of the train lulled him to sleep.

13

Indraneel

Mission Amritsar

Within a few months of joining the underground group of revolutionaries, Neel gained the attention of the local leaders. An astute organiser, he brought youthful optimism and enthusiasm to the meetings.

'To be effective, we will have to fight in unison,' he suggested during a meeting with the local leaders. 'There are over a hundred factions spread through the country, each of them waging an ineffective struggle against British rule. We can strengthen the fight for freedom by bringing the factions together.'

'It is easier said than done,' retorted a senior member. 'It is difficult to find a leader who will be acceptable to all the factions. Besides, it is easier to operate in small groups. A large and bulky organisation will attract the attention of the police.'

'I agree it will not be a simple task,' said Neel. 'But I believe it to be possible. Working in unison doesn't mean carrying out attacks in large groups. Let's not forget how Bhagat Singh and Batukeshwar Dutt got together to throw a bomb in the assembly house. Then there was Jogesh Chandra Chatterjee, who joined hands with the Hindustan Republican Association to carry out the Kakori train robbery.'

'Your argument does make sense. How do you propose we go ahead with the plan of uniting different factions?' asked the de facto leader of the party. 'There is no communication between the factions and groups. There is also the matter of ego. Every leader believes himself to be supreme and will not accept a secondary position.'

'As per my information, some of the most active revolutionary groups are working in Bengal, Bihar, the United Provinces, Punjab and Maharashtra. To begin with, we should target just a couple of groups. Let's send emissaries to Punjab and Bihar. If the experiment is successful, we could bring more factions under a united umbrella. We shouldn't give up for want of trying.'

The leader nodded. 'I have received feelers from a small group known as Inquilab. They are a group of young men based in and around Amritsar. The leader of Inquilab has sent a missive expressing the group's willingness to collaborate with us.' Turning to Neel, he said, 'Why don't you travel to Amritsar and speak to their leader?'

Neel was overjoyed. 'All I require is the contact person's name and address.'

'We will arrange to deliver a train ticket and expense money to your house within an hour. There's a train to Amritsar that leaves tonight. When you reach, contact a man called Gurmeet Singh. We will inform him of your arrival. Good luck!'

A few hours later, armed with a few clothes, some money and a pistol, Neel embarked on his journey. He knew the people of Amritsar were in a mutinous mood since the news of Bhagat Singh's hanging had reached the town. Every man, woman and child wanted to avenge the death of their hero. The number of attacks on police officials was on the rise.

In retaliation, the police had unleashed a frightening upsurge of brutality. They picked up and tortured able-bodied men at random, hoping to extract information about the revolutionary groups. They did not spare the women either. An atmosphere of fear hung over the town when Neel reached Amritsar. He was confident that Gurmeet would know of his arrival since the underground grapevine was quite efficient. The man, however, was impossible to trace. Neel's discreet inquiries led him nowhere.

Disguised as an aged Sikh, he walked into the Golden Temple where he had been told to meet the leader of Inquilab. It was noon and the pilgrims were being served food. The appetising smell of freshly made rotis reminded him it had been many hours since his last meal and he headed for the langar. Neel was handed a thali and glass, after which he joined the row of people waiting to be served.

A young woman, her head covered with a dupatta, dropped a couple of rotis on his plate, and a couple of women served dal and potatoes out of the large buckets they were carrying. Neel picked up a roti and found a small piece of paper stuck underneath.

He discreetly pocketed the note and continued eating. It was only after he had washed his hands and joined the devotees in singing the Gurbani that Neel took it out. Someone had scribbled an address on the tiny piece of paper. He was to reach there in an hour. Just as he was wondering how he would locate the place, the woman who had served the rotis emerged from the temple. Nodding imperceptibly, she beckoned Neel to follow.

Avoiding the busier parts of the town, they wound their way towards an arched gateway that led into a lane with a dozen houses on either side. The houses were of modest size, their roofs running contiguously. The woman disappeared into one of the houses as soon as they were halfway down the lane.

Neel was pondering his next step when the door of the house across the street opened and a man called out to him. Crossing the street, Neel entered the house and shut the door behind him. He was impressed by the manner in which the operation had been conducted.

Neel stepped into an open courtyard and scanned the place. The single-storey house, with two large rooms, a kitchen, bathroom and toilet, was sparsely furnished. There were a couple of string cots in one of the rooms and the other was furnished with a writing desk and some chairs. The kitchen contained a few utensils and a pitcher, and had a chulha that used wood and dried dung for fuel.

'Gurmeet Singh?' Neel asked the strapping Sikh standing in the courtyard and received a warm smile in reply.

'So you're Inderneel from Calcutta?' said the Sikh, pronouncing his name with a thick Punjabi accent. 'Welcome to Amritsar!' With that, he hugged the visitor. 'First, go and wash off that terrible make-up and change your clothes. Your disguise will not even fool an idiot,' Gurmeet said with a broad grin.

'It's a poor disguise, I agree. It fooled the police, though,' Neel conceded, returning Gurmeet's smile.

'They are not known to be too bright or I would have been dead by now.' The Sikh's eyes crinkled with amusement.

A couple of minutes later, discarding the fake beard and changing into his usual clothes and spectacles, Neel emerged from the tiny bathroom in the courtyard.

'That's much better,' said the Sikh. 'Now I know what you look like. But I won't have you wandering around Amritsar.'

Warming up to each other, the two men settled on a string cot discussing the latest situation in the country and Amritsar in particular, their passion for freedom overcoming all language and cultural barriers.

Neel was delighted to discover that Gurmeet too believed in unified action by different factions of freedom fighters.

'We can succeed only if we fight together,' said the Sikh. 'As we say, a fist is more effective than five individual fingers.'

'I agree. It is easy for the British to overpower small bands of freedom fighters but a cumulative effort could shake them up.'

'The distance and differences make the task challenging. We will have to overcome those barriers.'

'If Bhagat Singh and Batukeshwar Dutt could find a way, why can't we?'

Neel's words cheered the young Sikh, who was a devoted follower of Bhagat Singh's principles.

'Now that we agree in principle, let me share our plan with you,' Neel said, lowering his voice. 'The second round-table conference is scheduled for September in London. Many of our leaders, including Gandhi, will attend. Most of the freedom fighters in Bengal do not agree with the non-violent principles of the Congress. We want to send a powerful message before the conference takes place. My organisation plans to carry out a bomb attack on the Central Legislative Assembly in Delhi. The aim is to kill as many people as possible. Only then will it work.'

Gurmeet's jaw dropped with shock. It took a couple of moments for the enormity of the plan to sink in.

'That's an ambitious plan,' he said finally. 'It will throw a spanner in the works of the British government if it succeeds, but won't it kill our people?'

'There will be some collateral damage. A few sacrifices for the sake of the larger aim.' Neel had had ample time to think about the matter. 'After all, Bhagat Singh and Batukeshwar Dutt saw some logic in the plan.'

'But they dropped smoke bombs which didn't kill anyone,' Gurmeet argued.

'That is why it didn't have the effect it should have had. Our party has debated this for long.'

It took all of Neel's persuasive powers to convince the Sikh. 'So, how do you intend to carry out this mission?'

'That is where you come in,' said Neel, pointing his forefinger at Gurmeet's chest. 'The plan requires a lot of resources and has to be chalked out in minute detail. Calcutta is far from Delhi but Amritsar is close. Can we count on your support?'

'You need not ask that, Bhai,' responded the Sikh, thumping his chest. 'As long as Gurmeet is alive, he will take part in any plan designed to bring down the British.'

'We will need money, safe houses and transportation. And now that we are to work together, you must call me Neel.'

'Don't worry. I will help you in all possible ways. Although we can't give money, our lives are at your disposal. I have some contacts in Delhi who will be happy to house me for a few days. I will travel to Delhi for a thorough reconnaissance and work on a plan of escape after the attack.'

'That will be a big help, Gurmeet.' Neel shook the man's hand to express his gratitude.

'Why don't you accompany me to Calcutta?' Neel suggested after a couple of minutes. 'You are a hunted man and it is not safe for you to stay in Amritsar. In Calcutta, you can meet the senior members of my party and discuss the details of the plan. Together, we can work out the modalities and strategies of our action.'

'It is not possible for me to leave at the moment. The superintendent of police, John Burton, is coming here for the Baisakhi celebrations on 13 April. That man is responsible for the deaths of more than two hundred men in this town. I am planning to kill him during the celebrations.' Gurmeet paused and smiled. 'The young boys in my cadre are getting restless. They want action. If I disappear soon after the assassination, my comrades will assume that I have been arrested. Demoralised, they may disband and that would be the end of Inquilab. I have to remain here for a couple of weeks. Thereafter, I will hand over charge to my comrade and travel to Calcutta.'

'That seems sensible. My mission was to seek your cooperation in joint action. Now that we have agreed, I will leave for Calcutta as soon as possible.'

'Enjoy our hospitality for a few days, Bhai, while I arrange for your safe passage. The entire town is under strict surveillance because of the Baisakhi festival. They are taking no chances. Under these circumstances, it may be risky for you to embark on the journey,' said Gurmeet. 'You look like a visitor, and they suspect all visitors now. If by any chance you are followed while leaving this place, we will lose the safety of this house and my life will be at risk.'

'Where do you plan to house me until the arrangements are made? Wouldn't it be safer to remain here?'

'This house is used only for brief meetings and exchange of information. We can't risk keeping you here till the arrangements are in place. I will take you—'

Gurmeet suddenly stopped speaking and placed a finger on his lips to warn Neel. His alert ears had picked up something. Quick as lightning, he opened the door and dragged in the person leaning against it.

14
Peter

From the Frying Pan into the Fire

It was the end of March, and a warm wind was blowing through the town when Peter reached Amritsar. The railway station was crawling with police, and every person who arrived there was subjected to their scrutiny. Not wanting to attract attention, he merged with the multitude of passengers making their way out. His feet led him towards the market, hungry and bedraggled.

Destiny had chosen a strange place to unload Peter. The province of Punjab was in a state of turbulence ever since Bhagat Singh, Rajguru and Sukhdev had been arrested and hanged after a brief trial. Enraged by the incident, the youth had picked up arms against the British. Peter had read accounts of recent events in the newspapers that came to the orphanage library.

His mind crammed with worries, Peter shuffled along the road. A person who has neither money nor education has to perfect the art of survival and this came naturally to Peter. Sleeping under the open sky at night was not a comfortable option, so he searched for a safe shelter. A brief search around the town led him to a *dharamshala* near the Golden Temple. It accommodated dozens of homeless people at night but his looks made him stand out in the crowd of unkempt beggars. Though no one said anything, it was clear from their hostile glances that a single night was all he could risk there.

Peter wanted to leave Amritsar as soon as possible. The town was too close to Pathankot and he suspected the police might already be on his trail. After much deliberation, he decided to travel to Calcutta. The city, he had heard, was full of Anglo-Indians.

It wouldn't be difficult to lose himself in the crowded and narrow lanes of the city.

The next morning, he loitered around the railway station trying to find a train that would take him to Calcutta. Unfortunately, there was none. He would have to take a circuitous route through Delhi to reach his destination.

The platforms were packed with passengers. The uniformed guardians of British law were scrutinising all the passengers. The paperwork of those entering the station were checked, as were of those who arrived on the trains. Peter spotted a few men being taken into custody as soon as they disembarked. They looked harmless but the police were taking no chances.

A Delhi-bound train came to a halt at the platform and the crowd rushed forward. So did the police, marching away a couple of young men. Peter was just a few yards away from the train when his courage failed him and he slunk out of the railway station, convinced that the police wouldn't spare him. Retracing his steps to the dingy street in the bustling market where he had spent the previous day, he lost himself in the crowd. Crowded places, he knew, were his best refuge when hunted by the police.

Tongas, cycles and rickshaws crowded the entrance of the busy vegetable market. Men and women jostled each other, their bags full of fresh vegetables. Grocery shops lined another lane. Hungry and exhausted, Peter loitered around the bazaar, looking for an opportunity to earn some money. Spotting a couple of coolies unloading sacks of grain at a shop, the boy tried to join them to earn a quick buck but was shooed away.

It had been hours since his last meal. Peter hung around a vendor's cart, eyeing the hot puris and potato curry being ladled out on sal-leaf plates to the people who flocked around. Taking advantage of the crowd, Peter stole a few puris and took to his heels. After quenching his thirst at a tap in the public park, he stretched himself under a large peepul tree and fell asleep. He was awakened by a hard kick in the rear. The sun was still high in the sky and he had no way of knowing how long he had been asleep.

'Get up, *saala harami*,' a burly Sikh in a police uniform stood towering over him. 'This is not your baap's property.'

The abuse was followed by another kick and the policeman raised his baton to strike. Peter caught the man's baton before it could land on his head. Snatching it from the policeman's hands, Peter struck him with it and fled. His unexpected action took the burly man by surprise. For a moment, the fellow clutched his forehead. Then, he recovered and gave chase. The two of them left the bazaar far behind and entered a congested residential area. Peter continued running with the policeman on his tail till he reached a secluded lane.

The lane was so narrow that shadows of the houses on one side fell on the other. A couple of cows sat at one end of the street chewing the cud torpidly. It was siesta hour and the residents of the area were all indoors. Not a soul was around. It wouldn't be difficult for the policeman to spot him, Peter realised. But there was nowhere to go. He paused near a door to catch his breath. Pressing himself flat against it, he waited for the policeman who now stood at the end of the lane, unsure of the direction his quarry had taken.

The door against which the boy was leaning suddenly creaked open and a hand shot out. The next moment, he was pulled into the house. The action was so quick that Peter lost his balance and fell to the ground.

Brushing himself down, Peter got up and faced the man who had pulled him into the house.

'What the hell!' he glared at the two men standing before him.

'Why were you spying on us?' asked the tall and muscular Sikh who wore a saffron turban.

'Why would I spy on you? I was just leaning against the door.' Peter squared his shoulders. 'Why did you pull me inside?'

'Resting against the door?' asked the slender man dressed in a wrinkled white dhoti and kurta. A pair of metal-framed spectacles sat on his nose. His thick hair was parted down the middle. 'At this hour of the day? Why?' he continued in a silky voice.

Peter's eyes scanned the room in a quick sweep. A couple of string cots, a few *mooda*s and an earthen pitcher with a brass glass were the only items in the room.

'He's lying,' said the Sikh. 'I saw him leading a policeman to this lane.'

'The policeman was chasing me. I didn't lead him here,' Peter protested.

'Don't you dare!'

'Let me speak to him, Gurmeet,' said the shorter man. Turning to Peter, he asked, 'Would you like some water?' His voice was smooth and cultured. He sounded like a teacher.

'Yes.' Peter licked his dry lips. He was still panting.

Ladling out water from the pitcher, Indraneel offered it to the boy.

'Well, boy, let us hear your story. What are you doing here? You are not from Amritsar. Are you in trouble?'

Peter had no intention of sharing his troubles with the two of them. His eyes swept across the room and settled on the door as he weighed the possibility of making an escape.

'Don't even think about it,' warned the quiet man. 'Gurmeet is swifter than the policeman lurking outside the door. I am sure he has already called for reinforcements.'

Stuck between the devil and the deep blue sea, Peter stalled for time. He had no wish to run into the cops.

'Why did you pull me inside?' Peter repeated.

'We saved you from the police, you idiot,' thundered Gurmeet. 'Don't you realise that?'

'Well, I wasn't begging to be rescued.'

'Let us throw this ungrateful bastard out on the street, Neel,' said the Sikh, glowering at the Anglo-Indian. 'The police can deal with him.'

They scowled at each other like two mongrels fighting over a bone, ready to pounce.

'One moment, Gurmeet. Let me do the talking,' said the man called Neel. 'We have no intention of harming you. You are safer here than on the street but we want to know why the policeman was chasing you.' His voice was gently persuasive. 'All we have to do is throw you out on the street. I am sure you know they have locked up, tortured and killed several young men.'

The ominous implication of the words didn't escape Peter.

'I was scared, so I ran and the constable began chasing me.'

'You were scared of the constable and he chased you?' Neel mocked. 'Tell us the truth if you want us to help you.'

'I didn't ask for anyone's help.'

'Let him go, Gurmeet,' Neel said with a sigh. 'He doesn't seem to need our help.'

The brawny Sikh propelled Peter towards the door and opened it. Peeping out, the boy saw that the lane was teeming with policemen. He shut the door quickly and stepped away from it.

'Get out!' Gurmeet hissed, making a move to open the door.

'No! Please don't open the door. They will kill me,' Peter begged.

'You are putting us in danger. The police don't spare those who shelter a criminal.'

'I am not a criminal. Please help me.'

'Then tell us the truth.'

'I was lying under a tree in the public park when the constable hit me with his baton. All I did was stop him from hitting me, and he began chasing me.'

'And how did you stop the cop from hitting you?' There was a look of incredulity on Neel's face.

'I did a bit more than that,' admitted the boy sheepishly. 'I snatched the baton and gave him a whack.'

Gurmeet burst into laughter. 'Well done! He must have taken you for a nationalist.'

'I don't want to be caught by the police,' Peter whined. The house and the two men were the only barriers between him and his pursuer. 'Please help me.'

'That's better,' said Gurmeet. Turning to Neel, he said, 'This fellow has brought the police to the lane. I suspect they will soon begin a search of all the houses in the area. We must leave this place immediately.'

'Please don't leave me here. Take me with you,' Peter begged.

'Then let's hurry. It is not safe to linger here.'

The three of them rushed up the ladder leading to the terrace. The houses were so close to each other that jumping over to the roof of the adjacent house was child's play. They moved stealthily, jumping from one roof to the other till they'd put enough distance between them and the police.

Weaving their way through the deserted lanes, avoiding the stray passers-by, Gurmeet led them out of the area. He seemed to know the escape route like the back of his hand. Moving swiftly like a panther, he guided them towards the outskirts of the city. Only after they reached a deserted area did he allow them to take a break.

15
Olivia

The City of Joy

Olivia had always been a shy girl with few friends but after her mother's death, she withdrew into her shell. Her disfigured face contributed to her reclusive nature. In school, a few classmates tried to bully her but she neither complained nor resisted. Tired of her stoic behaviour, the children gave up and stayed away from her. The few kindly ones that ventured to be friendly jettisoned the effort after a while. Her monosyllabic responses to their attempts at making conversation dampened their enthusiasm. Olivia was a dull girl, they decided.

Olivia was a mediocre student. She didn't merit praise or reprimand, so teachers ignored the girl who sat at the back of the class. Olivia bore her humdrum life with resignation. She had learned not to expect any excitement, though she secretly pined for a friendly shoulder to unburden her sorrows.

Irene had introduced her daughter to the wonderful world of books and the beauty of nature and music. In her loneliness, Olivia turned to them for company. Fairy tales, history books, romantic novels and adventure sagas—she devoured them all, spending hours in the deserted building that housed the damp library room. Loneliness provides immunity against many odds and, over time, she began enjoying the solitude. As long as there were books and gramophone records, she wanted for nothing.

Years glided by on well-oiled wheels, bringing no change in her life until one day she found herself on the brink of adulthood with no one to guide her through the strange changes in her body. Olivia had overheard discussions among the girls in her class. They spoke about bleeding and the discomfort they faced each month. She was terrified but didn't know whom to seek out for guidance. Books were proving a poor substitute for a mother.

In the end, it was the sweeper who worked in their house, who noticed the stained underwear. The kindly woman tried to help her as much as she could but it wasn't enough. Olivia was ill-equipped to handle the changes that had arrived with adolescence.

One day, while looking for a stray dog that often followed her home from school; she came across a quaint chapel hidden behind a grove of trees. It was in a state of disuse after the monks who had built it in the early nineteenth century moved away.

The mongrel had strayed into the chapel. Compelled to follow it inside, Olivia stood transfixed as she took in the place. It was an enchanting sight. Behind the altar was a set of stained-glass windows and the colours on the glass glowed brightly in the sunlight that filtered in through the trees. Bright colours seemed to spill out from the frames and fell on the floor in shimmering, dappled pools. Moved, she fell to her knees and clasped her hands. Unrestrained tears flowed down her cheeks.

Till then, she had avoided going to church. God had taken away all that Olivia loved, and she had found no reason to thank him for anything. But she felt strangely peaceful in the deserted chapel. She sobbed piteously and felt cleansed of all sorrows. From that day, she visited the chapel regularly, to complain, rant and rave about the injustices of her fate.

But she soon lost this comfort too as her father received a new posting yet again. Major Bradley was being transferred constantly, as his dedication to his service did not go unnoticed. From the scorching desert to idyllic hills, anywhere was fine for father and daughter who were now equipped to move at short notice. But no one thought to consider the toll it was taking on the young woman as she struggled to find her place in the world.

It was a tough life, requiring many adjustments. Olivia learned to move from school to school without complaining. There were no friendships to nurture and no warmth of familiarity. It was a nomadic existence. The changes were the only invariable element in her life.

The meagre communication channels between father and daughter were now completely choked. They rarely spent time in each other's company. Even mealtimes didn't bring them together.

An uncomfortable silence reigned on the rare occasions the two of them dined together. Apart from asking a few questions about her health and education, Major Bradley had nothing to say.

Often, the girl sat in the garden and dreamed of the happy days when they had travelled from Rawalpindi to Murree, recalling the scarlet of sunsets, the harsh cries of peacocks, the aroma of coriander and the taste of spicy curries. She had to only close her eyes to visualise the beautiful silk dress ordered for her fourth birthday. The flouncy lace frock stitched on their veranda by an old durzi remained her favourite for a long time. She had outgrown her old clothes but continued to hold on to them as they brought back so many memories each time she ran her fingers over the soft fabric.

Memories were all Olivia had now. It had been a long time since her mother died. Her father was now a senior officer. The years had peppered his hair and lined his face. From an easy-going and cheerful person, he had changed into an ill-tempered and sadistic man. Olivia could barely recognise him as the father she had once loved. He was insensitive to his juniors and boorish to the people around him, meting out severe punishments to the servants for the smallest lapses.

Olivia was delighted when her father received his posting orders to Calcutta. She looked forward to living in the city known as Bengal's nationalist and intellectual capital. For long, she had lived a cocooned life, a world restricted to pretty bungalows set in neat gardens, tall green hedges and reassuring tree-lined avenues. Calcutta held the promise of a large, bustling city and all its potential freedom.

16
Peter

Getting Away

Darkness fell over the town as Gurmeet led his companions to a house on the outskirts. What must once have been fields and orchards now had several large houses set far apart, distanced by orchards and fields that spoke of an agrarian past. Most of these houses were owned by wealthy farmers who spent their time in the city. The mansion before which Gurmeet stood was sitting on a large tract of land dotted with large trees, with a fruit orchard directly across a rutted path. Dark and silent, the mansion loomed before them like a phantom, the moaning wind adding to its menacing air.

Weeds and dandelions grew out of the cracks in the walkway leading up to the house, which appeared ghoulish in the pale light of the half-moon. Twisted trails of vines reached towards the roof. The balustraded balconies of the upper rooms overlooked a deserted road. The house had an unlived character, cold and neglected.

Gesturing to them to remain quiet, Gurmeet rapped on the metal knocker on the massive teakwood door. There was no response, so Gurmeet continued knocking.

'Who is it?' A tremulous female voice responded at last.

'Mai, open the door, it is Gurmeet.'

Minutes passed before the door creaked open and someone peeped through the crack. Throwing the door open, a shadowy figure melted into the depths of the mansion's cavernous interior.

They stepped into a spacious courtyard surrounded by rooms on three sides. Gurmeet led them into the central hall with a high ceiling. Remnants of past glory were peeling away from the walls and mouldy stains punctuated the plaster. A heavy chandelier with a couple of broken lamps shed dull light into the gloomy room. Brooding men in turbans and pearl necklaces stared down from portraits at the visitors, swords girdled around the waist. Outside, the wind intensified and the rustling of leaves grew louder. Peter shivered.

'Who owns this place?' asked Neel, looking around.

'It belongs to a wealthy landowner sympathetic to our movement. He's generous with his donations and the mansion. The location makes it a perfect hideout for our comrades but we use it sparingly.'

Exhausted after the hazardous escape, they made themselves comfortable on dusty couches. A little later, a servant came in carrying a tray with tea in chipped china cups and a plate of hot pakoras. Soon the tea and snacks disappeared inside their rumbling stomachs.

'Are you ready to narrate your story now?' Neel asked Peter after they had finished their tea.

The idea of escaping had not deserted Peter's mind. Now that they were far away from the watchful police, he debated the possibility of fleeing the place. The menacing look on Gurmeet's face put an end to that train of thought.

'We're waiting,' he reminded Peter.

Hesitantly, the boy began narrating his story. There were no comments during the brief pauses in the narration, just a quick exchange of looks between the men.

'Do you think the police are looking for me because I killed the missionary?' Peter asked anxiously.

'Who knows?' Neel shrugged his shoulders in reply, while Gurmeet pretended to inspect his nails.

'What will happen if they arrest me?'

'What do you expect, Anglo boy? They will send you to the gallows for murder.' The Sikh's voice dripped with sarcasm.

'Can you help me?'

'That depends on the situation,' Neel replied. 'Do you have any plans?'

He had no plan. An Anglo-Indian would stick out like a sore thumb in a town full of Sikhs. It was just a matter of time before the police found him.

Peter shook his head. 'All I know is that every minute spent in Amritsar is taking me closer to being arrested.'

'Would you like to go to Calcutta? I am going there tonight and you can give me company if you like.'

'I would like to accompany you but the police are crawling all over the railway station.' Peter looked expectantly at Neel. 'Is there any way to avoid them?'

'I am sure the police are not looking for a young Sikh boy.'

Peter's surprise must have shown on his face because Gurmeet burst out laughing. 'You couldn't pass him off for a Sikh,' he hooted.

'Let us not squabble,' said Indraneel, eyes flashing at Gurmeet. 'He needs our help.' He turned to Peter and said, 'We still don't know your name.'

'I'm Peter,' he said, making a decision to forgo his earlier self. What did it matter, anyway? There was no returning to that life. His mother's family had made certain of that. Instead, he asked Neel eagerly, 'When are we leaving Amritsar?' He wanted to get away from Gurmeet. It was evident that the two young men were accustomed to pulling the wool over the police's eyes. They were not thieves or petty criminals but they were not innocent citizens either.

'Are you involved in revolutionary activities?' Peter hazarded a guess.

Gurmeet glowered at the Anglo-Indian but Neel remained impassive. Unblinking and steely, his eyes glinted coldly, the effect more daunting than the Sikh's hostility. Gurmeet was all bluster and bluff; Neel was silent and menacing. The Sikh was brawny but the Bengali was brainy and that made him more dangerous. 'It will be better for you to keep your thoughts to yourself,' Neel warned.

'Anglo boy, don't stick your nose where it doesn't belong. Do you want us to hand you over to the police?' Gurmeet added.

It was Peter's turn to play his card. 'I don't mind,' he sniggered. 'You can imagine what will happen if you take me to the police. I will share my suspicions with them and you will never walk out of the police station. Ever!'

The three of them were on a par in this game of bluff.

A blow landed on the side of Peter's head and he reeled. The boy lashed out at the Sikh and received another blow in return. This time, he fell to the ground. Peter was strong and muscular but not trained in combat. Stunned, he lay on the floor.

'Don't make the mistake of challenging Gurmeet,' advised Neel in a bored voice. 'I think he is a trained boxer and wrestler. Am I right?'

Gurmeet's silent nod confirmed the assumption.

'Not now, maybe,' mumbled Peter, wiping his bleeding nose on his shirt sleeve. 'But one day I will make him pay for this.'

'Now that you both have finished with your fisticuffs, let's talk business,' Neel intervened.

'Let us throw the thankless rascal out of the house. He deserves no help,' Gurmeet raged.

Neel raised a hand to quieten the Sikh. 'Stop squabbling, please. We will transport you safely to Calcutta,' he said to Peter. 'It is a long way from here and our journey has to begin tonight. First, you must let Gurmeet help you with the disguise.'

'Not until he apologises,' Gurmeet resisted.

'Well, I am sorry,' Peter's words belied his tone. He resented the Sikh and made no bones about it.

Gurmeet summoned the servant and gave some instructions. A little later, he led Peter towards a room on the first floor. A kurta–pyjama set and a turban lay on the bed. There was also a kirpan and *kada* to complete the get-up. Once Peter had changed into the clothes, Gurmeet tied a turban around his head and fixed a moustache on the upper lip.

It was a clever job, the boy admitted after checking his reflection in an ornate mirror hanging on the wall. He could pass off as a Sikh from a distance but the make-up wouldn't stand up to close scrutiny.

Peter emerged from the room to find a sadhu seated on a cot in the dimly lit veranda.

It took a couple of minutes for Peter to realise it was Neel. With his head wrapped in a saffron turban, a *rudraksha* necklace around his neck and a string of holy beads in his hand, the Bengali looked nothing like his former self. He had a bulging saffron bundle on his shoulder, looking every inch like the holy men who roamed around the country.

'You could pass off as a sadhu as long as you keep to the shadows,' Peter chuckled.

'You will pass off as a young Sikh if you do the same,' retorted Indraneel.

'No policeman is foolish enough to be taken in by the clothes. My complexion and eyes will give me away.'

'That is just too bad,' Gurmeet sniggered.

A servant brought them a simple fare of rotis and potato curry. Unsure of when the next meal would be, the trio ate in silence. There was tension in the air. It would not be easy to slip out of Amritsar or into Calcutta.

'When do we leave this place?' Peter's tension grew as the minutes ticked.

'All in good time. Impatience often leads people to commit blunders,' Indraneel replied laconically.

Somewhere a clock struck eleven. An owl hooted ominously in the distance, interrupting the heavy veil of silence hanging between them. Howling jackals seemed to fill the forest beyond. Peter's heart thudded against his ribcage. His tongue felt like sandpaper.

17

Indraneel

A Wedding Party

'Time to leave,' announced Indraneel. Nervousness punctured his usual composure. It would take all his ingenuity to keep away from danger. The journey was long and the hazards many.

They exited through the back door which opened onto a deserted lane. A couple of abandoned huts stood mournfully along the furrowed path. There was nothing to illuminate their path save for the flickering lights far in the distance.

The three of them slid into the shadows and waited for a couple of minutes. They had to cross a small patch of vacant land to reach the thicket of trees that lay on the other side.

They crouched behind the crumbling wall of a hut, waiting to cross the rutted path and disappear into the dense orchard. The three men stood still and listened intently. Assured no one was around, Indraneel signalled to Peter to bolt into the orchard across the path. Fear clutching his heart, he ran, ducking his head as though expecting a volley of bullets. No one shouted out, nor did anyone shoot.

A minute later, Indraneel joined him behind the trunk of a massive tree. Gurmeet was the last one to cross. He took the lead and they began moving in a single file among the trees. The dead leaves on the ground crunched under their feet. Convinced that they could be heard a mile away, Peter kept glancing back fearfully.

It was a vast orchard and they walked for a couple of miles in the darkness until they reached a wide road snaking desolately ahead. Gurmeet brought out a tiny flashlight from his pocket and directed its beam into the darkness.

'I wonder where Bhola is,' he muttered impatiently, flashing the beam once again. Minutes ticked by before they heard the tinkling of brass bells tied around bullocks' necks. With loud groans from its wooden wheels, a bullock cart made its way towards them. It drew alongside the trio and the driver clambered down. He conferred with Gurmeet for a couple of minutes before lifting the burlap covering the rear of the cart.

'Jump inside,' he instructed. Peter was the first one to get in.

Indraneel lingered. The two revolutionaries hugged each other. They did not know if they would live to see each other again.

'Jai Hind!' The Sikh raised his right arm in a salute.

'May you succeed in your mission,' responded the Bengali, getting into the cart. 'Stay safe until we meet again.'

'Don't worry,' Gurmeet chuckled. 'I will be in Calcutta sooner than you expect.'

'We will wait for you,' Neel replied.

'All the best, Anglo boy.' Gurmeet waved one last time. 'Keep out of mischief. Don't create trouble for Inder-neel.'

A few minutes later, huddled amidst sacks of wheat, they were on their way. A quarter of a moon smiled overhead as, lurching and rolling, the bullock cart went on its way. Soothed by the rhythmic rolling and the musical tinkling of the bells, Peter nodded off.

It was difficult to gauge how long they travelled hidden between dusty sacks, going over bumpy roads and dirt tracks, passing over and under bridges, crossing railway tracks. Over the next six hours, the sun travelled languorously. The bullocks seemed to grow tired and the cart stopped to rest. The driver placed a bucket of water and some hay before the animals. Indraneel and Peter left their cramped hiding spot to straighten their backs.

'If you want to eat anything, there is a village nearby,' said Bhola, the cart driver. 'You can get some food while I tend to the animals.'

Indraneel was reluctant to venture into the village. 'Since you seem to know the way around here, why don't you get some food for all of us?' He handed Bhola some money. 'I'll take care of the animals.'

Fields of mustard nodded in approval as the sun came up in its full regalia. Enchanted, Peter ran his hand on the golden flowers.

'The leaves make an excellent dish, I am told,' Indraneel commented, walking alongside. He plucked a flower and bit into it before handing one to Peter. 'The flowers taste like horseradish.' Peter took a bite and spat it out, which made Neel laugh.

It took more than an hour for Bhola to return with several rotis, jaggery and bananas. Famished after the bone-rattling journey, they ate the simple fare with relish and hit the road once again. The discomfort of travelling seemed to increase by the hour. Every bone seemed to ache as they rattled along, wishing the journey would end.

Three times they halted en route. The animals had to be provided with food and water. While Bhola tended to the bullocks, they were happy to stretch their limbs.

At last, the bullock cart deposited them at Jalandhar railway station. It had taken them many hours to travel the distance, choosing circuitous routes to avoid curious eyes. Indraneel hugged Bhola and gave him some money.

The humble cart driver folded his hands and refused the money, shaking his head determinedly. 'I am glad to have been of help. This is the least I can do for the freedom fighters.'

'The money is for your bullocks. They have travelled a long distance and should be fed properly.' Neel pressed the money into the man's calloused hands.

'May god keep you safe!' An emotional Bhola wiped his eyes with his sleeve. He patted the bullocks and the cart began moving away.

They watched the cart trundle away slowly. The tracks were empty and train engines silent when Peter and Neel walked into the railway station. Even the vendors had not laid siege to the platforms. With just a few trains scheduled to arrive or depart so early in the morning, there was a languorous air around the station.

While Peter looked around for a place to relieve his bursting bladder, Indraneel disappeared to check the timings of trains leaving for Calcutta. Groups of people huddled together on the platform, some curled up under sheets, still sleeping. Cockroaches and rats scurried around the sprawled figures, hunting for scraps of food.

At the end of the platform, a hawker was doing brisk business pouring out hot tea into earthen cups from a large aluminium kettle. Indraneel brought two cups of tea and they settled down on a bench, enjoying the syrupy, cardamom-flavoured tea. It warmed their entrails and put a smile back on their faces. Things no longer appeared as gloomy as they had seemed the previous night.

A little while later, they breakfasted on hot puris and potato curry, which they bought from another vendor.

'How far is Calcutta from here?' Peter asked, polishing off the last morsel of food.

'I guess it is about a thousand miles.'

'That is a long way off. How are we going to reach there?'

'We will take a train from here to Mughal Sarai and change to another one going to Calcutta.'

They sat in silence for a while. Peter couldn't contain his curiosity and asked, 'Indraneel, why are you helping me?'

Neel turned to look at the Anglo-Indian and smiled at him. It lit up his face and reached his eyes. 'Is it necessary for every action to have a reason? You needed help and we helped you. It is as simple as that.'

'Life has taught me that no one helps anyone without reason. I will not be comfortable till I know what you expect in return.'

'Relax! We sometimes do things without any expectations. Besides, what can you give me in return? You have no home, no money, not even an iota of patriotism. What can I expect from you?'

His words irritated the boy. 'I know I have no home and money. As for patriotism, I don't believe in it.'

'Forget it, my friend. Take it as a generous gesture of a stupid and emotional Bengali. There is no need to feel indebted.' Neel patted the boy's hand kindly. 'We have a lot of time to kill. It will be a few hours before our train arrives. If you want to go around the town, you could do so.' Neel got up and stretched his arms. 'It seems like a safe place.'

The Anglo-Indian didn't want to gallivant around town attracting attention. It was much safer to wait at the station. 'I'll wait here with you,' he said.

It was hours before a train finally arrived at the station and they scrambled towards a crowded compartment. A peasant family seated on a lower berth shifted to make room for them and there they sat for the next twelve hours, sleeping on each other's shoulders, their noses filled with the stench of sweat. A thousand miles is a long journey when one is crammed into a bogey teeming with people.

The train finally chugged into Mughal Sarai and they joined the multitude of people alighting at the station.

Indraneel led Peter towards the deserted end of the platform. Once there, he pulled the Anglo-Indian behind a freight train parked on the adjoining track. Like a magician, he conjured a change of clothes from his voluminous cloth bag.

'Get out of your clothes and put these on,' he ordered and handed a pair of dark trousers and a blue shirt to Peter. In the bag was a topi, which was usually worn both by the British and anglicised Indians. To Peter's questioning look, he replied, 'It's safer to travel in different disguises.'

By the time Peter put on the new set of clothes, Neel had changed into a pair of trousers and a shirt. Extracting a tiny vial of oil from his bag, he applied it to his hair. Then, parting it in the centre, he combed it into a sleek style. His eyes sparkled from behind a pair of wire-rimmed spectacles.

'Quite a chameleon, aren't you?' Peter chuckled.

'Bundle up your clothes and throw them into the bushes along the track,' he instructed Peter.

Comfortable in clean clothes, they bought their tickets and strolled to the other end of the platform where some people waited for the train to arrive. There must have been at least two dozen men and women in the group, with several bags scattered around them.

Indraneel struck up a conversation with an elderly man who, having perched himself comfortably on a metal box, was reading a newspaper.

'Medical student hanged for involvement in terrorist activities,' Indraneel read out the headline on the front page. 'Tch! Tch! The situation is getting from bad to worse.'

The gentleman directed his eyes towards Indraneel. 'You look like a lawyer. Do you work for the British?'

'I practise in the district court,' bluffed the revolutionary and diverted the conversation to safer grounds. 'Where is your group headed?'

'We are going for a wedding in Chandernagore. The bridegroom is my nephew.'

A little later, the women produced packets of food from large wicker baskets and passed them around.

'What a coincidence! We too are on our way to Chandernagore,' Indraneel told the man.

He noticed Peter stare at him in surprise.

'Why don't you travel in our compartment?' asked the man, introducing himself as Rameshwar Dutta. 'We will be happy to have you with us.'

'Yes, why not?' added another member of the wedding party. 'The more the merrier, I say. A wedding is an occasion to enjoy and you are most welcome to join us.'

'We were . . .' Neel pretended to hesitate.

'There's no need to hesitate. We can continue our discussion during the journey.'

'You are very kind, Sir.'

'And who is this boy?' asked Dutta, directing his attention to the sniggering boy.

'Oh, this is Peter. He is an Anglo-Indian. His father works in the post and telegraph department. The two of us are travelling together.'

'That's nice. Come, share some food with us.' The generous man thrust a platter into Neel's hands.

'Thank you, Sir. We just had our breakfast.' Peter declined the offer.

'At your age, I could polish off an entire chicken and a mound of rice,' the gentleman chuckled.

Indraneel, however, displayed no embarrassment at enjoying the food.

'This is delicious!' he said, smacking his lips with satisfaction. 'It's been a long time since I enjoyed aloo sabzi. This tastes exactly like the one my mother used to make.'

The comment caught the attention of the lady who was serving food to the group. 'Isn't your mother staying with you?' she asked, loading his plate with more food.

'She passed away,' Indraneel replied. He wondered if his mother and sister were still alive.

'Oh!' the lady laid a sympathetic hand on his arm and doled out some more food, saying, 'I am sorry.'

The discussion soon veered to politics and freedom, drawing more people into its fold. It grew more animated by the minute.

'Gandhi and only Gandhi can get us freedom,' an elderly gentleman remarked, striking his walking stick on the ground to stress his point.

'Whoever heard of fasting resulting in freedom?' a youngster sniggered. 'Building castles in the air, that's what the Congress is doing. Pompous airheads, that's all they are.'

'Do you know what the problem is with your generation? You love violence. Why shed blood when one can get freedom without it?' The old man tugged at his earlobes and shook his head.

'And the problem with your generation is that you are too laidback. Little wonder Gandhi finds favour with you,' retorted the youngster.

'Frankly speaking, no one gained freedom with heated arguments,' laughed Indraneel, taking the heat off the argument. 'All it does is raise blood pressure.'

'Well said, son!' The elderly gentleman nodded his head in approval. 'If only these boys could understand that a cool head can take us a long way.'

There was silence for a while.

'One thing I can say with certainty is that the trains are becoming more and more unreliable,' Neel remarked, glancing at his wristwatch. The topic was guaranteed to provoke passengers.

'The trains are moody and unpredictable,' opined a gentleman. 'One is lucky if they arrive a few hours late. As for reaching one's destination, I am sure even god could not predict the day or hour.'

Within moments, trains and the railways bore the brunt of everyone's ire.

'Things are getting from bad to worse,' agreed another man. 'Apart from the unpredictability, one has to deal with the discomfort, filth and stench of overcrowded train carriages.'

As if in defiance of their argument, the train chugged into the station at that very moment and a scramble ensued as passengers picked up their bags and rushed for the compartments. The men led the charge while the women followed. Neel and Peter helped with the bags and the wedding party clambered into a compartment.

Once the bags had been placed under the berths and everyone had found a place to sit, they heaved a sigh of relief and order was restored.

During the journey, they discovered common friends and kin.

'That binds us into some kind of kinship, doesn't it?' said an old man, happy to have found a connection. 'It has been years since I laid eyes on that family. The lady was barely five years old when we last met. It is nice to know you are related to her. Why don't you come for the wedding?' said Rameshwar Dutta. 'You can meet some interesting people.'

The invitation came at the crucial moment when Neel had been wondering about his next step. He needed a safe harbour and it had been offered to him on a platter. Things had fallen neatly into place.

Turning to Peter, Dutta asked, 'Peter, would you like to attend a Bengali wedding?'

'It will be an honour, Sir,' the Anglo-Indian replied politely. 'I have never attended a Bengali wedding.'

It was a delightful journey. They shared food, jokes and anecdotes, played card games and debated over many matters. Being a part of the group made them inconspicuous to curious eyes and law-enforcement agencies. Indraneel was now singing along with the menfolk, clapping his hands to keep time. Relaxed, the Anglo-Indian began enjoying himself.

18

Olivia

Finding Friends

It was love at first sight for Olivia. She fell in love with Calcutta, as well as the beautiful bungalow allotted to Major Bradley.

For the first time in many years, she even made a friend, someone who didn't care about her disfigured face. Roma Chatterjee, a classmate, belonged to a progressive family. She was unlike anyone Olivia had met. The girl had a positive outlook and a good sense of humour. They laughed, teased each other and played pranks, enjoying each other's company.

Olivia loved everything about the Chatterjee house—the warmth and closeness among the family members, Roma's mother's cooking and even the pet dog, Caesar. In Roma's mother, she found the love she had been craving all these years.

In Calcutta, Olivia discovered that life could be fun. Thanks to Roma's company, she let her hair down for the first time since her mother's death. She looked at life differently and learned to laugh without restraint. It was like shedding a drab garment for a bright one.

She breathed freely now that she was in college. It was as if the clouds had parted and the sun was finally shining. The weight of decorum fell away from her shoulders and she brightened. Each day dawned with a fresh anticipation of happiness. Olivia's father had no idea of her college friends, nor was he aware of her growing closeness to Roma's family.

Romance suddenly unfurled its wings. Olivia, who had never been exposed to youthful romance, found herself drawn into its charming circle. Her friend, Roma, was in love. The girl's dreams sparked many desires in Olivia's youthful mind. For the first time, love seemed a distinct possibility. 'Not every boy is looking for a beautiful face,' Roma assured her friend. 'There are some who look for something beyond beauty.'

'Do you think I possess something beyond beauty?' Olivia laughed. 'My friend, I appreciate your loyalty but I am painfully aware of the truth. I have not known a man to look beyond beauty.'

'Well, I know of one.'

'And may I know who that saint is?'

'The one I love. The one called Rajat. I will ask Rajat to introduce you to his friends. They are quite different from the usual youngsters,' said Roma.

Roma's words planted a seed of hope in Olivia's heart despite her misgivings.

Rajat spent long hours at the Chatterjee abode where the three young people argued and philosophised on various subjects. The large terrace of Roma's house was their refuge. Olivia enjoyed listening to Roma and Rajat debate life, college and politics. The two of them were childhood friends and their marriage was a natural outcome of the long rapport between the two families.

Rajat promised to bring his friends along but that never happened. Olivia knew better than to remind her friend about her promise. Rajat was no different from the other men. Despite the many hours they spent together, he was never able to look Olivia in the face.

In college, Olivia barely paid attention to the lectures. Instead, she absorbed the information that came at her from all directions. She read the newspapers and magazines in the library and listened to the interactions between the students. There was no escaping politics. It was the topic of discussion everywhere. There were heated debates on whether Gandhi would be successful in getting freedom for the country. There were two factions and two schools of thought. While Gandhi had his followers, it was the firebrand revolutionaries who inspired the youth. The more Olivia heard about Gandhi, the more she wanted to learn.

Calcutta was a breeding ground for revolutionary thinking. Political discourse occupied a major part of everyone's mind, as did food. But there was also music, the arts and celebrations. People devoted time to them all. Olivia loved the vibrant city and the intensity of its residents. Her father's long absences, drinking bouts and foul language didn't disturb her as much any more. They existed in a different world, a world she left behind as soon as she stepped out of the house.

19

Peter

Chandernagore

The wedding party finally reached the neoclassical-style mansion located in the suburbs of Chandernagore, and a distinguished-looking gentleman came forward to receive the guests. Grey hair parted in the centre, polished ebony walking stick in hand, the man approached them with folded hands. Behind him were two young men who bore a strong resemblance to the gentleman.

'Welcome!' he said. 'My name is Narendranath Mitra and these are my sons. I am the bride's father.'

A prosperous business owner, Mitra was well known in the neighbourhood.

The guests were led through a large hall and up a grand staircase with brass railings and shown to their rooms. The room assigned to Neel and Peter lived up to the standards of the stately mansion. With a huge four-poster bed occupying the centre, it had large doors and windows opening onto a veranda. Enchanted with the splendidly furnished bathroom, Peter wallowed in the warm-scented bathtub after many days of unwashed living.

In the evening, dressed in silk kurtas and pyjamas graciously gifted by their hosts, they joined the other guests walking towards the mandap which was swathed in strings of fresh flowers and mango leaves. Mellifluous notes of the shehnai filled the air, adding to the festive ambience.

The celebrations lasted a full week. The guests gorged on seven-course meals and dozens of sweets prepared for the nuptials, ending it all with specially made paan. Each evening, the menfolk gathered in the *baithak khana* smoking hookah, chewing on paan and discussing politics or football.

One evening, at the gathering in the baithak khana, Peter decided to sample the expensive whisky being served to the menfolk.

'So, what are your views on freedom?' asked a young man bent upon teasing the Anglo-Indian.

'I don't believe in talking about freedom and revolution,' Peter replied dismissively. He extended his glass for another peg of whisky and continued, 'They are of no relevance to me.' He had no intention of ruining his mood.

'You don't believe in freedom?' the tormentor needled. 'Being half Indian, aren't you a part of this country?'

'I don't consider myself an Indian and I am not a part of this country.' Peter quaffed some more whisky. Ignoring Indraneel's warning looks, he stood up and, pointing dramatically at his chest, asked, 'You tell me. Who am I?'

Unfazed by the shocked looks around the hall, he repeated, 'Go on, tell me.'

'You are an Anglo-Indian.' The young man was amused by his question. 'Half British and half Indian.'

'That's right. Half and half.' Peter nodded approvingly. He took another swig of the drink and resumed his rant. 'Do you know what I am called? Everyone calls me a bastard. My kin . . .' tears began flowing down his cheeks. 'My mother's family . . .' Overwhelmed with emotion, he wiped his eyes.

Indraneel walked over to the boy and placed a comforting hand on his shoulder but Peter pushed him away and continued, 'No, Sir. I am not an Indian. But I am not English either. So, what am I?'

Shaking a finger in the man's face, he said, 'We are the nowhere people.'

'Do the British see their half in you?' asked the cocky young man.

'Yes, they do. Why else would they tutor us in their language, give us jobs and treat us better than they treat the Indians?'

'Why are you in India?' shouted someone. 'Why don't you go to Britain?'

'Indians are a bigoted and divided lot. No wonder the British rule this country,' Peter continued aggressively. 'You will never get freedom.'

There was a stunned silence in the baithak khana.

'All right, Peter, these are not the people who wronged you. Let us find the ones who mistreated you and we will deal with them.' Indraneel propelled the boy out of the hall. This time, the Anglo-Indian didn't resist.

The next morning, Peter was given an earful by the revolutionary.

'You deserve to be thrown out of the mansion,' he scolded. 'How dare you abuse the host who has treated you with generosity? He has gone against the norms of society to do so. Not only did you shame him, you shamed me too.'

Mortified, Peter apologised. 'I am sorry. It was the whisky speaking. I lost control.'

'There is no point apologising to me. It is to Mitra Moshai you should apologise.'

Ashamed of his conduct, Peter did not want to face the family. An hour later, when the Anglo-Indian didn't come down for breakfast, Narendranath Mitra went up to inquire.

'I couldn't face you after my misconduct last evening.' Peter hung his head.

'It happens to the best of men,' he said, taking a seat on the couch. 'Alcohol makes us utter words we would otherwise not dream of bringing to the lips.'

'I am truly sorry for the things I said last night. Please forgive me,' begged the remorseful boy. 'It was the first time I had whisky. It loosened my tongue.'

'It's all right,' consoled the gentleman. 'We will not speak of the incident any more. Let's join the others for breakfast.'

That evening, the men congregated in the baithak khana. Leaning against a bolster, Indraneel listened to the tirade of a young man seated next to him. Peter noticed that his friend rarely got into an argument or a debate.

'I do not doubt that the British will have to leave the country,' the man was saying. 'It's just a matter of time.'

The air was thick with tobacco smoke. While some enjoyed cigarettes, others indulged themselves with the expensive cigars offered by the host. There was also hookah for the elderly.

'How long do you think it will take for such a thing to happen?' Indraneel's question put an end to the man's spiel.

'Mark my words, it is the Bengalis who will force the British to exit this country,' a seemingly meek gentleman in a spotless white kurta and neatly pleated dhoti remarked as he pushed a paan into his mouth.

'I agree,' said Rameshwar Dutta. 'Swami Vivekananda, Sri Aurobindo, Rabindranath Tagore and Bankim Chandra have all tried to awaken public consciousness.'

'Don't forget the sacrifice of Khudiram Bose and Master Da . . .' interjected a boy of about seventeen.

'Master Da is the greatest revolutionary ever born. It is people like him who can free us of foreign fetters.'

As usual, Indraneel remained a silent listener.

'What about Gandhi?' asked Peter, trying to draw Indraneel into the debate. He knew how much the man hated Gandhi. But the chameleon refused to take the bait.

'Gandhi! Tch, tch, don't begin that topic. It is best left untouched,' grunted a portly gentleman with an authoritative look on his face. 'I do not believe in Gandhi's ways. We need a revolution to bring the British to their knees. Whoever heard of attaining freedom through peaceful protests?'

'True, there is no way to drive the British out other than to fight them,' opined a dapper gentleman. 'I believe in the power of the gun; no *satyagraha* for me. All this declaration of Purna Swaraj and peaceful marches and burning foreign goods is getting us nowhere.'

'Mark my words,' another gentleman announced pompously. 'It will be the guns and not hunger strikes that will liberate us.'

Indraneel could no longer resist the urge to join the discussion. Throwing a scathing look at the gentleman, he said, 'In that case, should you not be picking up the gun instead of sitting in a baithak khana while thousands are dying for the country?'

His words shocked the wimpish gentleman who was lighting his third cigarette. 'Not everyone can take up the gun,' he mumbled.

'Why not? You just said that you believe in the power of the gun. What stops you from fighting for the country's liberation?'

'Well, there are other things that need to be done, too.'

'Things like attending wedding feasts and debating the matter in the luxurious confines of a baithak khana?'

Sensing trouble, the host intervened, 'It is all a matter of opinion and everyone is entitled to their belief. How does it matter how we attain our goal as long as we get our freedom?'

'Anyway, I have burned all the suits that I had brought from London last year,' smirked a rakish gentleman. 'And now I have taken to wearing khadi and I must say it is quite comfortable in Indian weather.'

The conversation turned to khadi and its benefits.

'I have heard that Gandhi, Nehru and Subhas Chandra Bose have their differences.' A woman's voice broke through the din.

Everyone's eyes swivelled to the young lady who had strayed into the assembly of men.

She was more beautiful than any woman Peter had ever seen. Her eyes were dark and long-lashed, her skin was a radiant velvet of smoothness and her hair a tumble of dark, curly waves. Dressed in a white sari, she wore neither jewellery nor make-up. In her hands was a tray full of sweets.

A sudden hush fell over the gathering. 'You did not have to take the trouble, Ma,' said Narendra Mitra. 'The servant could have brought the tray.'

'It is no trouble,' she said with a smile, throwing a quick look at the men lolling around in the room. 'I hope I didn't interrupt a serious discussion.'

'You did nothing of the sort,' chuckled an elderly gentleman. 'We are trying to drive away boredom and nothing works better than a heated debate.'

'I thought working your brains so hard would make you hungry and so I brought some sweets to energise you all,' she said sweetly.

Peter's hand trembled as he accepted a sondesh from the bowl on the tray. 'Good god!' she exclaimed. 'We have a firangi in our midst and you all are speaking of revolution,' she teased. 'We will soon have the police here to arrest us.'

'Oh, don't worry, he is a friend,' replied Mitra. 'Besides, our discussion cannot be called treason by any stretch of the imagination. Don't you agree, Peter?'

'Treason is a much-abused word these days,' commented the woman.

'Coming to the point you raised,' continued the old gentleman, 'I too have heard that the Congress is not thrilled with Subhas Bose's radical views.'

'Subhas Chandra Bose is a born leader. He is courageous and intelligent. The rest of the leaders merely raise slogans and mouth words for self-benefit,' said the woman.

A murmur of voices followed the statement. The wimpish gentleman was the first to protest.

'I feel that the matter of revolution is best left to men.'

Eyes blazing, she turned to him and said, 'Indeed! Why should women debate such a serious matter when brave men like you inhabit this country? Did you know that Pritilata Waddedar laid down her life for the country while you are lounging on silk cushions and opining on liberation? You have certainly heard of Kalpana Datta, Surama Mitra and Bina Das. Oh, I could go on and on. There are scores of women who have done more for the country than you could ever dream of doing.'

A slow blush suffused the gentleman's face as everyone broke into a peal of laughter.

'Talking about freedom while reclining drunkenly on silk cushions will never bring freedom to this country.' Throwing a contemptuous look at him, she exited the room.

'Is she a revolutionary?' asked Peter, his eyes following the departing woman.

'Of course not,' Narendranath laughed. 'Devyani is the daughter of my eldest brother. She is a child widow and an educated one at that.'

A widow already! Peter was stunned. That explained her white attire and absence of jewellery. She couldn't have been more than sixteen years old. But she didn't look like a widow. He knew Bengali widows were forced to shave their heads and live in seclusion. They were not allowed to attend auspicious events like marriages either.

'My brother is a liberal man and Devyani is the apple of his eye,' Mitra explained in reply to Peter's unspoken query. 'He does not want the girl to be treated like a typical widow.' Narendranath shook his head.

Devyani's words had left an impact on the gentlemen in the baithak khana. There was silence after she left the room, and no one spoke of politics or the freedom struggle. It was as though the men had reached an agreement to avoid controversial matters.

The forced effort to lighten the atmosphere wasn't very successful until Heerabai made an appearance. Dressed in a bright royal-blue silk lehenga over a pair of tight red pyjamas and a sheer *odhni* of embroidered gold gauze, her hands and feet hennaed and lips painted a bright red, she sashayed into the room.

Peter was not the only one unable to tear his eyes away from the woman. She was sensational.

Flanked by her musicians, Heerabai settled in the centre of the room and began to sing. Strong and melodious, her voice rang around the baithak khana, drawing murmurs of appreciation from the audience.

It was past midnight by the time she ended the performance with a scintillating dance. It was much later that Peter learned the woman's role in the freedom struggle. Heerabai was much more than a *nautch* girl. She was an informer and operated as a messenger for freedom fighters.

20

Indraneel

Calcutta

The wedding festivities concluded and Indraneel and Peter were ready to depart for Calcutta carrying baskets laden with food from their generous hosts.

'Let this not be your last visit,' said Narendranath Mitra as he hugged Indraneel. 'Think of me as an eccentric uncle who loves visitors.'

Indraneel bent to touch the gentleman's feet, promising to visit as often as possible. 'Don't offer unconditional hospitality,' he joked. 'I am a shameless sponger. You won't be able to get rid of me.'

'I love entertaining spongers,' laughed the host. 'And I have no wish to rid myself of them.'

Most of the wedding guests had already departed, leaving a vacuum in the large mansion. The mirth, laughter and merriment had ended. Indraneel had grown fairly close to the Mitra family in the past forty-eight hours. In those two days, he had spent some time with Devyani as well, discussing political events. She was a woman of substance, quite different from the ones he had met in college and elsewhere. Her uninhibited laughter sounded like a gurgling stream, unrestrained and free. She was malleable as quicksilver, serious one moment and sparkling the next. The two were now thick as thieves.

The intense chemistry between Devyani and Neel didn't escape Peter's keen eyes.

Girish, the youngest son of Narendranath Mitra, offered to drop them off at the ghat from where they could take a boat to Calcutta.

'Being the youngest, I have inherited the worst automobile in the family. The only thing I can promise is that the car won't let us down,' the young man joked as he turned the ignition on and the car obliged with a jerky movement.

'I think it is an impressive car,' said Indraneel, running his hands on the dashboard of the old Chevrolet Master Phaeton.

'Well, it moves, so it is an automobile,' quipped Girish as he drove the jalopy, pointing out the landmarks en route. Chandernagore, a French enclave, was a thorn in the Britishers' flesh. Long before the English set up shop and took over the reins of Calcutta, the French had established a trading port at Chandernagore, reaping profits from indigo, jute, saltpetre and rice. The confluence of French and Indian architecture was visible prominently in the structures around town.

'Next time, I promise to take you on an excursion around town,' Girish said as he dropped them off at the ferry.

Promising to visit soon, Neel bid goodbye to the effervescent young man.

'Where do you intend to go after we reach Calcutta?' Peter asked as the ferry made its way to the city. 'I should say goodbye to you.'

Leaning against the railing on the deck, Indraneel stared pensively at the rippling waves of the river. 'Are you tired of my company, Peter?' he asked. 'I thought you had nowhere to go.'

'You are right, Neel. I have nowhere to go. Isn't it strange? All these years, I dreamed of being free from all restrictions and the watchful eyes of the Irish Brothers and now I don't know where to go. But I cannot be a burden on you any longer.'

Neel raised an eyebrow quizzically and stared at the boy. It seemed as if the boy was afraid to be spotted with a revolutionary.

'So be it,' muttered the Bengali as he went back to gazing thoughtfully at the lapping waves.

He had hoped that over the past few days, living with Indians at Chandernagore, Peter would alter his views.

The boat reached Calcutta and they joined the crowd of people spilling out of the ferry station. Indraneel gave away the baskets of food to a beggar. 'They need it more than us, Anglo boy,' he said in response to Peter's unspoken question. 'Have you been to Calcutta before?' He cleaned his glasses with a handkerchief. 'It's a large city. I hope you realise that.'

'Oh, don't worry about me,' Peter replied flippantly. 'I know there are over thirty thousand Anglos in Calcutta. Surely one more wouldn't matter to anyone.' He laughed.

Neel knew it would be tough for the young man to survive with no money, shelter or acquaintances in the city, yet he continued to bluster.

Calcutta was teeming with people. The wide roads, criss-crossing electric trams, surging rickshaw wallahs with their hand-pulled contraptions, confusing traffic and loud vendors could have a dizzying effect on a newcomer. Neel could see the enormity of his decision strike Peter as he stepped into the chaos. He had lived a protected life at the orphanage. Amritsar, with its busy market and large population, had daunted him but Calcutta was in a different league altogether.

Peter's bravado seemed to drain away as the two of them walked along the road.

'I have lived in an army cantonment for the first few years of my life, so I am familiar with cantonments. Maybe I should go where the army is garrisoned,' Peter blabbered.

Indraneel was curious to see how the boy would fare by himself. 'You'll have to go to Fort William for that. But what will you do there?'

'I could get a job as a servant with one of the officers.'

'There are thousands of unemployed boys loitering in the city. People can't just walk into the fort and get jobs. Let us get something to eat and then we can discuss the next step.'

The relief was visible on Peter's face. Neel had given him time to take stock of his surroundings and reflect upon his future.

They walked through a residential area with labyrinthine lanes flanked by houses that seemed to crowd into each other. An hour later, the two of them sat on the floor of a tiny eatery in a narrow alley off Bowbazar, enjoying a meal of rice and fish curry. Wrapped in their thoughts, they ate in silence. Indraneel had always been a good judge of character and he could see now that Peter's fears had turned into a conviction. The boy wouldn't survive the city without his help.

21

Peter

A Taste of Calcutta and Beyond

After the satisfying meal, Indraneel led Peter through a maze of narrow lanes. Scores of tiny shops crowded the lanes, which were rendered almost impassable with ear cleaners, food vendors and fish, meat and vegetable sellers who had set up their shops on both sides while open nullahs overflowed with garbage on either side of the lane. There were shoemakers, dentists, tailors and traders plying their trade from little cubbyholes. They were all talking at the top of their voices in a dialect he had never heard.

'What is the name of this place?' Peter was exhausted by the never-ending walk. He felt nauseated by the strange smell around him.

'This is Tangra, the China Town of Calcutta.'

'Why are we here?'

'You will know soon enough.' As usual, Indraneel was his reticent self.

They skirted the shanties and rickshaws. The lanes carried the distinctive smell of Chinese food and life. Narrow and dark even in the daytime, the streets buzzed with activity.

Stepping across an open drain, Indraneel halted before a tiny shop selling dried herbs and animal parts. A wizened man sat behind a counter, with a pair of round-framed glasses perched on his snub nose.

'Ni Hao, Neel Babu,' he greeted, waving a hand for them to come closer.

'Ni Hao, Xiang,' replied Neel.

'You have not come here for a long time,' complained the Chinese.

'I was away, Xiang. How are the missus and the grandchildren?'

'Ah, the missus is as garrulous as ever and the grandchildren annoying as always,' responded the Chinese, flashing a gummy smile at them.

'This is my friend, Peter. Please look after him if he needs help.'

'Englishman?' The old codger directed his unblinking eyes at the boy.

'No, Xiang, he is an Anglo-Indian.'

'Same thing. I don't like this.'

'Peter is a nice boy,' Indraneel insisted. His eyes twinkling mischievously, he added, 'He will not chase your girls.'

Xiang guffawed at his comment. 'Young men always chase girls. Peter is no different.'

'No Xiang, Peter is different. He is an orphan. No family.'

The information seemed to touch the old man.

'That's too bad! You come to Xiang when you get in trouble.' He said after subjecting the boy to prolonged scrutiny.

Thanking the old man, Neel led the boy towards another lane.

'You will find the best Chinese food in these alleys and if you are looking for opium, you could find it in these little opium dens.' Neel circumvented a rickshaw puller who was heading straight towards them. 'I love this place because the British rarely venture into these streets,' he continued. 'They hate the filth and the smell. I suspect they haven't developed a taste for Chinese food, either.'

Indraneel waved at a young man and pinched the cheek of a fat toddler who crossed their path. By now, Peter knew enough of him to realise that the chameleon did nothing without reason.

'If ever you are in trouble, this is the best place to seek refuge,' Neel finally said. 'The Chinese don't entertain strangers. Neither do they make friends easily. Now that I have introduced you to Xiang, you can depend on him for help.'

At last Peter realised the purpose of the tour. 'Thank you, but I can do without Xiang's help.'

'One never knows when one may need help,' was Neel's cryptic reply. 'And now, I will take you to Fort William.'

Minutes later, Peter took his first tram ride with Indraneel pointing out the landmarks.

Soon they were standing near Fort William.

The fort differed vastly from what Peter had imagined. Stern-faced, gun-toting soldiers guarding the barricaded gate were checking everyone's identity before allowing them through. Those without an identity card were lined up on one side.

How will I enter the fort? What will I tell the guards? Peter swallowed the lump in his throat.

His courage failed him and he walked back to where Neel was waiting. 'Can I stay with you for a couple of days till I find a way to enter the fort?'

A smile played on the Bengali's lips. It appeared as though he had been expecting such an outcome.

As a young boy, Peter had been reassured by his mother that his fair skin and grey eyes did not mean he was any less Indian. She had taught him all about the Indian gods and goddesses. But his time with the Irish Brothers had left him confused about his identity. *You are more Anglo than Indian,* they had said. *The natives are inferior to you. Always remember that.* They had discouraged the stories of demigods and demons and instead insisted that Peter and the other orphans adopt Christianity. The years of indoctrination had left him jaded, wary of Indians and the British alike.

However, that day, as the boy stood near the fort, all his misgivings evaporated in a trice. The crazy Bengali seemed far superior in thought and deed to any White man he had ever known. Suddenly, the guards patrolling the fort grew hazy as tears stung his eyes. He meekly followed the man who had repeatedly come to his rescue, not once demanding his pound of flesh.

It was dark by the time they reached a tiny two-room house in one of the poorer parts of the city. Indraneel knocked three times on the door and waited. A few minutes later, the door was opened by a frail widow. Neel touched her feet and she drew him into an embrace.

'It's been long,' she said. 'Let me look at you.' The lady held him at an arm's distance and nodded. 'You look good.'

'I had to go out of the city for some time.' Neel gave her a disarming smile and continued, 'Mashima, this is Peter. We need a place to stay.'

It was as simple as that. No explanations as to how long they would stay. The woman did not seem to need any.

'The two of you are welcome to stay as long as you wish. You must be tired and hungry. Let me bring you something to eat,' the woman said, spreading a mat on the floor.

Indraneel seemed at home. He sat on the floor and hummed to himself while Peter looked around the tiny room. Plaster was peeling off the walls. Save for a bed and chair, there was no furniture. He paused before a garlanded photograph on the wall.

'Mashima's husband was the founder-editor of a newspaper. He was jailed for sedition,' Neel informed. 'The unfortunate man died soon after his release. This is now a safe house for revolutionaries. We can't stay here for long, so we will leave for Medinipore as soon as possible'.

The two of them stayed there for a couple of days. Neel sneaked out for a few hours every evening, leaving Peter by himself.

'We have to leave tomorrow,' announced Neel, one night. 'It is not safe to stay here for long.'

'But, where will we go?' asked Peter.

'You ask too many questions.' Neel snapped.

Early next morning, setting aside some money for the journey, Neel placed all he had next to the widow's deities and the two men stole out of the house. The city had just started stirring as they began their journey towards Medinipore.

'How do you survive? Where do you find the money to eat and travel?' Peter asked as the train chugged towards their destination.

'We have many benefactors. Hundreds of businessmen, zamindars, landed gentry and high-ranking people all over the country donate money to the cause.'

There was so much he didn't know, Peter realised. He had been looking at India through a pair of coloured glasses provided by the Irish Brothers.

The train was not very crowded and the journey to Medinipore was not too long. It was noon by the time a tonga transported them to the sprawling mansion of the local zamindar, Madhusudan Chowdhury, one of Indraneel's maternal uncles. A long driveway fringed with ornamental trees led to a double-storeyed mansion that loomed majestically.

'My uncle is a rich man,' remarked Indraneel, amused by the awe in Peter's eyes.

'It is nice to live in such luxurious settings.' Peter rubbed his hands with eagerness. It would be a repeat of the good times spent in Chandernagore. The days spent in the poor woman's cramped quarters had been far from comfortable.

The grand hall with polished wooden beams and marble floors was decorated with magnificently carved Chinese furniture and Belgian mirrors. An impressive Venetian chandelier hung from the centre of the ceiling. Velvet curtains held with golden silk tassels, marble pedestals with bronze statuettes on them, crystal vases, tiger skins, grandfather clocks, ornate decorative pieces—it was an opulent setting.

'All these things were not bought in a day. Everything you see here was collected over three generations,' Indraneel informed the boy. 'Some of the expensive things are heirlooms.'

Soon Peter discovered that the house had umpteen rooms, dozens of residents and servants, and yet old Madhusudan Chowdhury was a lonely man.

With two of his sons studying in England and his daughters married off, he had a brood of relatives trooping in and out of the mansion. An army of servants and his ailing wife occupied the ground floor of the mansion. The house was a welcome haven for more than a few poor relations who lived on his charity. With the ownership of vast fields, orchards and property, Madhusudan had enough money to feed all of them. Scores of farmers laboured in the fields to harvest enough grain and fruit to feed the relatives who, more often than not, were parasites.

Neel and Peter were allotted a room in a corner of the first floor. The room, with its windows looking out onto the fields, was comfortable but not extravagant. Two beds occupied opposite sides of the room, with a few chairs arranged in the centre. There was a massive wooden almirah to hold their few clothes.

After a couple of days of idleness, during which they did nothing but eat, drink and enjoy long walks around the mansion, Indraneel took the Anglo-Indian to survey the fields. It was the sowing season for paddy and work was on in full swing.

'This is where we can make ourselves useful. We must help the farmers in whatever way we can,' he suggested.

'Why should we do that?' asked Peter, the idea of toiling suddenly repugnant. 'Your uncle can afford to employ labourers.'

'Didn't you promise to earn your keep?' Neel asked sternly. 'Don't go back on your word.'

'I am not going back on my word. When you said I would have to earn my keep, I did not know your uncle was so rich.'

'My uncle's wealth is no reason for laziness. Everyone must work for a living. A person who lives off others is a parasite. Do you want to be called a parasite?'

'Could you stop being nasty?' Peter protested.

'All right, do you have any plans? You can't just move around like a rudderless ship. An entire life lies before you,' said Indraneel as they walked through the field.

'I have heard that the British have reserved jobs for Anglo-Indians and one doesn't need to be highly qualified to get them.'

'For instance?'

'I could get a job as a railway engine driver or a guard or work in the postal department or join the military.'

'It's not as easy as you think. Besides, the British won't be here forever.'

'They don't seem to be going anywhere any time soon,' Peter countered.

'You will be surprised,' he said. 'India may become independent before long. Even the Anglo-Indians, who are the wheels, the cranks, the levers of the British machinery, won't be able to stop it from happening.'

'Why do you insist on clubbing me with the other Anglo-Indians? I am an orphan with no knowledge of the behaviour of other Anglo-Indians.'

'Have you not a drop of patriotism in your veins, Peter?'

Neel's homily angered the boy. He halted in his tracks and faced the Bengali.

'Patriotism? That's just a hollow word used by those who have no other purpose in life,' Peter snorted derisively. 'You don't have to worry about your next meal and so you think of words like country, patriotism, freedom. Ask the poor who can't manage two square meals a day and they will tell you that the word means nothing to them. Empty bellies can't be filled with words and sermons.'

'Bravo!' Neel clapped his hands. 'You are an opportunist who changes sides to suit himself.'

'You may call it opportunism but it's about identity. You are fighting to protect your identity and I am still struggling to discover mine. The day I find it, who knows, I might join your battle. As for your revolutionary activities, I feel it is futile to fight with crude weapons against a disciplined army.'

'Have you heard of David and Goliath, Peter?'

'Don't give me that crap about David and Goliath. It is a fable, and this is real life.' Peter was in no mood to relent.

'Don't lecture me about life. I have experienced enough tragedy to last a lifetime.' Neel took out a crumpled packet of cigarettes from his pocket and lit one. The tremble in his hands as he lit the cigarette gave away his emotions.

'Let me tell you why I believe in David.'

Reclining against the thick trunk of a tree, Indraneel narrated the story of his life. The sun had set quite some time back. Even the birds roosting in the trees had fallen silent. The croaking of a few frogs was the only sound around them. In the distance, a jackal howled ominously. The river flowed gently, unmoved by the tales of deprivation and misery.

The contradiction in Indraneel's personality continued to puzzle Peter. *Is he a cold and calculating nationalist or a sentimental Bengali?* Neel would speak about politics, freedom and friends. He recited Rabindranath Tagore's poetry, sang Nazrul's compositions and spoke of his love for literature but couldn't help being sarcastic about Anglo-Indians.

'You are a selfish lot,' Neel remarked one evening. 'You kowtow to the British to lead a comfortable life, so you don't want the country to be rid of them.'

'The freedom fighters are a supercilious lot,' Peter retorted. 'They wear a halo around their head and think themselves superior. Lobbing bombs does not make you a saint.'

Although the boy respected the Bengali's warmth and compassion, his arguments for freedom didn't find favour with him.

The relationship between the two swung like a pendulum and the equilibrium shifted as Indraneel distanced himself from the

Anglo-Indian. This disturbed Peter. Over time, he had anchored himself to the Bengali and looked to him for direction.

Weeks slipped by and the season changed. Summer gave way to moody monsoon and unexpected torrents of rain washed the fields, but the distance between the Anglo-Indian and the Bengali didn't reduce.

They were insulated from the disturbing events that were taking place elsewhere in the country. Spoilt by the comfortable life in Medinipore, Peter had no wish to involve himself with distressing and unpleasant happenings. He kept busy recording the animal feed delivered to the storehouse.

Neel spent long hours in the zamindar's office going over the land accounts and managing the financial aspects of the household. Although there was an old *munshi* who looked after the accounts, the revolutionary's interest in the financial affairs of the estate pleased his uncle.

A thunderstorm woke Peter one night. A torrential downpour lashed the mansion, pelting the roof like a hail of bullets. He rushed to close the window which was slapping wildly against the frame when he saw that Neel was missing.

Wondering where he had disappeared to, Peter went back to bed but found it impossible to fall asleep. An hour later, when the rain stopped and all was silent, he heard the sound of footsteps. Were thieves on the prowl or was it a police raid? Midnight raids were not uncommon in the country, nor were armed burglaries. An alarmed Peter emerged from the room to investigate.

As he walked across the passage, Peter noticed light streaming from under the door of one of the rooms. Curious, he crept closer to the locked door and peeked through the keyhole. There were eight people seated on the floor. To his surprise, Neel and Gurmeet were among them.

Pressing his ear to the keyhole, Peter tried to listen. At first, all he heard was a buzz of voices. Then, as his ears got used to the sounds, he caught snatches of the conversation taking place in the room.

Twice, Peter heard Gurmeet ask 'When?'

'There's no delay,' the Sikh said.

A few words reached Peter's straining ears.

'Saturday, at five in the evening . . .' the rest of the words were lost.

'Gun . . . after the assassination . . . safe house.'

Peter had no doubt that the men belonged to the revolutionary groups operating around Medinipore. The reason for Indraneel's presence in the town was suddenly clear to the boy. They were planning an attack on the British. Nothing Neel did was unplanned.

That night, Peter decided it was time to leave Medinipore. There was no point in remaining in a house that could be raided by the police at any moment. He could not afford to get involved with the revolutionaries or be arrested.

The next morning, immediately after breakfast, he announced his decision to return to Calcutta. Neel did not question him. All he said was, 'Let me know if you need help.'

'Do I have an option?' replied Peter, his eyes twinkling. 'There is no one else in the world for me.'

And then, Neel dropped a bombshell.

'There is good news for you. Gurmeet discovered that Barry Collins is alive. So you don't have to be worried about the police any more. You are a free man, Peter.'

Stunned at first, and then overjoyed, Peter hugged the man. 'Thank you, Neel. I am free!' he shouted. 'I don't have to live in fear any more.'

'All the best, Anglo boy. Try to stay free.'

As the train moved towards Calcutta, the boy mulled over the rush of events that had taken place over the past six months. His life had changed forever.

The time spent with Indraneel had given him a new lease of life. Despite the differences in their opinions, Peter respected the chameleon's mission. He had seen the generous side of the Bengali's personality. Neel could be cold, calculating and dangerous but his human values were intact. He was a balanced and intelligent person with a compassionate nature.

Perhaps, in his shoes, I would have made the same choices in life.

Despite an intention to stay clear of the revolutionaries, Peter sympathised with the young men who thought they could win freedom with a few rudimentary weapons, an attitude of optimism and unwavering dedication.

Looking back, he realised he had come a long way from being the unsure orphan back in Pathankot. It seemed like a lifetime since he escaped from the orphanage. The last few months had been tumultuous. They had taught him more lessons than a score of books. He felt like an old man trapped in a young body.

Back in Calcutta, Peter made his way to Fort William. On his previous visit, fear had fettered his feet but this time there was nothing holding him back. He had not murdered Barry Collins.

What he needed immediately was a roof over his head. With just the two rupees Neel had given him, it was impossible to find food and shelter. All these months, the boy had allowed his life to meander along as dictated by destiny. It was time to take charge. Living with Neel had taught him two things. One was to spot an opportunity and the other was to adapt to any situation.

Peter didn't know of a way to enter the fort and find a job but that didn't dampen his enthusiasm. After a brief spell of rain, the sun came out and the day turned clammy. Sitting in the shade of a large mango tree across from the fort, Peter contemplated his next step. Soon, lulled into a quiet lassitude, he nodded off until the drone of voices woke him up. He saw two men in uniform.

An intelligent person can learn a lot by eavesdropping, he had once been told by Neel. He strained his ears and picked up scraps of information that were to change his life.

'You had promised to find a helper within two days,' one of the men berated the other. 'It is now three days and there is a party in the officers' mess tomorrow. What am I to do now?'

'I tried,' said the other man earnestly. 'Honestly, Ismail, I did. But the chap let me down at the last moment.'

'Just my luck. Isn't there anyone else to take up the job? I want a reliable person, not someone who will disappear leaving me in the lurch.'

'Let me see what I can do.'

'Find me a *masalchi* by this evening,' warned the man called Ismail.

Hurrah! Peter wanted to shout. As soon as the two men left, Peter ambled up to one of the gates and tried to walk past the guards. The sentry shot him a suspicious look and shouted, 'Where do you think you're going? Show me your identity card.'

'I am to be the new masalchi in the officers' mess,' lied the boy. 'Please direct me to the mess.'

'I have no orders to let you in.'

'Well, I have been summoned by Ismail. There is a party in the officers' mess tomorrow and he needs a masalchi urgently,' Peter bluffed, hoping Ismail was important enough to recruit kitchen staff.

'Since when have *kaccha bacchas* started working as masalchis?' grumbled the sentry.

The insult didn't faze Peter. By this point in his life, he had heard all the derogatory terms there were for Anglo-Indians. His concerns were more immediate. *Would the guard check with the officers' mess?* Peter hid his sweaty hands behind his back and waited.

After a brief hesitation, the guard consulted his senior. There was a long moment of suspense as the senior scrutinised the boy. Although he was quivering with anxiety, Peter forced himself to meet the soldier's eye. A few heart-stopping moments later, the guards waved him in.

Within the next half-hour, he was standing before the head cook, having bagged the job. The interview was the briefest ever. Desperate for a helping hand, the cook ignored the lack of references. The previous masalchi had suddenly upped and left. With a party the next day, the cook was willing to recruit anyone who could do the job.

When asked if he had ever worked as a masalchi, Peter had no qualms about lying. A large stone grinder, a mammoth chopping board and a set of knives were assigned to him by Ismail. With no idea about the job, the boy stood gaping at the assortment of knives. He had never worked in a kitchen before.

Ismail, the head cook, proved to be a short-tempered and much-harassed man. His vast bulk restricted his movements, so he relied on Peter's quick feet to take care of errands. As a result, the boy was at the cook's beck and call throughout the day. His sharp wit made up for his slow hands. Although he couldn't chop to save his life, Peter's rippling muscles proved to be an asset while grinding the spices needed to prepare the special dishes. With curries, koftas, biryani, cutlets and desserts, the kitchen smelled of delicious food throughout the day and Peter enjoyed the perquisites of the new job.

Although Ismail's temper was on a short leash, he was a generous man. He fed the boy like his kin. Peter was given a cot in the corner of one of the barracks. The job was temporary but that didn't bother Peter—he had learned to live from day to day.

One fine morning, an excellent opportunity emerged out of the blue. Rashid, a bearer, had taken off suddenly to another city in pursuit of his lady love.

'The rascal knew we are short of help, yet he disappeared without permission.' Ismail was livid when he learned of Rashid's misconduct. 'He won't get his job back, that's for sure! The sahibs here are very strict.'

Rashid's job fell into Peter's lap. The timing was perfect. Nothing could have been more suitable. Handsome in a bearer's uniform, he stood proudly before a mirror. Rashid never returned and Peter continued to work as a bearer. It was a good job with a smart uniform, plenty of food and decent wages.

The officers' mess in Fort William was a haven for the bachelors. It also hosted married officers who wanted to play cards or billiards. Riotous dinner nights were very common and the parties would go on till three in the morning.

It was Peter's job to serve the officers. They kept him on the run between the kitchen and the lounge from the moment they trooped in.

Peter was quick on his feet. His smiling face and bright eyes drew a lot of attention and tips from the officers. He could crack jokes and make them laugh, lay a table to perfection and serve with a flourish. Some of the officers joked with him and others made jokes about his mixed blood. Most officers called him eight-anna or kaccha baccha.

Witticism became a part of his survival kit.

Peter had food in his belly and a place to rest his head at night but there was a gnawing emptiness in his heart. He would never be more than an eight-anna who could be kicked around and mistreated. His white skin and grey–green eyes didn't make life easier.

The acceptance he was seeking eluded him. A good life had once meant satisfying meals, a comfortable bed and some clothes. These came with the job but what he truly craved—acceptance—would never come.

It was an old server who introduced Peter to cocktails. The wizened man was addicted to alcohol and made his cocktail by collecting the remnants of drinks in glasses. Each drop counted. A little gin, a little vodka, a little rum and a little whisky—he made himself merry on the concoction.

'Try it, son,' he goaded one night. 'It is the only antidote to every problem in life.'

Peter took a sip and gagged. It tasted horrible.

'It always tastes bad the first time,' cackled the chap.

He was right. Soon the boy looked forward to their drinking sessions. When there was not enough left in the glasses, the two of them poured water into the empty alcohol bottles to get their fix.

Peter felt lightheaded after a few sips, carefree after some more. With half a glass came a feeling of invincibility. Comfortable in his job and surroundings, he no longer thought of Indraneel.

PART TWO: 1936–44

The year was 1936, a leap year. It was also a year of turbulent events that would shake the world. Adolf Hitler was on a roll. Britain and Italy, who had pledged help to France, did nothing to stop the German troops from entering the demilitarised Rhineland. The horrific Great Purge, a brainchild of the dictator Stalin, had begun in the Soviet Union. Millions of people were executed or sent to labour camps in Siberia. In Italy, Mussolini proclaimed the creation of a Rome–Berlin axis.

The British had promulgated the Government of India Act of 1935 which introduced provincial autonomy and, for the first time, direct elections were allowed. This had far-reaching repercussions. As expected, the Congress party rejected the Act, but a few positive changes took place. The dissenting voices found sympathetic ears. Many political prisoners were released and some civil liberties were recognised. A Federal Court was also established. It was the beginning of the end of British rule in India.

In the midst of all the turmoil, King George V had died, making way for his eldest son.

India now had a new emperor.

22

Olivia

Some Good and Some Bad

Olivia felt as if she were straddling two worlds, each distinct from the other. There was the world outside her home, where she smiled, joked, shopped and behaved like girls her age. Her senses came alive, absorbing the beauty of myriad colours, sights, sounds and smells. It was a world full of sunshine. And then there was the world inside her home, one she didn't want to inhabit. Dark, gloomy and depressing, it was a world filled with dark memories and silence.

At Roma's house, she found love and freedom. For those few hours, she forgot her miseries and losses. Each day, she dragged her reluctant feet towards the Bradley bungalow, wishing she didn't have to return home.

The house was large enough to keep her out of her father's way. Her father had taken to drinking throughout the evening and the rare dinners they used to share were now rarer. Olivia dreaded the nights when he went on a crockery-breaking spree in a drunken rage, leaving the servants to gather the shards of broken plates while she gathered the shards of her shattered life. On such nights, her father skipped his dinner and had to be carried to bed.

The Christmas celebrations had ended with a grand welcome to the New Year. In the cantonment, no one was in the mood to stop merrymaking. The gala nights, balls, picnics and parties continued unabated. Notwithstanding the unpleasant incidents of rebellion, all was well with the British residents in Calcutta. And then, the tragic news of a royal death brought to a halt all celebrations in the city. King George V had died in London. The loyal subjects of His Imperial Majesty went into mourning and an ominous silence spread over the cantonment.

Schools and colleges expressed their solidarity with the rulers by declaring a holiday. For Olivia, it was a day to make merry. She spent the day in Roma's house, where Mrs Chatterjee prepared her favourite fish curry and payesh. A few of their college friends had dropped in for tea. The discussions centred on revolutionary activities in their college. There had been a meeting of the radical elements a couple of days ago and when the police stormed the hostel later, they found incendiary pamphlets and took the boys into custody. The arrests had led to protests and violence on the campus.

'This couldn't have happened without inside information,' said Roma's friend.

'True! The police had no way of knowing who was involved in the recent meeting,' said Roma.

Although Olivia had nothing to contribute to the discussion, she enjoyed listening to the many views. The boys spoke of the growing disenchantment with the British. There was optimism and dejection in equal measure. The animated debate was fuelled by hope, energy and platefuls of snacks. Olivia lost track of time until the servant switched on the lights.

It was late by the time she returned home. She was about to walk into her room when her father's voice arrested her steps. He was sitting in one corner of the long veranda with a drink in his hand.

'Where have you been? And don't even think of lying. I know your college was shut today.' His harsh voice rang down the corridor. He rose from his seat and staggered towards Olivia.

She was unprepared for the slap that landed on her cheek. With a sob, she fled to her room and threw herself down on the bed.

'I know you are up to no good. You owe me an explanation,' shouted her father, lurching into the room.

Olivia didn't know what gave her the courage but she stood up and faced him. Her voice steely and steady, she asked, 'Have I ever asked you for explanations? Have I ever complained about your drinking? Why do I owe you an explanation when you owe me none?'

Bradley was not an easy man to shock but he was taken aback by his meek daughter's sudden transformation. He couldn't remember a single time she had talked back to him.

'Yes, I have faulted in my duty as a father.' He lowered his head contritely. 'You are a young woman and have every right to blame me for negligence.'

His words failed to provoke Olivia. Frustrated, he continued, 'I intend to make up for the lapse. It's time to think of your marriage.' He smiled cunningly. This was his trump card. 'In fact, I have an officer in mind.'

Olivia was dumbfounded. Her father's words echoed unpleasantly in her head. 'You have found a husband for me?' She stared at her father in disbelief. Till that moment, she hadn't realised how much she had come to hate him.

'Yes! My colleague.'

Even before he uttered the name, Olivia knew the officer her father wanted her to marry. A widower with an eight-year-old daughter, the Major, her father's drinking partner, was a debauch. 'How could you?' She spat out the words.

'What's wrong with him? He's an up-and-coming officer and earns well. He can keep you in comfort. Besides, he is the only one who doesn't care about your pockmarked face.'

Olivia had heard rumours about the officer and his search for a bride. Her shoulders straightened; she faced her father. 'I would rather die than marry that drunkard,' Olivia warned. 'You have caused me enough grief, but I won't allow you to add to my misery.'

Bradley stepped back, as though slapped. 'By God! I will find a way to cow you down,' he threatened before walking out of the room.

That night, Olivia stole a bottle of whisky from her father's bar. She locked her room and let the tears fall. The grief she had dammed for years broke loose. She cried for the mother she had lost. She cried for her innocent little brother. She cried about the unfair treatment destiny had dealt her. She cried till her brain was numb and her heart was empty of all pain.

23
Peter

A Trip to Chandernagore

A year had passed since Peter had come to Fort William. He had a cushy job, ample food and a roof over his head. But he was growing restless. Among the British officers, he felt the Indian side of his identity start to assert itself. In an effort to build connections, he wanted to reach out to Neel but was unable to locate him in the bustle of the city.

He also could not stop thinking about Devyani, the child widow who had enchanted him that long-ago evening in Chandernagore. Determined to seek out an adventure and a change of pace, Peter took a day's leave and caught the ferry to Chandernagore. During his brief stay at the Mitra mansion, he had made friends with the entire family. It was a large joint family with innumerable aunts, uncles, nephews and nieces. He was sure they would be happy to see him again.

Just as Peter had expected, the family was delighted to see him. Narendranath Mitra was his usual affable self. 'Where did you disappear to, young man?' he inquired, embracing the Anglo-Indian. 'We were wondering if you'd landed in prison along with the other revolutionaries.'

'I am working at the officers' mess in Fort William,' Peter admitted. He was embarrassed to confess he worked for the host's enemy. Mitra, however, displayed no surprise.

'That is smart. There is no point in going to prison if you can remain at liberty. You are going to stay with us for a few days, I hope,' he said, drawing on his hookah.

'Thank you very much for your invitation but I can only stay a night. I am on duty tomorrow.'

After dinner, the men gathered in the baithak khana. Feeling languorous after the heavy meal and paan, Peter reclined on a silken bolster. The discussion, as usual, revolved around the latest arrests. A couple of hot-blooded young men deliberated on how they could help the freedom fighters.

'This young man can help us since he's working for the goras right inside their bastion,' said a bespectacled man.

Several eyes settled on Peter. They were curious to see his reaction to the suggestion.

Peter had no desire to get caught in the maelstrom of nationalism just when things were looking up for him.

Narendranath Mitra, realising his dilemma, came to Peter's defence. 'There is no point in involving a person who doesn't want to be caught up in your movement.'

Sarcastic comments followed Mitra's statement. 'Yes, of course. Why would Peter want to be a part of the movement?'

'One should have the wisdom to spot which side of the bread is buttered.'

Peter blushed with embarrassment.

The host came to his rescue. 'Peter is a guest. It will be good if you can remember that.'

Chastened, the young men changed the topic of their discussion. It was late at night when the party broke up.

Eager to seek information about Devyani, Peter cornered one of Mitra's many nephews. 'Where is Devyani?'

'She has joined the freedom movement and doesn't stay here any more,' responded the fellow.

'When did this happen?' Peter felt his heart sinking. *Why does everyone have to join the movement?* 'Where does she stay now?' he asked.

'She lives somewhere in Calcutta but you will have to ask my uncle for the details. I don't have her address.'

The next morning, the host entered Peter's room. 'I wish you could stay longer,' he said.

'If only that were possible. You have been very kind. It is unimaginable for an orphan to find such warmth.' Propelled by gratitude, Peter touched the gentleman's feet.

'You are always welcome here.' Mitra patted his shoulder. 'I will look forward to your next visit.'

It was time to leave, but Peter had not achieved his aim. He gathered courage and said, 'I heard Devyani has joined the freedom movement. Is it true?'

'Yes,' replied the elderly man after a brief hesitation. 'Why do you ask?'

Peter's mind raced for an appropriate answer. 'Last evening, someone suggested that I can help with the movement. I can contact her in case I decide to help the revolutionaries.'

The reply did not fool the wise man. 'It is of no use. Devyani does not want anyone to contact her.' Mitra patted the young man's hand to console him.

Peter's face fell at the news.

'I will tell her to get in touch with you in case she requires anything,' added the shrewd man.

His shoulders drooping, Peter began walking away from the mansion. He had barely gone a few yards when Mitra called him back.

'Wait here,' he ordered before ducking into the house.

A few minutes later, Mitra returned and thrust a piece of paper into Peter's hand. 'This is her address.' He doused Peter's excitement saying, 'Let me warn you, Devyani is committed to the cause of freedom.'

'All I want is to meet her once. Just once,' Peter promised.

Keeping the little piece of paper safely in his pocket, Peter travelled back to Calcutta, his heart singing with joy.

It was a few months before Peter could find the time to slip away to the remote part of the city where Devyani lived. The address led him to a narrow lane in a crowded residential area. The neighbourhood was an immense warren of brickwork bisected by filthy drains. Most of the houses were old and reflected the limited income of the residents. It took the Anglo-Indian some time to locate the address given by Mitra. The nondescript house looked forlorn and neglected. Its cracked walls and warped door had seen happier days.

His heart lurching, Peter rapped the metal knocker on the door. There was no response. Impatiently, he rapped again. It was several minutes before he heard someone approaching the door.

Suddenly, Devyani opened the door and stood before him, more beautiful than he remembered. A wave of hair cascaded down to her waist; a white sari clung to her body.

'What do you want?' she asked in a sharp voice. Her face showed no sign of recognition.

Sensing that she was about to bang the door in his face, Peter moved quickly and put his foot in the gap. 'Devyani, it's me.' He looked into her eyes, willing her to remember him. 'It's Peter. I met you at Narendranath Mitra's house. Indraneel and I were there to attend your cousin's wedding.'

A light of recognition flickered in her dark eyes. After a brief hesitation, she opened the door and stood aside.

'I thought you had lost your way,' she smiled. Her eyes twinkled mischievously. 'A gora rarely loses his way in these lanes.'

'You are wrong on two counts. First, I have not lost my way. Second, I am not a gora.'

'Well, who could have imagined that you, of all people, would make your way here!'

Stepping into the house, Peter noticed the stamp of poverty all around. The walls were peeling and the floor was uneven. The only pieces of furniture in the room were a wooden almirah and a pair of rickety chairs. A rolled-up mat propped against the wall probably served as her bed. A solitary metal trunk occupied one corner of the room. On it was a pillow and a couple of neatly folded sheets.

He planted himself on a chair and studied the woman standing before him. There was an awkward silence as they grappled for words.

'What made you move to this dilapidated house?' he finally found his tongue. 'Your uncle's mansion in Chandernagore is large enough to host a marriage party.'

'I'll bring you some water,' she deflected, disappearing into the dark kitchen to avoid his question.

She placed a glass of water and a plate of sweets before him. Then she sat on the mat and watched him eat.

'It's my turn to ask the questions,' she said as soon as he had finished eating. 'What are you doing here? Who gave you my address? Does my uncle know you are here?'

And so, he started narrating his story, right from the day he entered the orphanage. He spoke about the sorrow of rejection. He told her about his journey to Amritsar and back.

Devyani sat motionless for a long time without speaking. 'It has not been easy for you,' she said, finally. 'Destiny deals us all different hands. How we play them is up to us.'

'Well, now I have a job in the officers' mess inside Fort William. So, life is looking up.'

'Why did you want to see me?' she probed.

'I've been trying to contact Indraneel but no one will tell me where he is.' In Chandernagore, Peter had noticed the growing camaraderie between Devyani and Neel. The two of them had discussed their views about the freedom struggle at every available opportunity. One evening, he had found them wrapped in a passionate discussion under a mango tree in a corner of the garden. Perplexed, Peter had observed the two from the balcony upstairs. From what he knew of Indraneel, the revolutionary was not a man who expressed his emotions freely, yet he was holding Devyani's hand familiarly. The intense chemistry between the two young people didn't escape his eyes.

'They have arrested Indraneel for the murder of a British officer and for conspiring against the British regime. We might never see him again.' She sighed and looked at him with sadness in her eyes.

'When did this happen?'

'A couple of Indraneel's comrades had let slip his name when they were tortured by the police. Although he was not directly involved in the British officer's murder, he was implicated in the bombing plot that eventually killed the officer. The police spread its dragnet and arrested him as soon as he stepped off the train in Calcutta.'

'Can't he prove his innocence?'

'Don't be stupid. Half the young men languishing in the jails would be free if they could prove their innocence. Mere suspicion is cause enough for a life sentence. Indraneel was actively involved in several cases of plotting against the regime. Besides, he comes from a family of revolutionaries. They will never let him go. His comrades suspect that the case against him is too strong and he may be sentenced for life and sent to Kala Pani, the Cellular Jail in the Andaman Islands.'

'Where is he now?' Peter was agitated to hear of Neel's arrest. He shuddered to think about the Bengali revolutionary's fate. 'I would like to meet him. That's the least I can do for the man who came to my rescue during my time of need.'

'No!' Her voice was sharp. 'You'll do nothing of the sort. Your visit may land him in deeper trouble. How will you explain your friendship with him? What if they interrogate or torture you? Besides, you will lose your job.'

Peter's heart sang with joy. She wanted to protect him. 'How does it matter?' He angled for her sympathy. 'I have no one to cry for me.'

'You can be of help to us, Peter.'

'How?'

'You are working in the officers' mess. You can bring us information.'

'I am not sure I want to get involved in these seditious missions.' Peter paced the floor in the tiny room.

'You are Indraneel's friend.' Devyani rose and faced him. 'Wouldn't you like to help him?'

'I want to, but I am not ready to spy on the British officers. Do you realise how dangerous that is?'

His refusal angered her.

'I thought you cared for Indraneel and his ideology.' She looked at him scornfully.

'I do care for Indraneel but not for his ideology.' He was determined to stay away from the police. 'I am sorry but I can't take the risk,' he said, spreading his hands in a gesture of helplessness. 'Other than spying, I am ready to do whatever you want.'

'I see.' Devyani curled her lips in derision.

'Please try to understand. For the first time in my life, I have a job and a semblance of security. All my life I've lived in fear—of going hungry and being imprisoned.' He tried to hold her hand but she pulled it away. 'You don't know what insecurity can be like. You don't understand—'

She cut him short. 'Don't you dare talk to me about insecurity! Do you know what it's like to be a widow? You can't even imagine. I guess you are more of a coward than I'd thought. You may leave now. And don't ever come back here.'

Walking to the door, she opened it and stood waiting for him to leave.

'Devyani, I am sorry,' Peter grovelled. 'Please try to understand my situation.'

Her silence was a thick wall separating them.

Peter returned to his little room at the fort, angry at her stubbornness. Throwing himself on the string cot, he cursed himself. Calcutta was filled with Anglo-Indian girls and he had to go and fall in love with a freedom fighter.

Over the next few weeks he found himself obsessed with Devyani. The memory of her blazing eyes haunted his nights. Reckless and uncontrolled, she was like a cyclonic storm. And that made her irresistible.

I will not grovel before her, he decided.

But finally, his resolve weakened, Peter found himself at Devyani's door once again. This time, she was neither cold nor distant. Her mood was, in fact, light and gay.

They spoke about the Calcutta weather and the rising price of rice. They reminisced about the wedding at Chandernagore. She updated him on the latest goings-on at her uncle's house. Not once did she mention the revolution or anything connected to it. It was frustrating to discuss nothing other than the weather and spiralling prices. Her behaviour confounded him. It was becoming impossible for Peter to continue the charade.

He worried about what the police would do if they learned of her involvement with the revolutionaries. Peter decided to distract her from the dangerous path. He would keep trying until he succeeded.

The season of festivities swept through Calcutta, bringing a sense of well-being. Even the revolutionaries took a holiday from their plans to celebrate the annual event.

A month later, unable to keep away, Peter was back at Devyani's house. His insistent knocks brought her to the door. 'I am sorry, I couldn't keep away,' was all he said as she closed the door behind him. A couple of tendrils had escaped the hair tied at Devyani's nape and her upper lip was beaded with perspiration.

She wiped her hands on her sari and turned towards him.

'Why are you back? What is it that you want, Peter?' asked Devyani. 'People are taking notice of your visits.'

'I will do nothing to harm you,' he replied.

'Then stop coming here.'

'I can't do that.' Peter looked at her helplessly.

Devyani went to the window and unbolted it. It opened with a protesting creak and bright sunshine flooded the room.

'Let me tell you a story.' She began speaking in a dull voice. 'I was married to a brilliant young man who was ten years older than me. Although my father did not believe in early marriage, he yielded to his ailing mother's wish. It all seems so long ago, almost like a half-forgotten nightmare.'

Devyani's eyes strayed towards a lizard on the wall. 'Like many young men, my husband was a part of the local youth group. He was in and out of prison all the time, so I hardly got to know him.'

'Didn't he come back to you when he was released from prison?'

Her eyes misted as she continued, 'No. He went underground. It was too risky for him to visit us. The police had declared a reward of five hundred rupees on his head and our house was under close watch. He was finally shot while lobbing a bomb at the magistrate who had sentenced one of his comrades to death. I was widowed at fifteen.' She straightened her slumped shoulders with resolve. 'I decided to continue my husband's work and started helping the freedom fighters.'

Peter's heart went out to her. He wanted to take her in his arms and soothe the lines of sorrow on her face. Devyani got to her feet and took out a photograph from under some clothes. She handed it to Peter, saying, 'This was taken on our wedding day.'

The young man was smiling broadly while Devyani looked shyly at the camera.

'He was a handsome man,' Peter said, handing the photograph back to her.

She wiped the photograph reverently with her sari and placed it back inside the almirah.

'Why don't you hang the photograph on the wall?' asked Peter. 'I'll help you drive a nail to hold it.'

'I don't want to give the police any reason for suspicion. I have locked away the painful memories. Let them remain there.'

A silence fell over the room.

'I respect your feelings but I love you, Devyani.' Peter liked the feel of her name on his tongue. 'Will you not consider an easier life?' he asked finally.

She remained silent for a moment. His confession didn't surprise her. Instead, she appeared to be amused.

'All right, let me test your love for me,' she teased. 'Can you join our party and work for the cause?'

He felt trapped. 'Have you ever heard of an Anglo-Indian joining the freedom movement? We are part British, aren't we?'

'But your mother was Indian. Wasn't she exploited by an Englishman? Why, then, do you side with the British?'

'I hate the English as much as I hate the Indians. I am a bastard and nothing will ever change that. Will the Indians stop thinking of me as a bastard if I join the revolutionaries? Then why should I risk my life for freedom? At least I am assured of a job as long as the British rule this country.' He paused briefly before continuing in a softer tone, 'Don't misunderstand me, Devyani. I love you, but I don't love India. It has given me nothing but shame.'

'Do you think you will be better off in England? Do you think they will treat you any better?'

'No. I have no such illusions. I will continue to live and work here while praying that the country never gets its freedom.'

Her lips curled with contempt, and she said, 'In that case, we have nothing in common. I don't wish to see you ever again. Please leave.'

There was no hope for the two of them. They went over and over the same track like a worn gramophone record.

24

Olivia

A Daring Adventure

A year had rolled by. The gloom in Olivia's life had taken a back seat. She had been able to foil her father's plans to get her married. Much to her relief, he had finally given up. In any case, he had much to keep him occupied. Bradley had been promoted to the rank of colonel and with the higher position came more responsibilities that left him with little time for his recalcitrant daughter.

Eager to grab happiness with both hands, she hurtled from one day to another. Monsoon quietly slipped away and autumn tiptoed in with much fanfare. At Kumartuli, the skilful hands of sculptors gave shape to the idol of Goddess Durga and an air of festivity flowed through the streets and lanes.

One morning, Olivia and Roma returned from shopping to find a commotion in the Chatterjee residence. Roma's mother rushed out and wailed, 'They have arrested Rajat.'

Roma turned pale at the news. 'Why?'

Rajat was in his final year at the medical college and stayed in the hostel. The police, tipped off by an informer, had raided the hostel. They had taken the boys to the Alipore police station for interrogation.

'He is not a revolutionary,' said Roma, aghast at the thought of her fiancé being tortured by the police. She flopped down on the couch.

'The police found anti-British leaflets and pamphlets in his room,' her mother informed.

'That doesn't prove he is a revolutionary.'

'They don't need evidence to prove his involvement. Their suspicion is enough.'

'We have to get him released.'

'It's been hours since your father went to the police station.'

There was nothing to do but wait. By evening, Mr Chatterjee returned, exhausted and dejected.

'There is no hope for him,' he said. 'Rajat's friends and roommates have been found guilty. No one is ready to believe Rajat is not working with the revolutionaries.'

'We must not give up. I will meet the inspector and plead for his release.' Turning to Olivia, Roma asked, 'Will you come with me to the Alipore police station? You are British. You can convince them of Rajat's innocence. Your word will hold more weight.'

As much as she liked Roma's fiancé, Olivia knew she couldn't vouch for him at the police station. She was afraid the news of her visit would travel to her father.

'Please, for my sake,' begged Roma.

'I don't know. My father . . .' Olivia hesitated.

'Your father will not know,' insisted Roma. 'Why should the police inform him?'

'They will ask for my credentials. They will definitely check with him once they learn I am Colonel Bradley's daughter.'

'How does it matter if your father learns about your visit to the police station? It is a matter of life and death for Rajat. A word from you could make a big difference.'

Torn between her loyalties, Olivia wavered. An hour later, she sat before an insolent inspector, pleading for the young man's release.

'Miss Bradley, how long have you known the boy?'

'A little over a year.'

'A year? And you can vouch for his innocence? Even those who have known such people for a lifetime cannot be sure of their activities.'

'I know he is innocent,' she insisted in a cold voice. The arrogance of the inspector annoyed her. 'You cannot pronounce Rajat guilty just because his roommates possessed some pamphlets.'

'That is for the court to decide.'

'There are so many possibilities. Maybe someone planted those pamphlets in his room. Perhaps someone wanted revenge.'

'The police does not base its activities on presumptions. I would advise you to keep out of this, Miss Bradley. It is best not to trust the natives.'

'Rajat is an intelligent young man from a good family. He has a bright future. Besides, he is getting married shortly. Do you think he would risk his future by taking part in such activities?' Olivia tried one last time.

'Oh yes, he would,' sneered the inspector. 'The so-called young and educated men from reputed families are far more dangerous than the poor peasants who have no time to think beyond their daily bread. I suggest you go back home and I will not mention the matter to your father.'

He was threatening her.

'Please allow us to meet Rajat for a few minutes.' Olivia looked at Roma and added, 'This young woman is his fiancée.'

The officer scrutinised the girl squirming nervously in her seat.

'Please, officer,' repeated Olivia.

'All right! You may meet the detainee, but just for five minutes,' warned the inspector. 'Is that clear?'

Nodding obediently, the two girls followed the policeman down an aisle lined with cells on either side.

'Why have you come here?' Rajat cried on seeing Roma. 'You shouldn't have come.'

'Olivia is trying to get you out of this place,' whispered Roma, reaching out to touch the distraught man.

The lovers spoke in hushed voices while Olivia's eyes strayed towards a young man locked in the same cell who was trying to catch her attention.

'Your five minutes are over.' The policeman banged his baton on the bars of the cell.

'Just one minute, Sir.' Roma turned imploringly at the burly man. She clasped her fiancé's fingers protectively through the bars. 'I may not see him for a long time.'

The policeman hesitated. 'Not more than a minute,' he conceded, darting uneasy looks around. 'Bada Saab will not be happy if you loiter.'

Olivia moved away to offer privacy to Roma and her fiancé. Suddenly, a balled-up piece of paper dropped near her feet. Shocked, she looked at the young man in Rajat's cell. 'I am Indraneel,' he dropped his voice in an urgent whisper. 'Please warn the men staying at the address written on that paper. Tell them to escape immediately.'

It took a second for the stunned Olivia to reach a decision. Fortunately, no one had noticed the tiny scrap of paper lying on the floor. Bending down, she pretended to adjust the strap of her shoe. She picked up the crumpled piece of paper and thrust it inside her shoe. Her heart beating wildly, she nodded imperceptibly at the man called Indraneel.

'That's enough,' shouted the policeman and herded the girls towards the exit.

They left the police station, lost in thought. Olivia knew the news of her visit would reach her father. In the meantime, she had an errand to run.

'You shouldn't have accepted it.' Roma was aghast when her friend confided in her about the piece of paper. 'It's dangerous to get involved with the nationalists.'

'Don't you think we should deliver the message? It could save some lives,' Olivia declared. 'We will go to the address written on this paper and warn the men. That's it.'

'The police will not hesitate to put us behind bars if they catch us. Your father may save you but I won't be let off.' Roma shuddered at the thought of the consequences of this foolhardy mission.

'In that case, we will be careful not to get caught.'

'Oh Olivia! Just tear up the paper.'

'I can't do that, Roma. I have accepted the task.'

'How could you have done that? I didn't hear you speaking to the man, nor did I see the paper being passed to you.'

'That goes to show Indraneel's expertise, doesn't it?' Olivia laughed. 'Let's just hurry and get the message delivered before the police arrest the men.'

'You are a reckless girl.'

'And you, my dear, are a coward.'

'I would rather be a coward than a fool. You don't get it. These are terrible times and a tiny slip-up can lead to imprisonment.'

But Olivia was not to be deterred. At last something exciting was happening to her. It took a lot of patience and reasoning for Olivia to convince Roma before the two of them travelled to the crowded residential area at the other end of the city. There were three men at the address.

'Sister, you have saved our lives,' said a young man with his arm in a sling. 'We will never forget your kindness.'

'I will remember you in my prayers,' muttered Olivia, touched by his gratitude. It was not every day one found the chance to save lives. She felt strangely satisfied with her work.

Having carried out the task, Olivia returned home to find that the police had informed her father about her visit to the police station. He confronted her the moment she entered the house.

'Why did you go to the police station?' Bradley raged.

Olivia remained silent.

'Who is the young man you are trying to save? Do you know I can have him hanged just to spite you?'

'He is innocent.' She stared back defiantly. 'He doesn't deserve to be hanged.'

'How do you know that?'

'Rajat is the fiancé of my classmate Roma. The two of them are to marry shortly.'

'And since when have you been friends with this girl?'

'We have been friends ever since I joined the junior college.'

'And have you met the young man?' Bradley continued the interrogation.

'Yes, I have met him several times at her residence.'

'Oh, so you have been going to their house?'

'The Chatterjees are a nice family and I don't regret going to their house. Mr Chatterjee is a renowned doctor.'

'That has nothing to do with this case. How could you go to the police station to defend a man you know nothing about?'

'He is innocent,' she repeated.

'He is a terrorist. I forbid you from going to Roma's house. Do you understand?'

'Don't you want me to be happy? For the first time, I have found a friend and you want me to end my friendship.'

'I don't want you to have Indians as friends. Why can't you find friends in the cantonment? There are dozens of girls here.' Bradley felt cornered. Much as he hated the idea of his daughter associating with the natives, there was little he could do about it.

'All right, let's make a deal,' said Olivia. 'I will never go to Roma's house if you promise to have Rajat released.' It felt strangely satisfying to be defying her father.

'Do I have your word?' he asked resignedly.

'I believe in keeping my word.' Olivia's lips were pressed together in a thin line. 'I will disassociate myself from the Chatterjees if Rajat is released,' she reiterated.

Rajat was released. The police produced his friends in court and the boys drew six years of rigorous imprisonment. The provocative leaflets were produced as evidence against them. The defending lawyers pointed at the flimsy reasons for the arrests but could not get them released.

Olivia kept her word but Bradley wasn't sure how long his daughter would keep away from her friend if they remained in Calcutta. He asked for a transfer. Months passed, but the orders for his transfer didn't arrive. The wheels of bureaucracy moved slowly and frustratingly for the desperate man.

It was almost the end of summer when Bradley came home with the news of his transfer. Menacing dark clouds announced the advent of the monsoon. He had been transferred to Ross Island in the Andamans.

The Andaman Islands were a punishment posting for British officers. News of Olivia's visit to Alipore Jail had reached the authorities and they were none too pleased about her association with a man suspected of being a nationalist and his subsequent release after the colonel's intervention.

With a heavy heart, Olivia bid farewell to Calcutta, taking with her a host of happy memories.

25

Peter

A Man Spurned

Do I love Devyani enough to join the revolutionaries? Peter asked himself repeatedly but found no answers. The more she rejected him, the more he wanted her.

The miasma lifted suddenly. Peter had been roaming aimlessly on the streets when he saw Devyani exiting a restaurant with a British officer. Surprised, he watched her smiling coquettishly at the officer. This woman, who professed to have dedicated her life to the cause, had rejected his love for that of a British officer.

Worse, Peter knew Major Robert Adams was a womaniser and an alcoholic. The staff at the officers' mess had noticed the women who stole into his room. The philanderer had an enormous appetite for women.

Forty, balding and overweight, Adams was an ill-tempered officer posted at Fort William. What was Devyani doing with that scoundrel?

The officer held her arm and steered her across the road. Seething with rage, Peter followed them into a nearby theatre.

The next morning, taking leave from work, Peter made his way to Devyani's house to warn her about Adams.

She stood at the door, blocking his entry.

'Let me enter, Devyani,' he begged.

'Why are you here, Peter?' Worry lines creased her forehead and she appeared exhausted.

'How can you flirt with a British officer? What happened to all those sermons about your dedication to the country?' Peter shouted. His loud voice was drawing the attention of the neighbours who were now peeping from their windows.

'You are making a scene. People are watching us.'

'Why don't you let me enter the house?' Pushing her aside, Peter stepped inside.

'Have you been spying on me?' Her face was flushed with anger.

'There is no need to spy. You aren't discreet, Miss Lily White.'

'Are you drunk, Peter?'

'No, I am not drunk. I am celebrating my frustrations.'

Their relationship was far from comfortable at the moment. They had parted on a discordant note. Shrugging nonchalantly, Devyani stepped away from him. In a quick move, he grabbed and pinioned her against the wall, and kissed her on the mouth. For a moment, she was taken aback by his boldness. Then she began hitting and scratching him.

He swore and released her. She wiped her bruised lips with the back of her hand and tears filled her eyes.

Regretting the impulsive action, Peter grabbed her hand. 'I am so sorry, Devyani,' he muttered.

'How dare you?' she cried, slapping him hard across the face.

'I love you.'

'I don't want to see your face. Don't come here ever again,' she hissed.

'If I see you with Adams, I swear I'll kill him.'

'Get out!'

Peter's nights were haunted by thoughts of Devyani and Adams. Obsessed with jealousy, he shirked work and lurked around her house to keep watch. He followed her everywhere. Ismail's warnings had no effect on him. He no longer cared about the job or himself. He wanted to kill Adams.

A week later, he applied for leave and went to Chandernagore. A dangerous plan took shape in his mind as he travelled to the Mitra mansion, where he was greeted with the usual warmth.

After dinner, the menfolk gathered in the baithak khana to enjoy their session of hookah and gossip as usual. Predictably, the discussion veered to the political rumbles that had grown serious enough to disturb the British rulers.

Peter joined the group of young men who were engaged in an intense conversation about Gandhi's politics and the fallouts thereof. Patiently, he waited for his cue to barge into the conversation.

'Is it true that the slow pace of activity and the delay in attaining freedom has disillusioned many young men?' He nudged the discussion on a provocative path.

'The young are impatient,' agreed Srikant, a teacher in the local government school.

'The basic problem is the lack of courage. Most Indians prefer to leave everything to their gods and destiny,' Peter stoked the embers.

The teacher threw him a sweltering look. 'It is not the lack of courage but the lack of resources that is holding us back. As for the Anglo-Indians, I think they are nothing more than self-serving cowards.'

'Not every Anglo-Indian is a coward,' retorted Peter. It was the opening he had been waiting for. 'I am ready to take up any challenge to prove otherwise. In fact, I will join the revolution and undertake any task that is assigned to me.'

His bravado was greeted with silence. No one believed him.

'Enrol me in your ranks and let me show you what I can do,' Peter challenged.

The silence lasted for a few seconds. Then, someone sniggered. More people joined in and soon the baithak khana was reverberating with laughter.

'Peter, we believe you. You don't have to join a revolutionary group to prove yourself,' Mitra reassured him.

'I meant what I said,' Peter reiterated.

Srikant walked towards Peter after the gathering broke up. 'Let's go to the garden,' he suggested. 'I want to speak to you.'

A full moon flirted with the clouds in the sky and its silvery beams danced down. They passed a huge peepul tree and took a seat on a bench.

'Did you mean what you said in the baithak khana?' Srikant lit a cigarette.

'I meant every word of what I said,' Peter confirmed.

'How can you help us?'

'I have noticed that alcohol loosens tongues. The officers who drink in the mess discuss many official matters. It's easy for me to eavesdrop on their conversations.'

Srikant looked impressed with Peter's access to information. 'That's an excellent idea,' he admitted. 'You can be our eyes and ears inside Fort William.'

'I can give weekly reports to you. But first I want to kill Major Robert Adams.'

'Who is Major Robert Adams? And why do you want to kill him?'

'I have to settle a score with him.' Peter set his jaw and stared back.

'My, my, what has he done to deserve death?' Srikant asked. Taking a last drag on his cigarette, he crushed the butt under his heel and continued, 'Young man, your personal vendetta does not concern our party. Your commitment has to be tested before we can trust you.'

'Give me a pistol and I will prove my commitment,' Peter gnashed his teeth at the thought of pulling the trigger on Adams.

Srikant's eyebrows shot up in surprise. His intuition picked up the desperation in the Anglo-Indian's request.

'What makes you think I have one?'

'Will you get me one? In return, I will do whatever the party orders.'

'Prove yourself first and then I'll get you a weapon. Provide us with useful information. Once you have won the trust of our leaders, they will not hesitate to hand you a pistol.'

'What kind of information are you looking for?'

'Find out where our comrades are locked up and when they will be presented in court. That information can help us plan an ambush for their escape. We also need information on the number of officers and men inside the fort. You could provide a layout of the fort and point out the locations of the armoury and supplies. There are a hundred things you could do for us.'

'I will try to gather the information but I can't promise anything,' said Peter. 'Also, I can't tell how long it will take me.'

Srikant patted his shoulders patronisingly. 'It is risky business. Just remember, they will hang you if you are caught. There are no simple paths to freedom.'

The prospect of hanging terrified Peter but his hatred for Adams overrode his fear.

Over the next few months, Peter made a few trips to Chandernagore, ferrying information. His efforts failed to make an impression on Srikant. Spying was serious business and Peter lacked the skills required for the job. It was difficult to collect intelligence without raising suspicion. Information had to be ferreted carefully from officers who were drunk enough to blabber and not remember it the next day. He had to make his questions appear innocent. Peter tried to eavesdrop on the conversations while serving drinks. He picked up stray information at the bar and pieced them together.

'You must not be seen here too often,' Srikant warned him one day. 'Unless it is urgent, give all the information to a person at this address every week.' He wrote down an address on a piece of paper and warned, 'You must ensure that you are not followed to the address. Your carelessness can put many lives at risk.'

'I've been providing information for the past three months but you have yet to give me a pistol,' Peter complained.

'Have patience, Peter. Bring us some invaluable information,' Srikant encouraged him. 'You will get a pistol as soon as the comrades are satisfied.'

Another month passed before Peter realised that Srikant and his comrades would never be satisfied. He felt exploited. Yet there was little he could do.

Peter's fingers itched to kill Adams whenever he saw Devyani with the officer. Days turned into weeks, and weeks into months, but Srikant would not give him access to a weapon.

It was the monsoon once again. Heavy rains flooded the streets of Calcutta. The gutters were overflowing with filth as Peter picked his way towards the poorer part of the city, optimism quickening his steps. With him was a vital piece of intelligence that he hoped would change his life forever. One of the top revolutionaries was locked up in a cell inside the fort and the Anglo-Indian had discovered when the young man would be presented in court for a hearing. This was the only chance for the revolutionaries to free their comrade who was sure to be hanged.

Peter had no doubt the information was of utmost importance. This time, Srikant would have to provide him with a pistol. Drenched to the bone, he knocked on the door. There was a long delay before it was opened by a member of the group.

The man's eyes lit up with excitement on hearing what Peter had to say. 'I think the party will be pleased with this piece of information. You may just get that pistol you've been asking for,' he said. 'Meet me here in a week.'

Peter didn't have to wait that long. Three days later, while he was returning from the market, someone tapped him on the shoulder. Turning around, he saw two members of the group. Gesturing for him to follow, the men entered a shop and received an effusive welcome from the corpulent shopkeeper.

One of the revolutionaries placed an order for groceries after exchanging pleasantries with the man. 'Five *seers* of rice, two seers of masur dal,' he said, handing a list to the shopkeeper who ducked into a storeroom and returned with three jute bags.

'Take this with you.' The revolutionary thrust one of the bags into Peter's hands. 'Do nothing until we contact you. Now, turn left and keep walking till you reach the end of the road. Don't look back and don't hurry.'

'But . . .' Peter was unable to grasp what was happening.

'Not a word. Do as you are told.'

Clutching the bag, Peter left the shop. It was difficult to control the temptation to look inside. At the end of the lane, when he turned to look, Peter caught a glimpse of the two men melting into the darkness.

Once inside his room in the fort, he bolted the door and opened the package with trembling hands. Wrapped neatly in a newspaper was a gun.

Once the pistol was in his possession, Peter could wait no longer. He resumed spying on Devyani. The lovers had abandoned all caution and met frequently in parks, restaurants and theatres, unaware that they were being followed. Jealousy wrapped its talons around Peter's heart.

It was a Saturday night. Peter followed Devyani to Rivoli Theatre. He saw her waiting in the foyer. Almost everyone had entered the theatre by the time the British officer joined his paramour. After a quick greeting, the two hurried inside. Peter bought a ticket and slipped stealthily into the darkened hall as the usher led the pair towards their seats. The movie had already begun.

There was no time to lose. Under the pretext of searching for his seat, Peter inched closer to Adams who had snuggled close to Devyani and was trying to kiss her. *You are a dead man, Adams.* Peter gnashed his teeth and extracted the pistol from his pocket. With trembling fingers, he pulled the trigger. Devyani screamed as a bullet hit the officer seated next to Adams.

There was pandemonium in the theatre and the lights came on. Women screamed hysterically. People jostled each other to rush out. Stunned, Peter stood staring at the dead man, unable to believe he had missed his target.

Adams pulled Devyani towards the exit. An officer requested the restive crowd to remain where they were. 'Things are in control,' he tried to reassure them. Then, he commanded a couple of officers to take charge. 'Don't allow anyone to leave the theatre.' All the exit doors were closed immediately.

Soon Peter heard heavy boots running up the stairs and orders being shouted. The police rushed into the hall. His legs turned to jelly and he remained rooted to the spot. Adams had already reached the exit.

'What have you done, Peter?' Devyani yelled as she ran past him. 'Run. Go!'

Spurred on by the urgency in her voice, he ran towards the exit but it was too late. Several hands grabbed him and pushed him to the floor. Then the police slapped handcuffs on him.

An hour later, at the police station, stripped of all clothes and dignity, the Anglo-Indian stood crestfallen by his failure. Adams was alive. He had killed the wrong man. The mission had been a total failure.

What followed was inhuman torture. Every form of cruelty was used to extract information that he didn't possess. The police believed him to be a revolutionary and wanted to know the names of his comrades. Nothing he said could convince them otherwise. They rained blows on his head, knees and back; dragged him around the room by his hair; punched him on the nose; and then handcuffed and suspended him from the ceiling so his feet barely touched the ground. The more he denied being a nationalist, the more they tortured him.

'You are an Anglo-Indian. How could you join hands with the natives? It is not your war.' The British officer spat on him.

'I am not a revolutionary. It was a mistake. I killed the wrong man. All I wanted was to kill my rival,' Peter told them repeatedly but no one believed him.

He lost count of the days and nights. His body was black and blue, and covered in cigarette burns, his eyes swelled to twice their size. They had torn out a few nails and broken his nose.

Peter now knew the cruelty inflicted on the revolutionaries. He found courage in the thought that Neel would never succumb to their questioning. He modelled his reactions on what he assumed would have been his mentor's responses to the interrogators.

A week later, amidst a gaggle of curious onlookers, Peter was produced in court. The public prosecutor repeated the questions the police had been asking. Did he belong to a revolutionary group? Who had assigned him the mission to kill the senior official? How and where did he find the pistol?

Peter's legs buckled under the weight of his bruised body. Sobbing with desperation, he leaned against the dock. And then he spotted Devyani in the crowd of spectators. She had covered her head and most of her face with her sari but Peter had no difficulty in recognising the woman he loved. Her presence gave him strength. *Devyani loves me. Why else would she come to the court?* He saluted in her direction and she nodded.

The court was bursting with curious people. It was not every day that an Anglo-Indian was tried for treason. Newspaper reporters waited for his statement and composed headlines for the next edition. The crowd cheered and shouted slogans. Peter was a hero who had killed a British officer.

'I am asking you for the last time, young man. Do you admit to being a part of the radical group?' the public prosecutor asked.

Energised by the loud cheering, Peter spat in contempt and replied, 'I do not recognise this court. I have done nothing wrong. I am not a revolutionary.' He had been repeating the same words since his arrest. They slipped out of his mouth without effort.

'You are a young man with a bright future. If you name the leaders and members of your group, you will be released with minimum punishment,' said the magistrate, leaning forward. 'We are sure you have been misled by the radicals.'

Peter's head reeled. He felt weak and desperate. He had eaten nothing for the past fifteen hours.

'I have been cooperating all along, you bastards,' he shouted. 'I have been beaten and tortured. I am tired of repeating the same statement. I am not a revolutionary. Don't you understand simple English?' Peter wanted to impress Devyani. To prove he was not a coward.

The crowd tittered and the magistrate went red in the face. He banged the gavel. 'You will refrain from using foul language. I will consider it a contempt of court if you continue speaking in the same vein.'

'Foul language? I have not yet begun using the words that describe you. You bastards demand respect but you deserve none. You are thieves, murderers and rapists. I have no respect for you white monkeys.'

A stunned silence followed the outburst. The British were horrified by his words and the Indians lauded his courage. The crowd tittered and encouraged him to harangue the magistrate. He felt brave and didn't care about the consequences.

Peter observed a few Anglo-Indians in the crowd. They were listening to the arguments with attention. 'You are not white,' he said, pointing at them. 'You are bastards like me. So why do you dance at their bidding? Break free from your shackles. Show some courage.'

'You are forcing my hand,' declared the magistrate banging the gavel to bring order to the courtroom. There was pressure on him to make an example of the Anglo-Indian. 'Your attitude leaves no room for leniency.'

Pens poised over their notebooks, the reporters waited for the magistrate to announce his judgment. People leaned forward and held their breath.

'The accused has been proven guilty beyond doubt and this court pronounces a sentence of twenty years of imprisonment to be carried out at Port Blair.'

There was a shocked silence in the court. Peter heard the words coming from a distance. His bravado vanished at the implication of the verdict and his knees gave way. It had never occurred to him that the magistrate would sentence him to the notorious Kala Pani. His eyes sought Devyani who seemed shaken. He threw one last look at her as they dragged him out of the court into the waiting vehicle. The crowd spilled all around the police vehicle, shouting slogans and jeering at the policemen.

The next day, Devyani visited Peter in prison.

'I am sorry,' she said in a shaky voice, tears welling in her eyes.

'You should not have come here.' Peter turned his face away from her. She could be in danger if the police suspected her. 'Go away, Devyani. There is nothing anyone can do for me now.'

'I want you to know that I have nothing to do with Adams. My leaders want me to extract information from that man.'

'I thought you were in love with him.'

'Are you crazy, Peter?' she appeared aghast. 'You know I hate the British.'

'I went insane with jealousy. I wanted to kill him.'

'Oh Peter!' she wailed. 'I will never forgive myself for keeping the truth from you.' She held his hand and wept.

'Devyani,' said Peter, his voice gruff with emotion, 'do you love me?'

She hesitated and lowered her head in silence.

'Tell me the truth, please, Devyani. It will help me through my years in prison,' he begged.

'I care for you, Peter.'

It was not the reply he wanted. 'I will return once I have served my sentence and then we will marry,' he said. 'You will wait for me, won't you?'

Devyani didn't reply. Instead, she whispered, 'Indraneel has been sent to the Cellular Jail for his involvement in a bombing conspiracy and for killing a British officer.' Her eyes reflected intense sadness. 'I thought you should know.'

The message lifted his spirits. That night, lying on the hard prison floor, he chuckled. 'Bloody hell, I have a friend on that goddamned island.'

26

Olivia

Ross Island

Olivia stepped off the boat and turned to look around. The ocean swirled all around her—now blue, now green. The tangy smell of the sea mingled with the woody smell of the forest, and the azure melded into emerald green in the distance. Ross Island lay in a stupor under the scorching sun. This was exactly the way her dreams always ended. But this was not a dream. She was standing on the dock of what appeared to be paradise.

Drawing a deep breath, she took small, hesitant steps towards the high-wheeled rickshaws waiting to carry her to her new house. As the rickshaw trundled down the tree-lined road, Olivia noticed a gang of men chained to each other. They were breaking a huge rock with sledgehammers.

Paradise wasn't perfect.

The rickshaw-pullers grunted with exhaustion as they laboured up the gradient. Colonel Bradley had disembarked at Port Blair to visit a colleague, leaving Olivia to proceed to Ross Island with a staff officer.

'Welcome to your new home,' said the staff officer as Olivia alighted from the rickshaw.

A cobbled path led to a wide gate beyond which stood a charming bungalow. It was surrounded by laburnum and purple orchid trees. The front was a profusion of wildflowers. Olivia placed her hand on her heart, enchanted by the sight.

'The bungalow will require a lick of paint and some repair work,' the staff officer apologised. 'I will come around with the supervisor tomorrow. He will take care of all the requirements.' He scribbled a phone number for her. 'Please call me if you need anything.'

Olivia thanked the officer and entered the house.

The interiors were a contrast to the beauty outside. An air of desolation hung in the air. She walked through the house, making a mental note of the work that had to be done. There were four bedrooms. For herself, Olivia chose an airy corner room with a large bay window, which she flung open. The forested area at the back of the house and the sea beyond it gave the room a magical touch.

Sighing with pleasure, Olivia watched the rolling waves. It was perfect! The ideal place to start afresh.

The garden was in a terrible state. The lawn was a mass of overgrown grass and weeds that enjoyed unfettered growth. She knew that tropical weather encouraged the rapid growth of weeds but that still didn't explain the condition of the garden. Covered with vagrant creepers, a pergola stood at one end. The overhanging branches of the whispering willow trees needed trimming. It was clear to Olivia that she would need an efficient gardener to make the place beautiful.

Rosie and Faisal came with the house. The woman, a rehabilitated prisoner, was tall and wiry, while the cook, Faisal, was just the opposite. Overweight and lethargic, he dawdled around trying to wriggle out of chores.

The house needed a lot of work before it could become comfortable. A few leaky faucets had to be fixed, and the existing furniture and wooden floor would do well with a coat of polish. She would need new curtains and some additional pieces of furniture. The kitchen larder had to be replenished. Diligently, she made a list of the things that needed to be done. An electrician, a carpenter and a plumber were summoned and a workforce organised. While Bradley busied himself with official matters, Olivia refurbished the bungalow.

She didn't mind the work but the rains were a nuisance. Nothing dried; even the clothes carried a musty smell. Ugly green mould grew in every corner. Insects and vermin cropped up in the store, ruining the grain. Dark, threatening clouds covered the sky the entire day. The whining of mosquitoes was a constant bother. Each morning, Olivia inspected the rash of bites on her body and realised why so many people on the island died of malaria.

The gloom gave way to joy as the sun broke through the clouds one morning after days of endless rain. Seated in a chair on the veranda, Olivia supervised the household help as they went about their chores. Everything that needed sunning was brought out, dusted and cleaned.

Rosie and Faisal's refusal to live in the servants' quarters was an irritant. Nothing Olivia said would convince them to change their minds.

A couple of months passed and the house began to shape up but the garden remained unkempt. The sight of the overgrown trees and flower beds irritated Bradley but he was unable to find a good gardener. The weeds grew faster than the flowers.

They put Faisal on the task, with little result.

Once the house was in order, Olivia found time hanging heavily on her hands. Despite her frequent trips to the well-stocked library on the island, books couldn't fill the void in her heart.

A dog was what she wanted. Providence obliged. One morning, while at the bakery, she noticed a poster announcing the availability of puppies. On an impulse, she noted the address and called on the owner. She found four rambunctious puppies and as she neared them, one lunged forward, sniffing her outstretched hand with curiosity.

'Dotty likes you,' the lady beamed at her.

'I think she does.' Olivia cuddled the little pup. Its warm body felt reassuring. 'I will take her home.'

It was the last few weeks of the year. Preparation for Christmas was keeping everyone busy. There was a profusion of winter flowers all around the island but the neglected Bradley bungalow continued to look forlorn.

Then, one afternoon, just as she had given up on the garden, Colonel Bradley walked into the bungalow, a young prisoner in tow. The muscles in the prisoner's forearms tightened as he was pushed forward by a guard. His face seemed familiar. Had she met him somewhere? It didn't seem possible.

'This man is going to look after the garden,' her father informed Olivia. 'I found him in the Cell.' The Cell was how the jail was referred to.

Olivia was delighted at the prospect of a neat garden.

'He is good with plants, I have been told,' continued her father. 'He will work in the garden till sunset. His food will be brought here. I've instructed Faisal to keep watch on him.' Turning to the gardener, he said, 'My daughter will instruct you on the layout of the garden. I want you to turn it into the best one on the island. Understood?'

The young man lowered his head.

Having charged the prisoner with his duty, Colonel Bradley drove off in his official vehicle.

Later, Olivia learned the details. Her father had been visiting the Cell on work when he noticed the gardener.

'You seem to have an excellent gardener, Frank,' Bradley remarked as he stepped out of the jailor's office, his eyes arrested by the profusion of flowers flanking the path.

'Oh, he's got a green thumb, that lean one there,' said Major Frank, pointing towards a prisoner who was yoked to the oil press. 'Last week, I saw him revive a dying sapling. It is incredible; the chap seemed to be talking to it. These bloody Indians! I think he knows witchcraft and magic.'

'Why is he here?' Bradley watched the prisoner running around the large wheel of the oil press. It was one of the toughest chores assigned to prisoners.

'The bastard bombed the Central Legislative Assembly, killing a British officer. A killer with a green thumb. Isn't that something!'

'What do you know about gardening?' Bradley asked the young man who was brought before him by a cane-wielding guard.

'Nothing!' responded the prisoner.

Bradley noticed the irreverent note in the man's voice.

The guard raised his cane but Bradley held up his hand.

'Then how did you revive the rose sapling?'

'I touched the sapling and it sprang back to life. All it needed was a bit of tender care.'

'Tender care?' Bradley curled his lips in a sardonic smile. 'Well, I would like you to give some loving care to my garden.'

In response, the prisoner merely shrugged his gaunt shoulders. It was not for him to decide. In under an hour, the formalities were complete and the prisoner was transported to Ross Island.

From the veranda, Olivia watched the gaunt prisoner working in the garden. He had been clearing the weeds, digging the soil and preparing the ground for plants for over a week. His body was scarred, the eyes sunken and lips parched, but his expression remained insolent.

On the island, the prisoners walked at a slow and shuffling pace, their eyes vacant with hopelessness, and their faces reflecting the pathetic conditions of their imprisonment. Crushed, wretched and dispirited, they had resigned themselves to their fate. But this one was different. There was a fire in him.

Despite his soiled uniform, shaven head and bare feet, he was cloaked in dignity. Olivia couldn't shake off the feeling that she had seen the man before. Efforts at jogging her memory had been fruitless. Why did he look so familiar?

One morning, when her curiosity got the better of her, Olivia marched up to the man, Dotty in tow, and asked, 'What is your name?'

'Prisoner Number 7048. That's what everyone calls me.' He flashed the metal strip around his neck. Etched on it was a number.

'I asked for your name,' she persisted.

'Prisoners have no name. Now, if you tell me where you want the roses planted, I can start working.'

'That can wait,' Olivia said brusquely. 'I am sure we have met before.'

'You are mistaken. Our backgrounds and circumstances don't warrant a meeting.'

His voice was icy and his stare audacious. The scars on his body bore testimony to his impertinence.

'Since we will be meeting for many hours, every day, I thought it prudent to address each other by name.'

'I don't think that would be prudent at all,' he snapped. Dotty whipped up her head, her eyes alert at the sharpness in his voice.

Olivia was piqued by his audacity. It was easy to have him lashed and punished for insolence. Suppressing her irritation, she instructed him about the plants. His body bent against the scorching sun, he toiled for the next three hours without a break. She watched his muscles ripple and strain as he dug and levelled the earth.

It came to her in a flash one night. Indraneel! That was his name. Along with the name came the memory of that eventful morning when Olivia had visited Rajat at the Alipore police station. Indraneel had handed her a slip of paper with an address and requested her to warn the residents to flee.

The next morning Olivia buttonholed the prisoner. 'Isn't there a word like gratitude in your dictionary, Indraneel?'

Surprised by her words, he looked up from the rose saplings he was transplanting.

'Gratitude?'

'Yes, gratitude,' she stressed. 'Do you have no recollection of our meeting?'

'I do not know what you are talking about,' he replied, turning back to his plants.

'Let me jog your memory. Some months ago, you handed me a slip of paper at Alipore Jail on which was an address. You requested me to warn the people staying there.'

Shocked, Indraneel dropped his tools and turned to look at her. In his eyes, Olivia saw the light of recognition.

'It was you?' he stood up and faced her. Dotty, who had been digging up earth, bounded up to them. 'I have much to thank you for. You saved the lives of my comrades.'

'So, you remember the incident?'

'I am sorry for being rude. I hadn't realised you were the person who helped us.' There was remorse in his voice.

'You are not the only one. Not many people want to look at my face.' Olivia laughed.

'You are a courageous woman and I salute you. Now that I know you are Colonel Bradley's daughter, I am doubly grateful for your help.'

'Since the misunderstanding has been cleared up, may I call you by name?' she asked with a smile.

'Please call me Neel. It's what all my friends call me.'

'So, we are friends?' Olivia looked archly at the unsmiling man.

'Your father is a British officer and I am a revolutionary. We stand on opposite sides of the fence,' he said sarcastically. 'It wouldn't be wise for us to be friends.'

Olivia knew her father wouldn't hesitate to punish the man if she befriended him. 'Leave that to me to decide, Neel.' She stared back, challenging him.

'Bravo!' His eyes twinkled with mirth. It made him look youthful and good-natured. 'You will be my first British friend. The only other white-skinned friend I had was an Anglo-Indian.'

'An Anglo-Indian? That's interesting.'

'His name is Peter and he is a highly confused fellow.' Neel smiled at the recollection of their first meeting.

'Confused?' Olivia shaded her eyes with her hand and looked at him.

'Peter is confused about his identity.'

'How did the two of you meet?'

'That's a long story.' Indraneel sighed and bent down to continue working.

'I have all the time in the world.' Olivia smiled encouragingly.

'Peter and I met in Amritsar. . .' There was a distant look in Indraneel's eyes as he began narrating the story.

'You miss your friend,' Olivia murmured.

27

Peter

A Prisoner in Paradise

Peter's journey to the Andaman Islands was fraught with suffering. The prisoners were packed into the hold of an ancient ship that seemed to float on prayers and hope. There were more than a hundred of them crammed like sardines in a can. They were a mix of murderers, felons and freedom fighters.

The dark and wet hold barely offered enough space to sit. Peter was lucky to find a spot near the ladder that led up to the hatch. Each time the hatch opened, he glimpsed the sky and got a whiff of the sea breeze.

By his side, a young boy sang patriotic songs. His voice was strong and youthful, ringing with courage and hope. By the third day, his voice had weakened and, on the fourth, he stopped singing. He was pulled out of the hold and thrown overboard.

In the bowels of the vessel, the prisoners felt their innards churning violently. An ink-black, overcast sky made visibility poor and the ship bobbed up and down on a steadily swelling sea. There was mayhem all around. Even the atheists began praying for deliverance. As the ship crossed the black waters, the journey seemed endless, with the prisoners locked in the hellhole with nothing but the fetid air of hopelessness all around them. Some, weak with hunger and disease, died during the voyage and were tossed overboard. Within a couple of days, the hold had lost five prisoners. Selfishly, the survivors welcomed the additional space.

Days later, the shipload of prisoners reached their destination, ill, hungry and exhausted. Peter's legs gave way as he straightened his body after the long days of crouching in the hold. Blinded by sunlight, a spell of dizziness hit him as he walked.

At the port, the prisoners were subjected to a medical examination to segregate the sick and infirm from the able-bodied.

While the freedom fighters were sent to the Cellular Jail, Peter, to his surprise and delight, was singled out for Ross Island.

'Lucky white shit!' remarked a Bengali activist. 'They have made concessions for the colour of your skin.'

Despite Peter's rudeness and posturing during his trial, the magistrate could not overcome his bias towards Anglo-Indians. Besides, there was no precedent of an Anglo-Indian being sent to the Cellular Jail or even the Andaman Islands for revolutionary activities. Behind this leniency lay the fear that Anglo-Indians too might turn against the British.

As the manacled freedom fighters were led away to their doom, Peter couldn't help rejoicing. He decided he would do everything to remain on Ross Island for the rest of his sentence. He would do nothing to rock the boat.

Ross Island, the power centre of the British in the Andaman and Nicobar Islands, was heaven compared to the Cell. Flanking the open sea, it was a flourishing township, a miniature England.

The luxurious bungalows, clubs, paved paths and swimming pools were built by calloused hands, chained legs and tortured bodies that had been shipped in the hundreds to cut down the ancient trees, clear the jungles and pave the way for the construction of a comfortable haven for the British. Hundreds of prisoners had worked to transform the island into what was fondly known as the Paris of the East.

The seventy-acre island was divided by a wall. Sited on the hilltop towards the north of the wall were sprawling bungalows for the British officers. Fringed with lush gardens, they commanded a spectacular view of the sea and beyond. The northern part of the island also held comfortable barracks for the white troops. The Indian soldiers, servants and convicts were housed on the southern end of the island.

Ross Island was proud of its amenities. It offered the officers and their families shops, a printing press, a hospital, a post office, a treasury, tennis courts and even a water filtration plant. And then, there was Farzand Ali's store, which stocked every necessity for the five hundred-odd residents of the island.

The comforts enjoyed by the troops on Ross Island were impressive. There was a plush subordinate's club for non-commissioned officers, fitted with a revolving, teak dance floor mounted on springs.

Compared to Ross Island, life for prisoners in the Cellular Jail was nothing short of Dante's inferno. Peter was thankful he had not been sent to the Cell even though he knew that somewhere in the Cellular Jail, there were revolutionaries locked in a solitary cell, suffering a fate worse than death. Was Neel one of them, he wondered.

Aware that many prisoners were worse off in lock-ups on another part of the island, Peter was thankful for the small mercies that came his way. During the day, the prisoners laboured in the gardens and swept and cleaned the streets, only to be locked up in filthy and damp cells in the evening.

While the prisoners were assigned menial tasks such as cleaning the lavatories, sweeping the roads and removing garbage, Peter was given easier chores like polishing, cleaning, sweeping and swabbing the floors and balustrades of various buildings to keep them gleaming. Sometimes, he was sent to work in the printing press, bakery or library. Each morning, a guard read out the chores assigned to them for the day and Peter endured the envy and abuse of the other prisoners.

Peter's movements were restricted but he soon created a favourable impression on the guards. His witty repartee, jokes and fluency in English came in handy once again. Within a few months, he had earned the guards' goodwill and roamed unescorted around the island. The guards allowed him more privileges than the other prisoners and he did his best to keep them in good humour.

One morning, the guards ordered Peter to report to the library. The job was heaven-sent. It offered flexibility and a little dignity. Samuel Jones, the elderly librarian, was a kind soul. He was learned and compassionate, two qualities that were scarce on the island. Learning was something most British officers lacked and the word compassion didn't exist in their dictionary.

Peter was happy to work in the library. He enjoyed the quiet atmosphere and the librarian's benevolence. His cheerful and diligent nature created a favourable impression and soon Mr Jones became his friend and mentor.

The librarian was a lonely man who loved pottering around his domain. A modest man, Mr Jones had two obsessions—the library and Shakespeare.

The library, with a few thousand books, some of them tattered and beyond repair, became Peter's refuge. There were few borrowers amongst the officers and troops. It was the women who loved reading and most of them restricted themselves to romance novels.

Peter's job was to dust the books, place them in the right cabinets and keep the area clean. Sometimes Mr Jones asked him to make the entries in the register.

There was binding, tabulating, organising and dusting to be done, besides categorising new books. In a short time, Peter learned the art of bookbinding and became indispensable to the librarian. Their busiest time was when the much-awaited shipload of magazines and books arrived from Port Blair. The rest of their days passed quietly, giving Peter enough time to read while also tending to his duties.

On one such day, heavy clouds had been gathering over the island all morning. By late morning, it had started pouring. Seated near a window, Peter was trying to repair the pages of a damaged book when a woman arrived. It wasn't often that a woman came to the library. Most preferred to send a note for specific books and magazines.

She shook the water from her umbrella and ran a hand over her tousled auburn hair that fell around her slender shoulders. Then the girl turned, and he noticed her pockmarked face.

Pushing open the door, she entered and stopped at a table near Peter. Just then, the librarian strode up and exclaimed, 'Miss Bradley, you shouldn't have ventured out in this terrible weather. Had you sent word, I would have had the books delivered to you.'

'That's very kind of you, Mr Jones,' she said. 'Bad weather doesn't worry me. Coming to the library is an excuse to get out of the house, anyway.' Her voice was soft and pleasing.

'Well, it isn't much of a morning,' he said with a laugh. 'The rain gods are making merry.'

'They make merry too often for comfort.' A smile lit up her face.

She selected three books and paced the veranda, waiting for the rain to stop. Peter watched her as she stuck her hand out to feel the drops. Then she leaned out and looked up into the rain. He watched her delighted expression as she closed her eyes and enjoyed the raindrops falling on her face.

Peter chuckled.

Embarrassed at being caught in this childish game, the woman took her hat from the hatstand and determinedly placed it on her head, only to have it blown away by a sudden gust of wind. Still chuckling, Peter ran to retrieve her hat. 'Thank you!' She rewarded him with a smile.

And then she was gone, leaving Peter with the image of her upturned face awash with raindrops.

'Poor girl! Who would have thought that a young girl like her could be so lonely and neglected,' said the librarian as he watched the rickshaw disappear around the corner.

'Doesn't she have a family?' asked Peter.

'The only family she has is a father and he is too busy to bother about her.'

'But a young girl like her must have a lot of friends.'

'Unfortunately, she has no friends. The young men keep away from her because of her pockmarked face and she is too proud to ingratiate herself to the hoity-toity women on the island. Olivia Bradley is a sensitive creature.'

Miss Bradley, Peter learned over the next few days, was one of the few people who visited the library. 'She has fine taste in literature. Surprisingly, she reads a lot of books on India and Indian culture. It's certainly a departure from the others on the island,' said Mr Jones. Struck by a sudden idea, the librarian continued, 'You could deliver books to her. That way, she wouldn't have to take the trouble of coming here in bad weather.'

'Yes, I could do that,' volunteered Peter, only too glad to see more of the island.

'Here are some books from her list.' Mr Jones handed him a few tomes. 'Remember to use the servants' entrance at the back of the bungalow. Don't make the mistake of going through the front gate,' warned Mr Jones, just as Peter turned to go.

From that day, Peter walked regularly to the Bradley residence to deliver or collect books. He took care to enter the house using the rear gate and exchanged the books with Rosie or Faisal. This continued for a couple of weeks until Olivia summoned him to the front of the house.

He found her reading on an easy chair behind the bougainvillea-laden screen on the veranda.

'Come here, Dotty,' Olivia called to her dog, who was sniffing him suspiciously.

Once the books were exchanged, she instructed him to go to the kitchen at the back, where the cook had been told to provide him with tea.

Olivia was a kind soul who never allowed Peter to leave without having a glass of lemonade and something to eat. Sometimes it was a piece of cake or scones, at other times it was sandwiches. On most days, he lingered outside the kitchen, waiting for the treat. It didn't take him long to ingratiate himself with the staff. His efforts often resulted in an extra piece of cake or sandwich from the cook.

28

Olivia

Love Is in the Air

Dreaming suited Olivia. It brought a glow to her face and a softness to her eyes. Sitting in the bower, she dreamed of a cottage with whitewashed walls perched on a craggy hilltop by the seashore. There were roses in the garden and geraniums in pots on the windowsills; the air was thick with the scent of flowers, and butterflies flitted about freely. The sky was so blue that it hurt the eyes.

In Roma's company back in Calcutta she had begun dreaming of love. Watching Rajat and Roma had kindled a strange fire in her. She had not missed the mischievous look in Rajat's eyes whenever he looked at Roma. The unspoken message of sensuality between them didn't escape her either and feelings she didn't know she had, began surfacing. A pleasurable tingling beginning in the pit of her stomach spread downwards in an ache. She dreamed of a man's arms around her. Touching, caressing and comforting.

These days, in all her dreams, she had a man by her side, and he looked like Neel.

Like the moss sticks in the potted plants, Indraneel was a fixture in the garden. He neither spoke nor showed any inclination to strike up a friendship with the servants who hated him for his arrogance. Unlike Peter, he refused the food and drinks Olivia sent through the servants.

'Why didn't you take the tea?' Olivia asked one morning. 'You must be thirsty.'

'Can you offer tea to all the prisoners in the Cellular Jail?'

'Why should I offer them tea? They are not working in my garden. Besides, will it help them if you refuse the tea?' she retorted.

'It is a matter of principle.' He stood upright, his shoulders straightening from the usual stoop. 'Just forget it. I don't expect you to understand,' he said scathingly.

'I think you will serve your country better if you keep in good health. I am sure you don't want to die on this island,' Olivia pointed out.

Her words struck a chord with him. Neel was thoughtful as he went back to work. An hour later, he approached Olivia. 'May I have that cup of tea now?'

Surprised, she raised her brow.

'You are absolutely right.' His eyes crinkled with amusement and he continued, 'I don't want to die on this island.'

Perhaps it was thirst and hunger that forced him to drop his arrogance. Perhaps he thought her advice made sense. He no longer refused the tea and snacks offered by her. It was strangely satisfying to feed his hunger and subdue his arrogance at the same time. Olivia had never been in a position of power. She had always played a secondary role in everyone's life but now she felt a sense of power.

Soon the weeds had disappeared and tiny saplings flourished in the well-laid beds, their tiny leaves nodding in the breeze. Neel rejuvenated the lawn and there was exuberant foliage near the gazebo. He had planted fragrant lavender in the beds flanking the pathway leading to the porch. Even a chance brush against the blossoms released a pleasant fragrance.

The change did not escape Colonel Bradley's eyes. Drawn by the neat landscaping and beautiful flowers, he took to spending more time on the veranda. Not much of a reading man, he sat with a glass of beer while going through his official *dak*.

The gazebo, with its beautiful climbers, was Olivia's refuge. With Dotty at her feet, she spent hours watching the butterflies that flitted around the flowers, listening to the birds or reading a book. The trees were nested and life pulsated in them.

Gradually, Neel's tea breaks became longer as the tea was accompanied by sandwiches or fruit. It was Olivia's way of acknowledging his contribution to the garden. The weather changed, as did the flowers in the garden. It had been several months since the prisoner had come to work for the colonel. In that time, much had changed, apart from the weather and the flowers. Olivia's feelings for the man, for instance.

She often heard him crooning to the plants, praising a plant for its growth, rebuking another for laziness, tending to the ones stricken by pests or running his calloused hands tenderly on another. She struggled to believe Neel was capable of violence.

Not just the plants, even animals took to him in a big way. For Dotty, it was a case of love at first sight. The dog loved hanging around the garden, staring at Neel with limpid eyes.

Olivia watched the man as he toiled. His face had dropped the lean look and his features had softened. The tea had done its trick. Sitting in the shade of the flowering creepers on the veranda, Olivia noted his biceps moving rhythmically as he worked with the heavy shears, trimming the hedges. Watching him, she felt a warmth coursing through her. It left her with a beautiful tingling sensation and deep longing.

Neel was the only person who looked into her eyes. The marks on her face made no difference to him. Like any woman in love, Olivia found excuses to be with him. Sometimes she joined him in planting the saplings or pruning the roses. Together they created bird baths and put up bird feeders.

Every morning, Olivia took a seat on the veranda pretending to read, while her eyes followed his movements. A strange longing consumed her nights. She was frustrated by Neel's dispassion. He was a taciturn man and the only conversations between the two of them were the ones engineered by Olivia. Was this love? Neel's dark and brooding eyes left her mind spinning with possibilities. If this feeling was love, she had not the voice to express it.

Why did I have to fall in love with him? He is impudent and unresponsive. There is an unbridgeable gulf between the two of us.

Olivia tried countless times to remain aloof but her resolve would last just a few hours. She hung around Neel the way Dotty did, seeking a smile or a touch.

29

Peter

An Unexpected Encounter

The *Triumph* docked that morning, bringing its cargo of goods and tales for the waiting porters.

The ship's arrival was an exciting event for the islanders, especially the prisoners. Each vessel sailed in with tales of heroism and hope. Along with supplies, it brought whispers of liberation and the latest political accomplishments. It also brought heart-rending tales of brutality and oppression.

Several months had passed since the day Peter had first brought books for Olivia. He knew the authors she liked and carried a book list to help her choose the ones she wanted. The kind girl had insisted that he use the front entrance of the bungalow. Although he was curious about her father, Peter had not yet come across Colonel Bradley since his chores took him to Olivia's house after the colonel had left for work.

One morning, as he was leaving the bungalow after delivering some books, Peter noticed a prisoner working in the garden. The man was hunched over a bed of roses, pruning them. There was something familiar about the stooped figure. Peter halted.

'Good morning,' he called out to the man.

The man turned and looked at him. The next moment, Peter rushed forward with a cry. Surprised, Olivia watched the two men from the veranda.

'Peter! Is it really you or am I dreaming?' Neel stared at the Anglo-Indian in disbelief before enveloping him in a bear hug. Tears ran down their eyes as they clung to each other. 'It's so good to see you, Peter. How the hell did you land up in this hellhole?'

'That's a long story, brother. First, let me catch my breath.' Peter was laughing and crying at the same time. He had thought

Indraneel was in Port Blair, in the Cellular Jail. Not in his wildest dreams had he expected to meet the chameleon on Ross Island.

'Peter!' the happiness in Neel's voice was unmistakable. Throwing a cautious glance around him, he caught his friend's hand and led him to the bougainvillea-covered gazebo at the far end of the garden.

'Peter,' he repeated, as though he couldn't get beyond his name. 'It's really you. I still can't believe you are here.' Neel squatted near the Anglo-Indian.

'Destiny wanted us to meet, so here I am.' Peter searched the Bengali's face. He was a skeleton of the youthful and energetic man Peter once knew. 'How have you been, Neel?' he asked gently.

Neel looked down at his calloused hands and smiled. 'I am alive.' A wheezing cough shook his body.

So much had changed in the past few years. It had been worse for the revolutionary, Peter realised. They sat on the grass and wrestled with a flood of emotions.

'How did the bastards get you?' Peter finally asked. There was so much he wanted to know, so many gaps that had to be filled.

'That's another long story,' Neel said with a sigh. 'We are the thorns in the crown, to be removed, one by one.'

'Where is Gurmeet?'

Neel's eyes misted at the mention of his comrade. With a heavy sigh, he replied, 'We had plans of bombing the Legislative Assembly but the mission failed. After that, we tried assassinating the Governor but he escaped unhurt. However, we did manage to kill a British officer who was accompanying him. But then someone sneaked on us and we were arrested. Gurmeet was carrying a gun and that gave them a reason to hand him the harshest punishment. He suffered inhuman torture before being hanged. Having been involved in the plot, I was already a hunted man. The judge lost no time in pronouncing a life sentence and I was sent to the Cellular Jail.'

'The bastards!' Peter clenched his fists.

'Few can withstand their barbaric torture but Gurmeet was different. They broke his bones, knocked out his teeth and gouged out an eye but he refused to speak. That fellow was made of steel.'

Peter shuddered and his nostrils flared with anger. 'If the police can resort to such torture in Calcutta, I shudder to imagine the treatment meted out in the Cell.'

'It's nightmarish.' Neel's eyes hardened as he recounted the inhuman cruelty he had faced. 'The solitary confinement and torture have driven many young prisoners to insanity. We are ill-fed, skeletal beings trying to survive the indignities heaped on us. With our food and water rationed to an unimaginable extent, we somehow survive. Can you imagine being yoked like a bull to a press to extract oil from mustard seeds or having to pound coir endlessly till your hands bleed? The quota assigned to each prisoner is beyond any man's capability. Any protest lands a prisoner on the whipping post. Fettered and shackled, we spend each day wishing for death. I can't describe the torture. All I can say is that I won't wish it upon my worst enemy.'

For months he had suffered in the hideous hellhole, marking each day on the wall with his nails. 'My luck changed the day Colonel Bradley visited the Cell,' he continued. 'The colonel was there on an official visit but he used the occasion to pick up a few prisoners to work on Ross Island. Four prisoners were selected and I was one of them.'

'There must have been hundreds of prisoners lined up for his inspection. How did he select you?'

'It was simply one of those things we call luck. I was yoked to the oil press. It was physical torture that carried on for hours while, whip in hand, a warden sat watching, ready to flog the laggards.' Neel clenched his jaw at the memory. 'I learned to switch my mind off. I focused on the good things about my life, forcing my mind to go back to the happy days of my childhood.'

'How did Bradley settle on you?' Peter brought him back to the subject.

'As I was running around the oil press axle, the warden took me off the yoke and I thought he was going to flog me. But all he asked me was if I knew anything about plants.'

Neel paused for a while and stared at his hands.

'I was brought to Ross Island and asked to look after Bradley's garden.'

It was noon and the sun was blazing overhead. The two of them had spent a lot of time talking.

'I should get back to work,' Neel remarked.

Peter learned that Neel lived with five other convicts in a derelict structure close to the forested area. The leaky roof over their head exposed the prisoners to the elements throughout the year. Cold, biting winds chilled their bones and rats plagued them at night. The gruel supplied twice a day was not enough to keep hunger away. It was Olivia's charity that had kept Neel alive. Peter and Neel both depended on the favours doled out by the colonel's daughter.

Now that he knew Neel was working at the Bradley bungalow, Peter began looking for excuses to visit the place. They spoke of many things—the past, the present and the future. Working in the library provided Peter an opportunity to read the newspaper and he relayed all the news to the revolutionary. Although the newspapers printed censored news, the two were happy to keep abreast of what was happening in the country.

Over a few weeks, Peter realised Neel had changed. He had given up all hope of returning to Calcutta.

'You are not the Neel I knew,' Peter told him one day. 'That Neel was an optimist.'

'Does that surprise you, Anglo boy? Some of the young revolutionaries in the Cellular Jail have gone insane. It has taken much determination to keep my sanity.'

'I think you are a much stronger man.' Peter thumped his friend's back. 'You must not give up, Neel. We will go back to Calcutta soon.'

'They will never let me go, just as they won't let go of the others. In those six hundred and ninety-eight cells of that jail, they have locked up honourable men—men who have done no wrong.'

Unknown to the two men, Olivia listened to every word they spoke.

30
Olivia

A Challenging Man

It was well past spring. The trees glowed in the light of the setting sun. The lawn looked tired and the trees were ready to shed their leaves. Even the tall palms had a drooping look about them. The evergreens looked morose and the cluster of bamboo plants stood like a posse of guards ringing the little kitchen garden at the back. Bradley's garden was the envy of many.

Praise for the garden and its architect fuelled Olivia's desire for Neel, but the man remained aloof. The only verbal exchange between them was the morning salutation. 'Namaste, Memsahib' or 'Good morning, Madam'. The greeting depended on his mood. It could even be 'Jai Hind' when he was feeling rebellious. Olivia shuddered to think about the consequences if her father were to hear him.

It was a Sunday morning and the colonel was in his study. Book in hand, Olivia settled on her favourite chair in the veranda, watching Neel working in the garden. Bradley emerged from his study and caught her staring at the prisoner.

'Don't you have anything better to do than to ogle the gardener?' he shouted at his daughter.

Stunned at his outburst, Olivia stared at her father. He seemed to be in a foul mood. She was confident that a servant had complained about Neel to her father.

'Go inside, right now!'

With a loud sob, she rushed into the house. The colonel strode over to Neel and slapped him hard. Watching them from the window, Olivia saw the gardener stiffen with resentment. Tears ran down her cheeks. Neel was being punished for her indiscretion.

'Bloody blackie! I shall have you flogged if I catch you speaking to my daughter. Is that clear?' Bradley bellowed.

His fist clenched, Neel lowered his eyes. He did not want to go back to the Cell but he was determined to defy the colonel by becoming Olivia's friend. He took pleasure in rebelling against the British any way he could. Neel's defiance was encouraged by a mutinous Olivia.

Over the next few days, their closeness grew, monologues turning into dialogues and discussions. Olivia was keen to know about Neel's past, his people, his village. Their discussions ranged from India's history and culture to the current national mood.

Each morning, after her father left for work and the servants got busy with their chores, Olivia sat near Neel while he worked.

'How can you work sincerely for my father, a man who hates you?' she asked one day.

'You forget, my dear. I hate your father, too.' Neel continued shovelling the flower bed. 'I do it for my pleasure. Gardening is a balm for lacerated souls.'

'Would you like to continue this work when you are released?'

'Do you think they will ever release me?' he countered, amused at the suggestion. 'I am a convicted murderer. Worse, my victim was a white man.'

'Tell me about the Cell. Is it really a hellhole?' she egged him on.

His mocking laughter angered her.

'You must be the first white woman to display so much interest in Indians and their wretchedness. Most white women are content being served by their slaves.'

His words stung. 'Aren't you being judgemental? All British women are not prejudiced and unsympathetic.' Olivia stomped off to her room. But she had lived in India long enough to know the truth of his words.

The midday sun was at its peak but Indraneel continued to work in the garden. Olivia peeped from behind the chintz curtains of her room and stared at his bent back. He must have sensed her presence, because he turned unexpectedly and bowed mockingly in her direction.

Ordering the servant to fetch a jar of lemonade and cake, Olivia sauntered towards the gazebo. Armed with a novel, she settled down on the white wicker chair while Faisal spread a lace tablecloth on the rattan table. From her vantage point, Olivia had a full view of the garden.

From the corner of her eye, she saw Neel pause for a moment and wipe his brow. Olivia pretended to be engrossed in the book till Faisal had left.

'Come here, prisoner,' she called out to Neel. 'Why don't you have some lemonade? I do not want you to faint in this heat.'

'Memsahib, your father would have me shot if he saw me sitting there with you. Don't worry. I will not faint nor will I stop working.'

'Don't be stupid, Neel,' Olivia scolded.

Smiling, he ambled up to the table and picked up a glass of lemonade. His dark eyes danced with devilish glee as he smiled. His smile smoothed the deep furrows on his forehead, making him look younger.

'I wonder why you are so kind to me. You are not so kind to the other servants in the house.'

Neel never minced his words. She was impatient with the grovelling servants. Faisal and Rosie were oily and treacherous. She didn't trust them. Olivia threw him a condescending look she normally reserved for the others.

'That's more like it.' He saluted cheerfully and returned to his task. Neel's impertinence was delightful.

He was a challenge and she liked challenges.

31
Peter

Hopes Rise

The club was a popular place in the evenings. Most officers gathered there for a drink or a game at the end of the day, and the ladies joined them occasionally. It was also a place where most rumours originated and romances developed. Peter was sent to work there whenever there were parties and extra hands were needed. He enjoyed listening to the gossip and sharing it with Neel.

One day, Peter overheard some disquieting rumours about Bradley's relationship with an officer's wife. It was whispered that the colonel had deputed the husband to another island so he could spend time with the woman.

'It is impossible to associate words like love and romance with that crusty and cruel man. It can only be lust,' said Neel. He was taken aback when Peter shared the gossip. 'I feel sorry for Olivia.'

'True!' admitted Peter. 'That girl could do with a little love and romance. She needs a man to share her thoughts.'

Soulful strains of music reached their ears as they stood talking. Olivia was playing the piano.

'You are right. Olivia is a nice person. She needs love.' There was tenderness in Neel's voice. 'It's not just her face that is scarred. Her soul is scarred too.'

Something in his voice caught Peter's attention. Was there something brewing between the colonel's daughter and the revolutionary?

He had noticed that Olivia rarely moved from her seat on the veranda when Neel worked in the garden. The look of longing in her eyes hadn't escaped Peter. He shuddered at the thought of the consequences of their romance. Bradley would not hesitate to kill Neel at the slightest suspicion.

Peter brushed away the gloomy thoughts. Knowing Neel's strong hatred of all things British, Peter knew the man would never reciprocate Olivia's feelings.

One morning, on his mission to deliver Olivia's books, Peter discovered her standing behind the vast mass of bougainvillea flowers near the gazebo. Neel was pruning the unruly branches. Moving closer, the Anglo-Indian eavesdropped on their conversation.

'Why don't you join me for a cup of tea on the veranda?' Olivia asked.

'I am sorry, Memsahib,' he replied. 'I have a lot of work to do.'

'Neel, the servants have gone on their errands. There is no one to spy on us. There are so many things I want to share with you.'

'I don't think that is advisable, Memsahib. I am a wild and dangerous animal that needs to be chained and locked up.' Neel's voice was laden with sarcasm.

'Please . . .' she replied. 'Call me Olivia.'

'Well, Olivia, let me get back to work.'

Sighing with relief, Peter quickly moved away. But he wanted to be sure Neel harboured no romantic feelings. So, on his next trip to the bungalow, he cornered his friend. 'I think she likes you, Neel.'

'I don't care whether she likes or hates me. I am here to work as a gardener. I am not here to entertain or amuse her.'

'I still don't see the harm in being nice to her,' Peter said, testing Neel's resolve.

'Do you know her father?' Neel asked, his eyes piercing.

'No, I have not met him yet but I have heard a few stories about the man.'

'He is one of the most sadistic people on this island—pompous, cruel and vindictive. There is so much blood on his hands that if he were to spend the rest of his life washing them, the rivers would turn red. He is the Lady Macbeth of this island and will spend his old age hounded by guilt and fear.'

'So, the sins of the father are to be laid at the daughter's door? Is he the reason you avoid Olivia? Or are you afraid of something else?' Peter continued to provoke his friend.

'Afraid of what?' Neel's voice was belligerent.

'Afraid of falling in love with her, for instance.'

'In love with Olivia?' Neel broke into laughter.

It was a long time since Peter had heard him laugh.

'You are a stupid romantic.' Neel thumped him on the back. 'Can you imagine me falling in love with her?'

'Is it the colour of her skin?'

'Isn't it all about the colour of our skin? You are a privileged prisoner on this island because of the colour of your skin. And I am treated like a dog because of my skin colour. My dear friend, don't delude yourself. It is all about skin colour.'

Peter left the bungalow, relieved by Neel's response.

As the season turned, there was no change in their routine. Occasionally, Peter came across some disturbing news about events taking place elsewhere in the country. Cut off from the mainland, they had only a sketchy idea about the turmoil and politics there. The newspapers, run by British editors, offered biased views.

Peter received information about the Cellular Jail from the librarian, which he faithfully relayed to Neel.

'The freedom fighters want to get back to the mainland,' Peter informed Neel one morning. 'They want to be a part of the upheaval that is imminent. A petition that all political prisoners should be repatriated to the mainland was sent to the viceroy a few weeks ago.'

'They are foolish to assume that the viceroy is interested in their petition,' Neel countered.

'According to Mr Jones, the prisoners have issued an ultimatum. They have threatened to go on hunger strike if their demands are not met.'

'I think a lot will depend on who blinks first. Let's wait and watch.'

As predicted by Neel, the viceroy had no time for their petition and so a hunger strike began on 25 July 1937 with almost all the prisoners in the Cell joining it. This was the second time they were going on a hunger strike.

The librarian greeted Peter excitedly when he arrived one morning.

'Peter, there you are! Do you know the latest? Political prisoners in jails across the country have joined the hunger strike to support the freedom fighters in the Cell. There are massive demonstrations of intellectuals and students on the mainland.'

He waved his hands expressively. 'Do you realise what will happen now? You could go home, my boy.'

'I can go home only if the petition is accepted by the viceroy.' Peter's voice was sceptical.

The waiting game continued as the British remained unmoved by the plight of the prisoners in the Cellular Jail.

In the meantime, the hunger strike entered its second week. Many prisoners were in a pitiable state, some of them on the verge of death. Telegrams and letters of support poured in from all over the country. They came from leaders like Jawaharlal Nehru, Subhas Chandra Bose and Rabindranath Tagore, each one imploring the freedom fighters to end their strike.

'This time, the viceroy will have to relent,' predicted the librarian. 'Things may change soon. Mark my words.'

'It may happen, finally,' Neel exclaimed on hearing the latest news brought by his friend. 'We might live to return to the mainland.'

Charged with excitement, they hugged and congratulated each other. The battle, however, was only halfway through.

32

Olivia

A Change of Heart

In a surprising turnaround, Olivia's father declared a truce with the young gardener.

'The fellow seems sincere, not like the other prisoners,' Bradley conceded grudgingly. Noting his daughter's surprise at the statement, he continued, 'He's done a good job in the garden. No doubt about that.'

It was a muggy Sunday morning. The colonel and his daughter were sitting in the arbour, the heady fragrance of frangipani flowers hanging around them. A delicately designed wrought-iron table was laid out with the finest Darjeeling tea and freshly baked cookies from the Farzand Ali store.

Olivia poured another cup of tea for her father. His shaky hands and flushed appearance didn't escape her. Excessive drinking was taking its toll on the once-handsome officer.

She wondered if the likelihood of repatriation of the Indian prisoners had anything to do with her father's change of heart. Like everyone else on the island, she had heard of the hunger strike and the demands of the prisoners.

'I am amazed at the size of those flowers.' Bradley picked up another biscuit and pointed at the bed of roses. 'Those roses are the envy of all officers on this island.'

'He seems to consider it a challenge rather than a task,' Olivia replied, flipping through a magazine that had arrived after a long voyage.

'I think you should feed him a bit. He looks famished. The prisoners get little food.' Noticing her raised eyebrows, her father explained, 'A starving man is of no use as a gardener. It is in our interest to keep him healthy. Our garden needs him.'

Olivia was surprised. She had not forgotten her father's reaction when he caught her looking at Neel. Her father was not a charitable person. She wondered if his words of praise stemmed from his anxiety that some other officer would take the gardener away. Good gardeners were in short supply.

Whatever the reason, the volte-face pleased Olivia.

'There is a masquerade ball at the club on Saturday.' Her father's voice sliced through her thoughts. 'You should attend. A mask is the best thing to hide your face.'

'Masquerading does not interest me. I would rather finish the book I am reading,' she replied, hurt by his comment.

'There are charitable men out here. They wouldn't mind a blemish or two if there is a big dowry to go with the girl. You should try your luck.'

Offended by his words, Olivia tried to concentrate on her book. It was best to ignore her father when he was in a spiteful mood. His moods were as unpredictable as the Andaman Sea.

The monsoon unleashed its fury once again. Volleys of unrelenting rain eclipsed the short-lived reprieve of sunshine. Sitting near the window, she watched Neel working in the slushy patch, unmindful of the rain. Olivia wanted to call him inside to discuss the latest situation in the Cellular Jail but her courage failed her. The man's moods were as unpredictable as her father's.

After a week of incessant rain, the clouds receded and a weak sun appeared in the sky. Her father was away in Port Blair on an official tour and unlikely to return soon. The servants had retired for their noon meal.

It was her mother's death anniversary and Olivia was in a terrible mood. Throughout the morning, her mood went through varying levels of melancholy. A photo album lay open on her lap and a picture of Irene Bradley with her two children stared back at her. Memories brought tears to her eyes. She wept for the lost days and the wasted lives. She wept for what her life could have been.

Tears cascaded down Olivia's pitted cheeks and her sobs grew louder. She did not notice Neel approaching.

'Memsahib!' His soft voice caressed her. 'I have finished my work. May I leave now?'

Colonel Bradley had issued orders that the prisoner did not need to be accompanied by a guard any longer.

Flustered by his sudden appearance, Olivia blew her nose into a handkerchief and looked up. The unexpected compassion in Neel's eyes tore at her heart and she broke into loud sobs once more.

'Is there anything I can do?' He looked confused and uncertain.

'No, no, please don't bother.' She waved him away. 'It's these blasted memories. They've ruined my morning.'

'Memories are best left in the cold till they shrivel and die,' he said in a gentle voice.

'Today is my mother's death anniversary, Neel.' Olivia raised her large, sad eyes and whimpered. She felt an overwhelming need to unburden her emotions. She wanted to be comforted. She wanted to be in Neel's arms.

On an impulse, he reached out and stroked her hair. His calloused fingers running through her hair were strangely soothing. Olivia closed her eyes. Sighing, she moved closer and placed her head on his chest. They stood like that for a few minutes, their hearts pulsating, and then he pushed her away.

'Get a grip on yourself, Olivia,' he said in a voice hoarse with emotion. 'I must go.'

'I am lonely and miserable, Neel. I need your company. Please stay,' she sobbed.

'Why don't you make some friends?' He stepped back from her extended arm. 'There are many young officers who will lend you a shoulder.'

'I don't want those young officers.' His words irked her.

'Why? You could find a kindly soul among them.' He spoke from a safe distance.

'Young men don't swarm around me. They avoid looking at my face. Do you think I enjoy sitting at home all by myself while the others are enjoying themselves at the club?' she responded with bitterness.

'I find nothing wrong with your face. I . . . I . . .' He searched for the right words.

'You are lying. Look at me and tell me the truth,' she said, throwing back her hair.

He lowered his eyes. 'Look at me, Neel,' she demanded, pulling at his arm. 'Do you think I am pretty?'

'You are Bradley's daughter and I am a prisoner. I don't want to think beyond that.' He forced his eyes away.

Olivia's eyes blazed with fury. She gripped his arms once again. 'No! Don't turn away like everyone else. Look at me and tell me the truth.'

He prised her fingers open and faced her. There was no mercy in his eyes as he spoke. 'You want the truth? I find you full of self-pity, which is a very damaging emotion. You deprive yourself of self-respect when you indulge in it. People are beautiful because of their thoughts. Your kindness and compassion are far more attractive than a pretty face.'

'Lofty words,' she snorted. 'I bet you don't even believe them. You are trying to console me.'

'I don't use lofty words.'

'Could you ever love me?' she challenged.

Her question stunned him. 'I am not allowed to fall in love. You forget, I am a prisoner.'

'There! I knew it! You are making excuses.' Her shoulders slumped.

'I am not making excuses,' he retorted. 'Love is a luxury for me. My present circumstances ensure it is an emotion I can never experience. May I leave now?'

'Not until you tell me I am beautiful,' she insisted.

'Don't be childish, Olivia.' His voice was gentle. 'You are beautiful and you don't need me to tell you that. Don't let anyone tell you otherwise either.' Neel began backing away slowly.

His words rang in her ears long after he left. They raised her spirits even if they were a lie.

Love is a strange emotion. The ways of the heart are complex and inexplicable. Why else would the frail fall in love with the powerful and the mighty with the vulnerable? For Olivia, it was a love born out of common suffering. Neel had nothing more to lose. Banished from the city he loved, brutalised and robbed of dignity, he had hit rock bottom. She found echoes of her own suffering in him.

Olivia's eyes sparkled with joy. She wouldn't give up. Neel would relent. He was a man after all.

Opening her wardrobe, she inspected the dresses hanging there. Brown, white, grey—the colours were dull, their designs conservative. 'It's time to get rid of these old clothes. I will get a new wardrobe in vibrant colours.'

It didn't take long for the colonel to notice the change in his daughter.

'You are looking nice,' he remarked at the breakfast table one morning. She was wearing a yellow linen dress, the colour of buttercups. The dress was a gift from Roma but Olivia had never worn it before, having rejected it as too bright.

'The dress suits you,' commented her father, picking up the newspaper.

'May I order a few dresses? All of mine are so old,' Olivia spoke quickly before her father could protest. 'I was leafing through the new catalogue and a couple caught my attention.'

The request surprised him. Olivia rarely displayed any interest in fashion. He stared thoughtfully at her. 'Of course, you may. Just mark your choices in the catalogue and send it to Farzand Ali's shop. He will have them delivered.'

'I will go there myself and select the fabrics,' she declared. 'While I am at it, I would also like to order a few pairs of shoes.'

'But dear, you don't need shoes,' the colonel protested. 'You hardly go out and I noticed at least four pairs in your room the other day.'

'Well, I think it is time I began going out,' she replied cheerfully. 'I won't spend too much, I promise.'

Her disarming smile took him by surprise. His daughter had changed, he realised.

'Buy whatever you want. Tell Farzand to send me the bill.'

Shaking his head in disbelief, he left for the club. Olivia wondered whether she should have shocked him some more by insisting on accompanying him to the masquerade ball.

But she would not go to the club because nothing had changed. She was still the scarred daughter of a pompous colonel. A gallant officer might take pity on the girl and dance with her but Olivia didn't want pity. She wanted love.

For the first time in many years, she looked at herself dispassionately in the mirror. Her desire to look good was amplified.

It was a pleasant evening and the promenade was dotted with a few young couples. Brightly clad girls chattered animatedly with their beaus. Olivia made a mental note of the latest fashion in hats as the rickshaw wound its way towards the Farzand Ali store. As she passed the Anglican Church, a few surprised looks came her way but she didn't try to pull her hat lower to cover her face. Instead, she met the curious looks with a smile or a nod. Love does strange things to people. It had brought a glow and self-confidence to Olivia.

Neel and Olivia struck a new balance in their relationship. The two of them could now speak without getting into arguments. They could banter without offending one another and speak about political events without bias.

Although Olivia had spent several months on the island, she was not used to its moody weather and constant rain. She had never been fond of the monsoon and, on the island, it seemed as if there were just two seasons—blazing hot or pouring rain. The garden was inundated and the plants flattened to the ground. Unmindful of the rain, Neel laboured in the garden and Olivia continued to watch him from the veranda. Sometimes, when no one was around, he came up to the veranda to have a cup of tea with her. They sat in silence, listening to the rhythm of the raindrops.

One morning, it was raining heavily and Neel rushed to the veranda for cover. Olivia was there already. He had moved back to escape the slanting shower and bumped into her. Standing side by side, they watched the rain.

'It's beautiful,' she murmured, conscious of the closeness of their bodies. If the rains were the only way to bring Neel close, she could come to love the showers.

'Yes, Olivia,' he remarked. 'Some day we will look back and remember these rare magical moments. It makes me believe every cloud has a silver lining. This, perhaps, is our silver lining.'

She stood silently by his side, unwilling to break the spell.

'I want this moment to last forever.' His voice was rough with passion. 'Oh! What bliss it is to live in the present, with no thought of tomorrow.'

'That sounds so poetic. If only this could last forever,' she whispered, leaning towards him.

The rain stopped as suddenly as it had begun and Neel walked away quickly, as if running from the possibility of love.

33

Peter

A Birthday Party

Even as the tempest of the freedom movement tore through the country, a storm was threatening to engulf the island. Disturbing news about the force-feeding of hunger strikers in the Cellular Jail spread through the country. There was indignation amongst the prisoners on Ross Island and they began expressing solidarity in many little ways. They lit candles and prayed for the hunger strikers and sang patriotic songs despite the punishment they received.

It had been a while since the freedom fighters had begun their hunger strike. Ominous dark clouds began to gather over the island and the sea rumbled discontentedly, its waves leaping higher every minute.

The hunger strike had far-flung repercussions and the inmates on Ross Island were not unaffected by the tremors. The wardens became stricter. Peter could no longer roam freely around the island. The frequency of his visits to the Bradley bungalow had also reduced considerably.

That morning, Olivia's father had gone to Port Blair for a meeting. The frequency of his meetings was increasing as the days passed. The prisoners were a determined lot and the British were using all imaginable punishments and methods to break the hunger strike.

Bradley's absence gave Olivia the freedom to talk with Neel and Peter, who had brought her some books from the library. An hour passed in the blink of an eye as they discussed the situation in the Cellular Jail.

'Is it true that the prisoners in the Cellular Jail are continuing their hunger strike?' Olivia asked. She couldn't believe the horror stories narrated by Neel and Peter.

'You don't believe it to be true?' Peter countered.

'I just can't believe a hunger strike can go on for so long.'

'Memsahib, every bit of what you hear is true,' Neel said. He gnashed his teeth in frustration. 'Some more prisoners will die and their bodies will be thrown into the sea.'

'I have heard that the news has travelled to the mainland and there are hundreds of petitions to support the hunger strikers,' Olivia said, her voice down to a conspiratorial whisper.

'Your father has been called to the Cellular Jail to help break the strike,' Neel said bitingly. 'So whom will you support? Your father or the strikers?'

Drawing herself straight, she replied, 'I believe in supporting the righteous.'

'That's very generous of you,' Peter said in a low voice. 'Let us all pray that no more lives are lost.'

'I have been expecting something like this for a long time.' Neel's voice was full of conviction. 'Mark my words. The hunger strike will have consequences for the entire country.'

Silence fell as the three of them pondered the possible outcomes.

'I wish they would end the strike.' Peter finally broke the silence. 'The British won't relent, and the jailors will use the opportunity to torture the prisoners.'

'That is true,' agreed Olivia. 'It will only lead to more deaths.'

'It's late. I must be going.' Peter got up to leave. Discussing the hunger strike depressed him. 'I don't want to be sent to the Cell.'

'Stay for a while,' Olivia held him back. 'Today is my birthday. I want to have a good time today.' Olivia was born in April. She lied in an attempt to get the men to stay longer, alleviating her loneliness.

'At last some good news! Happy birthday, Olivia!' said Peter shaking her hand.

'Happy birthday!' Neel smiled and held her hand. Smiling back, Olivia gazed into his eyes and squeezed his hand.

By god! She's in love with Neel. The realisation disturbed Peter. He feared the worst.

Forcing her eyes away from Neel, Olivia called out for Rosie and asked her to bring three cups of tea along with sandwiches and cake.

Peter was teasing Olivia when Rosie wheeled in the tea trolley with its elegant lace cover and embroidered napkins. Having fulfilled her duty, the ayah turned up her nose and walked back into the house.

It had been ages since Peter had enjoyed a cup of fine tea. He rubbed his hands with glee. 'I have heard that the bakery on the island turns out some of the most scrumptious patties and pastries in the world but this is the first time I will get a chance to taste them.' Peter chuckled as he took a bite. 'It's true! These are heavenly.'

Olivia smiled indulgently as Peter gorged on the food. Neel hesitated. It seemed blasphemy to have even a bit of the cake when the prisoners were on hunger strike in the Cell. But refusing the cake would hurt the poor girl.

'Go ahead! Have a piece,' Olivia beamed at him. 'It isn't poisoned.'

'Come on, Neel!' urged Peter through a mouthful of cake. He knew the thoughts going through his friend's mind. 'You can't be so boorish as to refuse the hospitality of this young lady.'

It was Olivia's disarming smile that made Neel pick up a tiny piece and peck at it.

'Actually, it is not my birthday,' confessed Olivia, sitting back with a satisfied smile. 'All I wanted was to share tea with the two of you, so I lied. Please forgive me.'

Neel couldn't help bursting into laughter at her expression.

'I don't mind you lying as long as you supply tea with it,' Peter said with a laugh.

'Just one minute,' said Olivia as they turned to leave. She rushed inside and returned with a camera. 'I want to take a few photographs so I can remember this day.'

She clicked a picture of the two men and then posed for one with Neel. A dozen photographs were taken, with the three of them taking turns to click.

'I want a copy of the photographs,' Neel requested. 'This may be our last tea together.'

'Please don't say that,' she begged. 'Let's hope for many happy returns.'

'Olivia, please give me a copy too,' entreated Peter before he left for the library. Spending time with Neel never failed to cheer him up. Little did he know that looming on the horizon was something that would alter his reality forever.

34

Olivia

The Storm

It was a rainy day in August 1937, and Olivia's life was about to change. Her father had left for yet another meeting in Port Blair. He would be gone for a couple of days, attending to official matters. After rummaging through old albums and drinking tea with Neel and Peter, Olivia retired to her room for a nap.

A sense of impending doom awoke Olivia. A storm was brewing. The dark clouds executed their dreaded repertoire of lightning and thunder. By late afternoon, a cyclone swept the island. Huge branches fell on the slate roof of the bungalow, breaking it in many places. Large drops of rain pounded the earth, seeking primeval retribution. A serrated bolt of lightning ripped the sky into half. The wind raged through the trees, making them bend and moan. It was as though the gates of hell had opened to swallow the earth into its infinite depths.

The fury of the sea compounded the din around the island, its waters transformed into mountains of angry waves, turbulent and unforgiving. The boats anchored at the port lurched drunkenly. Torn from their moorings, they began drifting into the sea. There was devastation all around. Doors were snatched from their hinges, windows were wrenched from their frames and walls collapsed into rubble.

Rosie rushed into Olivia's room, wailing, 'Madam, the storm! It is approaching the island. I have locked all the doors and windows.' She stood wringing her hands. 'Terrible storm. Sky is black. Sea roaring like giant.'

Olivia knew the woman wanted to return to the safety of her quarters.

'I will be all right, Rosie. You may leave. It is nothing we have not seen before.'

Relieved, the woman rushed out before her mistress could change her mind.

Storms and squalls were frequent on the island. This time, however, there was disquiet in Olivia's heart. The storm lashed mercilessly at the bungalow that trembled under the blitz, its walls and roof threatening to give way. Doors and windows rattled ominously.

A strong wind pinned Olivia to the wall as she approached the veranda to check for damage. Branches that broke off a huge padauk tree were carried by the wind, only to crash on the tiled roof of the bungalow. Upstairs, a window flew off its fastening and a door banged. The roar of the sea grew in intensity by the minute as the waves rode higher and higher, slapping the shores violently. The sky darkened, wrapping the island in a blanket of shadows.

Olivia hurried inside the house and switched on the lights. Just then, a loud explosion came from the direction of the power house and the next moment the island was plunged into darkness.

Fear gripped Olivia's heart. She called out to Rosie and then remembered that both Faisal and the ayah had left. Dotty was howling. The sound set her teeth on edge. The rain was blinding in its fury. Drops as large as pebbles hit the roof, and rain poured on Olivia's bed through the broken tiles.

Broken glass and objects littered the room. A thunderclap laid to rest her plan of reaching the neighbouring bungalow. Crouching in a corner of the room, she clung to Dotty, mumbling long-forgotten prayers.

And then she heard his voice. Neel was calling out to her. He limped into the bungalow, soaked to the skin. Sobbing with relief, Olivia stumbled through the room and flung herself into Neel's arms.

'I am so frightened, Neel.' Olivia clung to him. 'Please don't go away.'

'Hush, I am not leaving you.' Neel held her close to his chest.

She refused to let go of his hand as they groped their way around the house, their bodies warming each other. Neel ran a soothing hand over her damp curls. Outside, the tempest raged unabated. A terrifying clap of thunder shook the house and she clung to his dripping body.

What began as an attempt to comfort the terrified girl suddenly turned into an outlet for buried emotions. Neel's body reacted with unexpected passion. They were suspended on the brink of an abyss. There was just this moment, with no guarantee of the next.

Like marionettes dangling from silk threads, they moved together, their strings intertwined by emotion. Olivia slid her arms around his neck, her body moulding itself to his. The air around them smelled of fear and passion—a heady combination that robbed them of their senses. Carried away by the yielding warmth of her body, Neel bent down and kissed her. Their differences mattered no longer. They were just two individuals drawn together by irresistible force and hunger.

As though compelled by an unseen hand, they fell together on the living room carpet, tearing at each other's sodden clothes. An indescribable ecstasy raced through Olivia as Neel's hands moved over her body. He made love to her first with raw animal passion and then with the utmost gentleness. She had never felt this way before and sensed she never would again. Later, they lay spent amidst the rubble of their lives.

Outside, the storm continued to rage. 'If I were to die in the next minute, it wouldn't matter,' she whispered in the darkness. 'I now know the ultimate bliss.'

'Shh! Don't talk of death. Just enjoy these moments. Who knows what the morning will bring.' Neel reassured her, stroking her hair gently till she fell into a dreamless sleep, a contented half-smile on her face.

The storm finally died at dawn. Rosie and Faisal found Olivia in the morning, lying on the living room carpet amidst the debris, her clothes torn, dishevelled and dirty. If they suspected anything, they said nothing.

35

Indraneel

Trapped

Morning laid bare the effects of the storm. The signs of devastation were everywhere; even the chief commissioner's bungalow had not been spared. Nature did not differentiate between the master and the slaves.

A giant hand had uprooted everything that lay in its path. Trees and branches were strewn all over the island; many roofs had been blown off and glass shards lay all around. Debris littered the island. Several people, mostly prisoners and labourers, lay buried under the debris of their pitiful barracks. The morning also heralded the birds of prey. They circled the skies, waiting impatiently for a feast.

Gripped by remorse for his impulsive act, Neel picked his way through the debris and walked towards his barracks. *It shouldn't have happened*, he rebuked himself. *I shouldn't have lost control over my senses.* He remembered Olivia's warm body clinging to him and her pleas for love. But that didn't justify his actions.

He found debris and ruin everywhere. The prisoners were nowhere to be found; the hovels that housed them had turned into rubble. Forlorn, he continued to walk till he reached the forested fringes of the island. Almost unconsciously, his tired feet led him to the cemetery.

Wind whistled through the trees like the keening of mourners. The disembodied voices of souls that once inhabited the island whispered gloomy prophecies in his ears. Weathered tombstones, their engravings indecipherable, the only witnesses of his presence.

Sitting among the graves, he brooded over his actions. There would be repercussions, he knew. The sun was rising higher, its harsh rays lighting up the etchings on the marble tombstones.

He heard them coming from a distance. Armed with pickaxes and shovels, their feet trudging wearily, the gravediggers soon arrived. Behind them came the mourners bringing their dead for burial.

Neel hid behind a large granite tombstone etched with a warning:

Remember me as you pass by
As you are now, so once was I
As I am now, so you will be
Prepare for death and follow me

There, he stayed hidden through the day, hoping he wouldn't be discovered.

The processions of mourners continued. There weren't many casualties among the British, and the labourers and convicts bore the brunt of the storm. The convicts didn't merit a decent burial or cremation. It would be a shallow pit or a watery grave for them.

Thirst and hunger finally dragged Neel out of his hiding place. Darkness had fallen by the time he slunk out of the cemetery. Keeping out of sight, he made his way back towards Olivia's house. Guilt festered in his soul and he wanted to apologise for his conduct.

The Bradley bungalow was in darkness. The roof had been blown off in some parts; the windows were broken and there was debris all around. Olivia had moved to a safer place, he realised.

Pangs of hunger gnawed at his entrails. He felt weak with thirst. Cautiously, he walked along the service lane used by the sweepers. Shortly, he reached a row of houses meant for junior officers. These houses had weathered the storm far more efficiently. Neel was sure that Olivia had moved to one of these.

Praying that the colonel had not returned to Ross Island, he walked stealthily towards the rear entrance of one of the houses. Peeping through a window, he spotted no familiar faces. Neel continued to look for Olivia in each of the five houses, with no success. As he crept away from the last house, he was grabbed by a pair of brawny arms and pushed against a wall. In the dim light, he saw Faisal's grinning face. The cook tied his hands behind his back and gagged him before locking him in a dark room.

Hours later, Faisal returned with a loaf of bread and a bottle of water. He untied Neel's hands and removed the gag from his mouth. 'Eat,' he commanded. 'Colonel Sahib is back,' he added after a couple of minutes, rubbing his hands gleefully.

Dipping the dry bread in the water, Neel devoured the loaf hungrily. 'What do you want to do with me?' he croaked. 'You can't keep me here for very long.'

'So you think,' replied Faisal. 'Sahib will decide your fate now.'

'Let me go, please. You are an Indian. Don't do this to me.' For the first time in his life, Neel begged for release. He could expect no mercy from the colonel.

The servant threw a disdainful look at the man and turned to pick up the rope. In a flash, Neel hit him with the bottle. The sudden blow stunned Faisal. Recovering almost immediately, he fell upon Neel with a snarl. Picking up a stick, the cook clobbered Neel on the head until he passed out.

Just before dawn, when he came around, Neel found himself on a boat with Faisal and two other men. Horrified, he realised they were sailing towards Port Blair. An hour and a half later, gagged and tied, he was thrust into a solitary cell and the heavy metal door clanked behind him. Once again, he was back in the Cell.

This was Bradley's doing. Neel realised Bradley had learned of his indiscretion and would make him pay for it. This was just the beginning of the bad times.

Soon Neel lost count of days and nights. All he could remember was excruciating pain and humiliation. His fingernails were pulled out, bones were broken, and his body was a mass of lacerations and burns. He teetered on the verge of insanity.

36

Peter

Untraceable

It was difficult to restore the island to its former glory. Almost every structure had been damaged. Rebuilding would take months. Driven by their wardens, the convicts followed a punishing routine. Every spare hand was pressed into service. Along with the others, Peter laboured through the day and returned to the hovel to collapse in exhausted sleep.

The library was low down on the priority list as far as rebuilding was concerned. It had suffered extensive damage. Many of its window panes lay shattered and bookshelves had tipped over, spilling the books all over the floor. Several of the books were ruined and their pages were soaked to a pulp. It would require immense effort and expense to salvage them.

The old librarian was dejected. The work of a lifetime had been quashed in a single night but he wasn't about to give up.

A couple of days later, as they worked together to salvage the books in the library, Mr Jones told Peter about his meeting with the commissioner.

'You know how much I value the library,' said the librarian, making a pile of the books that could be restored. 'I couldn't let its precious collection perish. I know the commissioner is a well-read man, so I sought an appointment with him.'

'The commissioner is a busy man,' said Peter, assisting the old man.

'You bet!' the librarian chuckled. 'He looked up from the stack of papers on his desk and gave me a stern look saying, "I hope what you have to say is urgent, Jones. I am hard-pressed for time."'

Peter could imagine the scene. Mr Jones was a dogged man when it came to the library.

'"Thank you for seeing me, Sir," I said. "I won't take more than a few minutes of your time,"' Mr Jones continued his narration. 'I told him there are some rare books in the library. Any delay could ruin the priceless collection. The commissioner, being an erudite man, agreed it would be a pity to lose those books.'

'So he agreed to allow me to work in the library.' Peter tried to hasten Mr Jones.

'Not so fast, young man. The commissioner had to be assured that I might be able to save a few books with your help. I told him you have been working in the library for some time and you are well versed in the binding and restoration of books. You know what he said?' Mr Jones quizzed Peter. '"Well, what are you waiting for," he said and so here you are!'

'Happy ending to the story.' Peter chuckled.

'I wonder if we can rebuild this library in my lifetime,' he said, surveying the damage with sadness. 'Many of the books are beyond repair.'

'I am sure we can salvage some books. Don't worry, Mr Jones, we will have the library functioning again.' Peter's words sounded hollow.

Years of work had gone into collecting priceless books from various parts of the world. Many of them were now completely destroyed.

Peter was going through a heap of ruined books, sorting out the ones that could be salvaged, when Olivia burst into the library one morning.

'Where is Neel?' she asked.

Her question surprised the Anglo-Indian.

'Hasn't he been to your bungalow?'

'He hasn't come for many days,' she replied.

'Well, he must be busy with the rebuilding work. We have all been labouring over the buildings for the past few weeks. I guess he will return once the work is over.'

'No, I don't think he is on the island.' There was fear in her voice.

'Why do you feel he is not on the island?' Peter asked.

'I sent a couple of servants to look for him. They searched the entire island and asked quite a few prisoners about Neel. No one has seen him, Peter.' Olivia sobbed.

'Don't worry, I will find him,' Peter said, trying to sound confident. 'I will look for him the moment I have some time.'

He was uneasy at the news of Neel's disappearance. Was he buried under a collapsed building? Or had he been swept away by the storm? Would he attempt the impossible? He shuddered to think of the possibilities.

The reconstruction work had progressed at a good pace and most of the buildings were in a serviceable condition. As a gesture of goodwill for their labour, prisoners were given a day to rest.

Taking advantage of the unexpected holiday, Peter spent the day looking for Neel. The hunt for his friend led him nowhere. He met several wardens, prisoners and labourers, but no one knew anything about Neel.

Even Neel's barrack mates could give him no information. Some said he had been sent back to the Cellular Jail, others said he was dead. A couple of them were sure that the chameleon had escaped.

Peter was worried. There was no way to get away from the island. With his mind teeming with foreboding thoughts, Peter dragged his steps towards Olivia's house. What was he to tell her?

On his way to the bungalow, Peter saw Colonel Bradley being driven towards the headquarters. Olivia was sitting in her usual place on the veranda, a ghost of her former self. Her eyes lit up in anticipation on seeing him. 'Did you find him?' she asked.

'He has disappeared. No one knows where he is,' Peter replied dejectedly.

She shook her head in disbelief. 'How can anyone disappear from this island? It is impossible. He must be somewhere.'

'Did you try to find out?'

'How can I go around asking about a prisoner? My father would kill me if he came to know.'

'But . . .'

'I inquired casually about the gardener and mentioned the wilting flowers to my father.'

'What did he say?' If anyone knew about Neel's whereabouts, it had to be Bradley. Peter was sure that the man had a hand in the revolutionary's disappearance.

'He shrugged off my question and said that a new gardener will come around in the next few days.'

'Didn't you ask what happened to the old one?'

'Yes, I did. He gave me a suspicious look and said, "The fool must have tried to escape the island and got drowned in the sea."'

The Anglo-Indian drew a sharp breath.

'I don't think Neel would do something stupid like that. Do you?' Olivia asked pathetically.

'Neel is an intelligent person. He knows escaping from this island is impossible. He didn't want to die'.

Olivia sank into the chair. 'Go away, Peter,' she said in a low voice. 'Go away before my father sees you here. I don't want you to disappear like Neel.'

September brought glad tidings. The viceroy had finally accepted the demands of freedom fighters. The prisoners languishing in the Cellular Jail would soon be repatriated. There was jubilation on the island, and Peter's hopes soared with the news.

Shiploads of prisoners were being sent back to the mainland in batches. He waited impatiently for his turn to leave the island.

'It's just a matter of time,' Mr Jones said, patting his hand, 'and I am not speaking of repatriation this time.' In reply to Peter's questioning look, the librarian said, 'India will soon be rid of its rulers.' His voice was low but the tone was confident.

'By the way, did you meet Olivia?' he asked after a few minutes.

Peter nodded.

'Poor girl,' Mr Jones continued. 'Things are not good at the Bradley residence. According to the grapevine, the colonel suspects Olivia was having an affair with their gardener.'

Peter was stunned. Fearing the worst, he tried to get some more information from the man. 'What happened to the gardener?'

The librarian shook his head sadly. 'No one knows for sure. It is said that the poor chap tried to escape from the island by using an old boat and was drowned in the sea. The sharks must have got him.'

Peter swung between acceptance and disbelief. The chameleon couldn't die. He was like a cat with nine lives. Sitting in his hovel, he grieved over the loss of his dearest friend. Nothing seemed right. Neel was missing and Mr Jones's library was no longer a happy place. Peter had enjoyed the company of Neel and Olivia, as well as old Mr Jones. They had given him hope. He felt lonelier with each passing day.

It was the beginning of October when Peter received the good news. Orders for his repatriation had finally arrived. He was to return home. Whooping and dancing with joy, the Anglo-Indian hugged all the prisoners in his barracks. They were all going home. It was time to celebrate.

37
Olivia

A Punishment

Olivia's nightmare returned to haunt her nights. Frozen with fear, her heart pounding, Olivia tried to scream but a strange paralysis seemed to grip her. She tried to escape but there was nowhere to go. No matter which path she took, it led to a hangman's noose. Gasping, she woke up, drenched with sweat, feeling as though her heart would burst with fear.

Several weeks had passed since the fateful storm but the nightmares would not let her sleep. It always ended with a hangman's noose and a dark hooded figure. She knew it was caused by her anxiety for Indraneel. Her sixth sense told her he was alive. It also told her he was in pain.

Bradley's visits to the Cell had grown in frequency and duration. The visits were invariably followed by bouts of drinking. It made Olivia wonder. *Was he visiting the jail to torture Indraneel?*

As the days passed, Olivia's apprehension that her father had some evidence of her indiscretion grew. Either Faisal or Rosie had stoked the fire of suspicion in her father's mind. They hated Neel and would condemn him. Fear gripped her heart with icy talons.

Olivia was convinced Neel's disappearance was her father's doing. But she refused to believe he was dead.

It was almost the end of October when Peter came to the bungalow. His face shining with excitement, he exclaimed, 'I am going home, Olivia, finally.'

'Congratulations! That's wonderful,' she said dully. 'Neel should have gone back with you.' She smiled ruefully and let out a deep sigh. 'Do you think he's hiding somewhere? Could he be waiting for things to cool down?'

Peter wanted to believe that but the idea seemed too far-fetched to be true. 'It is possible.' He didn't have the heart to sadden her. 'Things will work out. They always do.'

'I am being a wet blanket.' She forced herself to smile. Clasping his hands, she said, 'I am happy for you.'

'I know you are. God willing, we shall meet again in happier times.'

'That is not possible, Peter. Father has decided to send me back to England.'

'Why?' Peter was aghast.

'He has his reasons, I guess,' Olivia shrugged with a look of resignation. Her eyes were brimming with tears as they parted, knowing it was their last time together. 'Will you tell Neel I waited for him?'

All hopes of finding Neel had died when her father called her to his study two days ago. With his back towards her, he stood looking out of the window. His squared shoulders and hands clasped behind his back worried Olivia. Nervously, she waited for the words that would change everything for her.

'You will go to England,' Colonel Bradley announced his decision.

'Please let me remain here with you,' she pleaded. 'You need me here.'

Her pleas fell on deaf ears.

'You have disgraced me by socialising with Indians. Your friendship with the Chatterjee family in Calcutta and your closeness to the gardener have caused me enough trouble already,' he raged. 'You are going to England. Let there be no argument about that.'

Nothing she said could change his mind. Her passage was arranged. Olivia was told to pack her belongings and go to Bombay, from where she would board the ship for London.

A fortnight later, forlorn and unhappy, she stood on the deck, waving at her grim-faced father who had taken the time to see her off. Olivia knew he was there to ensure that she boarded the ship. For a long time, as they sailed away, she stood by the railing, a frail figure. Her eyes continued to scan the faces on the shore till all she could see were the swirling waves around the ship. In romance novels, the hero arrives at the last moment and rescues his beloved but nothing of the sort happened. There was no hero to rescue her as the rising waves drowned all traces of her love.

Her last thought as she left India was that she was carrying a part of Neel with her.

38

Peter

Back in Calcutta

One pleasant day in November 1937, a ship carrying freedom fighters from the Cellular Jail approached Calcutta even as German troops were preparing to march into Austria. Hitler's powers were growing and so were his ambitions. Ominous clouds of an imminent war threatened to disrupt lives across the world, and the British were a worried lot. They were facing antagonism in their colonies while trying to amass men and munitions to take on the Germans.

While journeying with the prisoners from the Cellular Jail, Peter discovered that Neel was locked in the Cell. He had faced brutal torture but was still alive. The prisoners also told him about Colonel Bradley's visits to the jail. Hope welled in Peter's heart. The Anglo-Indian was confident he would meet Neel one day.

The captain's announcement that they were approaching Calcutta was greeted with joyful cries. Eager for a glimpse of the motherland, everyone jostled for space at the railing. Many of the freedom fighters were crying, while some laughed hysterically. It was an immensely emotional moment for the two hundred and fifty prisoners on the ship that had brought them to the very harbour from where they had been despatched to Kala Pani. Tears of happiness flowed down Peter's cheeks.

An enormous crowd had gathered at the port to receive the prisoners. They waved and chanted slogans. The crowd swelled and the chanting grew louder as the ship docked. Peter found himself swept up in the tide of patriotism.

The police had cordoned off the area but the crowd surged forward with garlands. A group of khadi-clad men surrounded the prisoners as soon as they stepped off the gangway. A little girl, riding on her father's shoulders, reached out and garlanded Peter with a string of bright marigold flowers. Overwhelmed by emotion, he began to cry. At twenty-one, he was standing on the soil of Calcutta once again.

While living in Calcutta, Peter had never considered himself a patriot but his experiences on Ross Island had turned him into one. It had taken him a long time to realise on which side of the fence he belonged. Neel would have been delighted to learn about Peter's transformation. The spark of nationalism the Bengali had tried to kindle in the Anglo-Indian was finally ablaze.

No one knew why Peter had been sent to Kala Pani. No one cared to know. For the multitudes, he was one of the freedom fighters and a person deserving of their respect. They heaped garlands around his neck and hugged him.

Then the police took charge. Brandishing their lathis, they pounced on the crowd that had gathered to greet the prisoners. Peter saw a policeman raise his baton to strike the little girl who had garlanded him. Rushing forward, he took the blow on his head.

The police herded the prisoners into the waiting vehicles and they sped towards the Central Jail. They were prisoners once again.

The struggle for independence was at its peak and the jail was overcrowded with freedom fighters. Scores of people filled the jail. They shouted slogans and sang patriotic songs.

'*Andolan karo, jail bharo.*' Revolt, fill the jails. The slogan resounded throughout India. People were in an upbeat mood, confident that the days of the British Raj were numbered. But the rulers were not ready to give in. Not yet.

In the Central Jail of Calcutta, Peter found himself surrounded by curious prisoners who wanted to hear about life in the Andaman Islands and confirm the horror stories about Kala Pani. There were endless discussions about the impending freedom struggle and the prisoners chanted slogans despite the warden's threats.

Five months later, on a muggy April morning, Peter was released from jail with a stern warning to remain on the right side of the law. He was free to do what he wanted as long as he reported to the local police station every Saturday. His jail mates sent him off with warm embraces and good wishes. Some entrusted him with messages for their families. Some gave him letters of recommendation so that he could find a job. He was now a part of their fraternity.

Calcutta was readying itself to celebrate *Poila Boisakh*, the Bengali new year, when Peter stepped out of jail. The sound of music, laughter and merriment brought back many memories. It was nice to be back.

The euphoria of release from prison didn't last too long. Getting in touch with Devyani was foremost on his mind, but the immediate goal was to find food and shelter. The Mitra mansion in Chandernagore was the only place that came to mind.

The mansion wore a haunted look. Weeds and dead leaves covered the once-immaculate gardens. Mildewed walls and jaded wooden balustrades spoke of neglect. The gleaming metal of the gate was now rusted iron. The huge planter's chair on the veranda normally occupied by Mitra Moshai was now vacant. No one came out to greet Peter as he opened the gate and walked towards the house.

A servant answered the doorbell and requested him to take a seat in the hall. Minutes ticked by. The silence was broken by the striking of the hour by a grandfather clock in the corner. The hall, furnished with an expensive carpet with piles of silk cushions, which once echoed with laughter was now silent. Peter ran a finger over the dusty furniture.

The sound of footsteps echoed through the hall. It was Girish, Mitra's youngest son. He was clad in a crumpled kurta and dhoti.

'Namaskar, Girish. Don't you remember me?' Peter stood up and folded his hands in greeting.

'Oh, Peter, it's been a long time.' Girish's voice was dull and tired.

His unenthusiastic greeting dampened Peter's hopes. The family didn't seem to want him. Where would he go? 'Everything seems to have changed here,' he remarked.

'Baba passed away two years ago. Then the police arrested Dada and our business ran into rough weather. Most of our relatives and friends deserted the sinking ship like the rats they are.' There was bitterness in Girish's voice.

'I am sorry,' Peter was at a loss for words. 'Is there any news about Dada? Which prison has he been sent to?'

'He is in the Alipore Jail.'

'As far as I recall, Dada was not a nationalist. Why was he arrested?' Peter asked.

'The police arrested a couple of his friends who were involved in an armed dacoity. That was reason enough for them to arrest Dada. They need little reason to imprison young men anyway.'

'Do you go to meet him?'

He shook his head sadly. 'Dada doesn't want me to be noticed by the police. Besides, this place has to be looked after,' Girish said. 'Enough about us. Where were you all these years?'

'You didn't know?' Peter was surprised. 'I was sentenced to Kala Pani.'

Girish raised his brows. 'And what did you do to earn that distinction?'

'That's a long story.' Peter smiled.

'In that case, you better stay here till you've shared the story,' said Girish and led him up the stairs.

The Mitra family had fallen on bad times but the dinner was good. Girish told Peter that the old cook had refused to leave although most of the servants had gone away. The two men retired to the baithak khana which had once been the venue for lavish banquets and musical soirées.

'I rarely enter this hall now,' Girish confessed in a shaky voice. 'It reminds me of the good days. There was so much laughter and happiness.'

Their conversation meandered from family and common friends to business and national turbulence. Girish was curious to know about the infamous Cellular Jail and Peter was dying to know about Devyani.

Unable to restrain himself, he finally blurted out, 'What happened to your cousin Devyani?'

'How can you possibly remember her!'

'She is unforgettable.'

'Poor girl! Despite Baba's warning, she worked with a revolutionary group. Devyani was instructed to get close to one Major Robert Adams.' Girish paused for breath.

'What happened to her?'

'One night, she went to a hotel with Adams. The chap was drunk and tried to molest Devyani. She removed the pistol from his holster and shot him dead.'

'That's great! She finished the job that I had started,' Peter exclaimed, happy to know that Adams was dead.

'You knew Adams?' Girish shot an astonished look at the Anglo-Indian.

'Let's not waste time talking about the devil,' Peter said, curling his lips with contempt. 'What about Devyani?'

'Devyani shot herself. It was impossible for her to escape, so she took the only way out.'

Peter was aghast. Devyani was dead! The only woman he had ever loved was dead. The thought of seeking her out on his release had given him the courage to survive imprisonment all this while.

The pallor on his face alarmed Girish. 'Peter!' he exclaimed. 'You look unwell. Is it the food?'

Peter shook his head. 'I am fine.' There was no point in staying in Chandernagore any longer. 'I have to go back to Calcutta,' he said in a low voice.

'But . . .' Girish was surprised by the sudden decision. 'Why don't you leave in the morning?'

'Please don't stop me.'

'All right, let me drop you to the station,' Girish insisted.

Peter made his way back to Calcutta, unable to get over the shock of Devyani's death. Damn it! He was just twenty-one. Fate had no business robbing him of every happiness.

Calcutta was fast asleep when Peter reached the city. There was no sleep for him, though. In the dead of night, he tramped down the deserted streets in the company of mongrels, walking past the elegant Park Street, through the narrow Tottee Lane and on to Sudder Street. The dull yellow of the street lights threw ghostly shadows around the filth-strewn lanes, the nauseating stench mingling with the odours of the night. He passed Elgin Hotel and continued to walk all the way to Dhurumtollah. Finally, utterly exhausted, he curled up against the cold shutter of a shop and went to sleep.

Morning brought the realisation that there was no place to go. He had no home and no money. Worse, he had no inclination to hunt for a job. A voluntary organisation nearby was providing food, clothes and shelter to those released from jails. Eyebrows went up as he joined the queue. The young were not expected to live on charity. He had no option but to ignore the dirty looks.

The generosity of the political workers kept him going for a few weeks till the lack of finances brought the charity to a halt.

His experiences and the horrific tales from the Andamans were a powerful deterrent against any involvement with the revolutionaries. He was determined to keep away from the lot. But he needed a job to survive.

Employment was scarce and getting a government job with a prison record was impossible.

It took him a week to find employment. Using the references provided by well-meaning jail mates, he found a job as a clerk in a jute factory. They gave him a room and a salary that was just enough to keep him from starving. In a dingy office in one corner of the factory, Peter spent long hours bent over files and papers. He hated his job. He contemplated resigning but the thought of going hungry kept him glued to his chair.

His tiny room on the fringes of the mill was not much more than a hovel. Surrounded by smoke from the chimneys, filth and detritus, he felt more dejected than ever. The nights were lonely and miserable as he tossed and turned on the creaking bed, slapping away at mosquitoes.

Every evening, the mill workers drowned their frustrations in cheap local hooch and returned home for their nocturnal sessions of wife beating or sexual gratification. The thin walls of his room couldn't block the sounds of sighing or weeping that punctuated the silence. Theirs was an unenviable life with a never-ending cycle of poverty and debt, compounded by respiratory problems that spared few.

Much as he hated the surroundings of misery and squalor, there was no alternative.

It was the longest year in Peter's life, longer than the one he had spent on Ross Island. Time crawled at a snail's pace and his restlessness grew as the days passed. Every morning, he walked into the office in a dark mood; the sight of his rickety chair and desk irked him.

Peter's boredom led him to devour the newspaper. From news about the World War to happenings in India, he followed every piece of news.

Peter noticed recruitment posters everywhere he went. The British wanted young Indians to join the military services. In the cinema halls, documentary films about Hitler's evil forces and the war were shown to attract enlistment. But ultimately, it was the promise of food in hungry bellies that lured the young men.

It had been more than a year since he had returned from the Andaman Islands but Peter's life was stuck in a rut. Unable to reach any decision, he continued to work in a job that he hated, tapping away on an obsolete typewriter during the day and tossing around on a hard bed at night. It was a pathetic life but there was no alternative. Peter continued whining and ranting but he didn't quit his job.

Desperation makes people do unusual things. Some take to religion, others to alcohol. Both are addictive in large measures. Peter chose the lesser evil. That Sunday, he strolled to the nearby church, trying to recall the teachings of the Irish Brothers. Bored, he drowsed through the service.

On his second visit, he sat straight, paying attention to the sermon. On his third visit, Peter joined the others as they sang hymns and his tears flowed freely. Layer by layer, his pain and hurt seemed to peel away as he continued to sing. A healing light seemed to touch the scars that had accumulated over the years.

He started looking forward to Sundays. The church was specifically meant for Anglo-Indians and Indians who had converted to Christianity. After a while, Peter was on nodding terms with a few. The demons of the past were still at work. He shied away from a conversation. How would he explain the things that had happened to him?

A year passed, and then two.

The World War had opened up an unexpected opportunity. The British Army was desperate to enlist men. The army was so short of men that verifying the credentials of applicants was often ignored. The thought of fighting a war for the British was repugnant. They were responsible for the death of the people he had known and loved—first Gurmeet and then Devyani. They were also the ones who had sent Neel and him to the Andaman Islands. He couldn't find it in his heart to forgive the British.

An ardent believer in Bose's philosophy, Peter wondered if he should enlist in the Indian National Army (INA) which had been cobbled together by the charismatic leader. But he was an Anglo-Indian. *Will I ever be fully trusted?*

Apart from death and devastation, war brings misery and scarcity. It also brings insecurity and fear. People around the world reeled under crippling shortages, harsher working conditions and low wages. Another year passed with no reason to celebrate.

One morning in March 1942, Peter was surprised as he read the newspaper. The Japanese had occupied the Andaman and Nicobar Islands. The islanders had exchanged one ruler for another. What he had not anticipated was that the Japanese would become ambitious enough to bomb Bengal. By December, the Japanese made their intentions clear. The bombing started soon after.

Every night, after darkness fell, the sirens began wailing. Peter joined others in trenches dug up on the factory premises and waited till the all-clear siren was sounded. Black curtains, blackouts, sirens—people got used to them all. Everyone lived in the present. The future was uncertain.

One day, as Peter was hunched up in a trench, humidity seeping through his pores, a thought struck his mind like a flash of lightning. Why not join the air force? Like many of the boys at the orphanage, he had dreamt of flying an aircraft. It was more than four years since his repatriation and he was free from the bondage of reporting to the police station every week. Peter was eager to climb out of the hole he had dug for himself.

The very next day, Peter travelled to Ambala, where the Royal Indian Air Force was recruiting young men. Looking around the air force station, Peter realised he had made the right decision. This was where he belonged. This was the life he had yearned to live.

The interviewing officer was sympathetic.

'You are tall and can speak English. Had you completed your matric, you could have become a pilot. Unfortunately, you'll now have to join as an airman but I can send you for technical training.'

'Thank you, Sir, I will be happy to serve the air force in any rank or capacity,' Peter responded with enthusiasm. He was happy to get away from the miserable mill.

In a matter of a few hours, he joined the men who were billeted on the campus. Life in the air force suited him. The rigorous physical training and strict regimen which many young men complained about gave him a rush of adrenaline. Soon, he regained his physical stamina and his face filled out. Winning trophies in sports came naturally to him. Athletic and willing, his tin trunk was soon filled with trophies and cups.

A few months later, Peter was sent for an aircraft maintenance course and his life took a turn. The training exhilarated him. After years of aimless wandering, he had finally found an aim in life. Determined to do his best, he pushed himself hard. Ambala was teeming with airmen and soldiers but he made no friends. The only person he had kept in touch with was Girish. The postcards from Chandernagore lit up his lonely nights.

Girish Mitra's missives never failed to delight the Anglo-Indian. Along with the whiff of good times, they brought tidings, happy and sad. The strict censoring of letters resulted in some of the text being redacted with thick black ink and Peter spent hours trying to decipher the words.

One such postcard brought the news of Indraneel's presence in Chandernagore.

On his return to Calcutta, Neel had been imprisoned on the mainland for a couple of years. He visited Chandernagore the very day of his release. But according to Girish who had resorted to a crude code for his communications, he was a changed man, a shadow of his former self. They had crushed his spirit. His cold eyes had no feeling in them. Neel hated the 'doves' and spoke of going the other way. He also contemplated helping their 'silver-tongued friend in ousting the illegal tenants from our house'.

It took Peter a couple of minutes to decipher the letter. Girish was alluding to the Congress and Gandhi by referring to 'doves', but the words 'silver-tongued friend' baffled him. He couldn't help bursting into laughter when the meaning came to him a few days later. Girish could only have meant Subhas Chandra Bose.

Knowing Neel, it wasn't difficult to guess that he was planning to join the INA.

'I will visit you the moment I can get leave,' Peter wrote back. 'I am very keen to meet Neel and I hope he will successfully oust the unwelcome guests.'

'He is leaving Chandernagore in a few days and sends you his best wishes,' Girish replied.

Peter wished Neel would write him a letter instead of sending a missive through Girish. Perhaps the revolutionary did not like his joining the air force.

'I am sure he will be a dedicated and loyal worker,' Peter wrote in reply to Girish's letter. 'I hope to meet him soon.'

By the time the postcard reached Chandernagore, Neel had left for Calcutta and Girish had no further news of him.

That Sunday evening, Peter pedalled his bicycle towards the European cemetery. There, seated on the grave of one Corporal Arthur William Bailey of the 1st Battalion of the Leicestershire Regiment, he wrote in his diary: *I am not unhappy. It's just the suddenness with which I realised I wanted to be an Indian. For as long as I can remember, I had hated the idea of being an Indian, preferring to count myself as an Englishman.*

The diary was a receptacle of his thoughts and penning them down felt cathartic.

Why did I decide to join the air force? The answer is quite simple. I am convinced that India will soon be free. My aim is to fly aeroplanes. There are several Anglo-Indian pilots who will be my colleagues one day.

Dusk had fallen and the shadows got longer as he rode to Jain Soda Water Shop in Sadar Bazaar to indulge in his favourite ice cream before returning to the barracks. It was while he was spooning the ice cream that a couple of young girls entered the shop. They stared at the brawny, square-jawed Anglo-Indian with grey–green eyes. They whispered in each other's ears and giggled.

It would be nice to have a girlfriend, he mused as he pedalled back to the base. *Life has been lonely for too long.*

The war saw the fledgling air force, with its newly acquired Lysanders, performing with aplomb. Indian pilots made up for their lack of equipment with sheer daring. Just as war separates, it also unites. Comrades who fight together are knitted into an enduring fabric of brotherhood. There was a strong bond between the Indian pilots and the airmen but this couldn't be said about their British colleagues who continued to look down upon them.

Indian officers didn't flinch when it came to expressing resentment against the way they were treated by the British officers. It made little difference, though. The turmoil in Indian politics kept the hatred alive. The stories of discrimination were many as were the unfair policies and practices.

Once again, Peter found himself caught between two sides, trusted by neither the Indians nor the British.

Peter kept away from politics. His mind was set on flying the aircraft parked in the hangars. To do so, he had to pass the matriculation examination. Obsessed with the idea of educating himself, he began spending his free time in the library.

Peter's diligence didn't escape the notice of his seniors. Then, a senior officer gave wings to the Anglo-Indian's dreams. Impressed by the airman's interest in aircraft, he recommended Peter for the Y Cadets course which was a prerequisite for a commission in the air force.

The course earned him a commission and Peter Flynn packed for the Flying Training School at Risalpur. His long-cherished dream of piloting an aircraft became a reality.

39
Indraneel

Joining the INA

War was raging across the world and Neel was at a loose end. After leaving Chandernagore, he wandered around Calcutta, trying to decide his next step. He had lost touch with most comrades and stayed away from the ones who were still around so as not to get them in trouble. He had no money save a meagre amount pressed into his hands by Girish. It was a Sunday morning and traffic was lean. He was sipping tea in a tea shop when he saw a college mate.

'Is that you, Binoy?' He approached the young man.

'Indraneel?' the friend responded. 'I couldn't recognise you for a minute.' He ordered another round of tea for the two of them.

'It's been such a long time,' remarked Neel, taking a seat on the bench. 'You look good. What are you doing these days?'

'I am working at the Writer's Buildings. Where have you been, my friend? You don't look very well.'

'It's a long story,' replied Neel, taking a sip of the hot cardamom-flavoured tea. He had eaten nothing and the tea tasted heavenly. 'It's been an eventful life for me.'

'There were rumours of your deportation. Is it true?' Wariness had crept into Binoy's eyes and he lowered his voice. 'It is not safe to speak of these things here. Let's go to my place.'

Paying for the tea, he led Indraneel towards his house. They walked across the market and into a street lined by shops with residences above. Right at the end of the street was an old double-storeyed building. Binoy lived on the first floor.

'You must stay for lunch,' insisted Neel's friend. 'There is so much to talk about.'

'It would be too much of a bother.' Neel made a token protest. He had to save every penny of the tiny sum until he found employment.

'It's no bother at all. I insist.'

Over an elaborate meal served by Binoy's charming wife, they talked about common friends and recalled the joys of their college days. They also spoke of Neel's harrowing time in the Cellular Jail.

'Do you remember our classmate Talukdar who had an uncle in the Congress?' asked Binoy, extending an ornate brass paan *daan* to Neel.

Stuffing a paan into his mouth, Neel laughed, 'You mean the guy with the pimply face, who never tired of making eyes at the pretty girls in class?'

'The very same fellow. He has joined the Congress.'

'Wasn't he one of those who denounced Congress policies?'

'Well, we were all taken aback by his decision. One would think that he would opt for the Forward Bloc, the party formed by Bose after he resigned from the presidency of the Congress. Those disillusioned by Gandhi's policies are joining the Forward Bloc.'

'Do you know of anyone who has joined that party?' Neel's interest was aroused.

'There are a couple of friends. To be honest, I keep away from them. I will lose my job if my bosses find me taking an interest in politics. With a family to look after, I can't take chances with my job.'

'I understand.' Neel knew how difficult it was to find employment. Associating with a political worker could damage Binoy's reputation forever.

Noting Neel's interest, his friend asked, 'Do you want to join the Forward Bloc? Haven't you suffered enough already? Why don't you try to find a job and settle down?'

'My dear friend, India will never attain freedom if we take up British jobs to avoid hardships.'

The barb hurt. Binoy lowered his eyes and toyed with the paan daan. An awkward silence hung over the room for a few minutes.

'I must go now.' Neel got up. 'My presence in your house could land you in trouble.' His remark was loaded with sarcasm.

'Where will you go? Do you have a place to stay?' asked Binoy, genuinely concerned.

Binoy's wife called out to him and he left the room. There was a hushed conversation before the friend returned. Sheepishly, he continued, 'I would have asked you to stay . . .'

'No, my friend, I will do nothing to put you in trouble. Don't worry, I will manage.' Neel realised Binoy's wife was the cause of the sudden change in his friend's behaviour.

'Wait! I can give you the address of a friend who works for the Forward Bloc. He may be able to help you,' Binoy offered as they walked towards the door. He rushed out of the room and returned with an address on a piece of paper.

'This will be a big help,' Neel smiled and hugged his friend. 'Thank you for the delicious meal. God willing, we shall meet again.'

'Keep safe, my friend.' Binoy's eyes were moist. 'I wish I could help you.'

'You already did.' Neel hugged his friend. Binoy was a simple chap with a deep sense of familial duty. He would not rock the boat.

Late that evening, Neel found his way to the address. The fading letters on the wooden nameplate read Kamalakant Banerjee. He hesitated for a fraction of a second before knocking. He knew that once he walked through that door, there would be no going back.

The door was opened by a diminutive man in his late thirties. His thinning hair was parted on the left. 'Yes?' A pair of shrewd eyes stared questioningly at him.

'Binoy Haldar has given me this address,' Neel replied, his hands clammy behind his back.

The Forward Bloc member appraised the gaunt young man with hollow eyes standing on his doorstep. His sharp eyes ran over the intelligent forehead, prominent cheekbones, high eyebrows and square chin on the emaciated body of the young man. They took in the scruffy shoes and threadbare clothes and the alert eyes behind a pair of wire-framed spectacles. There was a dignity in the squared shoulders but the man's desperation was evident.

Banerjee had knocked about the world for several years. He was a man who had seen life and knew truth from tripe. The man standing before him was a strong and determined person.

'Come inside.' He led Neel to a small study and called for tea. The room was crammed with dusty shelves loaded with books, pamphlets and files, and papers lay scattered everywhere.

'Put those on the floor and take your seat.' Banerjee ordered, taking the only vacant chair in the room. Studying Neel over his steepled fingers, he asked, 'So what can I do for you?'

'I need your help.'

'First, let me hear everything about you. Leave out no details and hide nothing if you want my help.'

The tea arrived and Neel concentrated on devouring the deep-fried snacks that accompanied it, savouring each bite. He polished off the onion fritters and the biscuits on the platter, aware that the next meal may not come for a long time.

Patiently, Banerjee waited for him to finish his tea.

At last, Neel began to narrate his story. Omitting no details, he took Banerjee through the eventful journey of his life. The man was a good listener. He neither interrupted nor asked questions.

'I was released from the Cellular Jail only to be sentenced to imprisonment in the Alipore Jail in Calcutta. I dreamed of being released into a free country but nothing has changed. The British are still here.' Neel shook his head. There was disillusion in his voice.

'Freedom can't be gained in a day or two. It takes consistent effort and many sacrifices.'

'I wonder if I will live to see that day.' Neel's shoulders slumped. 'I have sacrificed everything. I have nothing more to give to the country.'

'I am surprised to hear that,' chided Banerjee. 'This is not the time to give up hope.'

Neel had never been so dejected, not even during his imprisonment in the Cell.

'What do you intend to do now?'

'I have heard a lot about the Forward Bloc. I want to join your organisation.'

Banerjee was aware of the appeal of his party. The Forward Bloc had received unprecedented support right from the day Bose had appealed to the youth to join his party. Bose's appeal had caught the imagination of young Bengalis who were disillusioned with Gandhi's appeasement policy.

'Have you not thought of joining the INA?' he asked.

Neel had seen enough bloodshed. He knew Bose had an agreement with the Japanese but he was not convinced that the Japanese were the right ally. Bose's appeal had drawn hundreds of men and women to the INA, each of them willing to lay down their life for Netaji.

'The INA needs young people who are ready to sacrifice their lives for the country,' Banerjee continued. 'You are a born leader, Indraneel. I can see the fire in your belly. The country needs you. You are an ideal candidate for Netaji's army.'

Silence fell between the two men in the small study as Neel dithered.

'There is a batch of men waiting to travel to Burma. They will be off to join the INA in a couple of days. I can arrange for you to go with them if you enrol,' Banerjee urged.

'Give me some time.'

Neel didn't trust the Japanese. *Didn't they destroy much of the infrastructure of Calcutta by bombing it last December?* He hadn't forgotten the nights of 20–21 December, when bombs had rocked the entire city. Their aim had been to cause as much damage as possible. 'I need some time to decide,' he repeated.

'Fair enough! Let me know once you have decided.'

Banerjee got up and began moving towards the door.

'Can you suggest a place where I can spend the night?' Neel asked. 'I have nowhere to go.'

Banerjee halted and contemplated the young man. 'Have you eaten?' he asked, taking in Neel's famished look. The long walk through the city had exhausted Neel. He nodded, unable to believe he was hungry already.

'Come with me.' Banerjee led the gaunt man through a narrow corridor towards the kitchen at the back of the house and called out to an elderly servant, asking him to give Neel something to eat. 'Take him to the hostel after he has eaten. He will stay with the other boys.'

Twenty minutes later, the servant led Neel to a hostel where he found three volunteers. They had joined the INA and were waiting for Banerjee to arrange their journey to Burma.

The volunteers, barely out of their teens, were brimming with optimism. Neel could detect a bit of himself in them. He had been like them before misfortune had stolen the gloss from his dreams.

'Dada, please tell us about the Cellular Jail and the Andaman Islands,' they begged. 'This is the first time we are meeting someone who was imprisoned there.'

The boys were awed by the story of his experience in the Cellular Jail. It seemed to strengthen their determination to do their bit for the country.

'We will avenge your humiliation,' they promised. 'No sacrifice will go to waste, no suffering will be unpunished. The British will pay for every tear shed by our people.'

Neel was touched. It was impossible not to be euphoric in their company. For the first time in many months, Neel slept peacefully, still undecided about his future course of action.

PART THREE: 1944–47

It was a turbulent time for countries around the world. Hitler was on the back foot with the Allies gaining ground. The Siege of Leningrad, one of the longest and most devastating in history, ended after eight hundred and seventy-two days. Over one million people died, mostly of starvation. Energised by their success, the Russian army advanced into Eastern Europe and defeated the Germans to liberate several countries.

In June 1944, Operation Overlord started with the Allied forces crossing the English Channel to land in Normandy. It signalled the end of Hitler's progress and heralded the end of the war in Europe. Things were changing rapidly across the world.

Closer home, the Japanese forces were planning to cross the Indian border at Imphal. In India, a rising crescendo of voices clamouring for freedom was making the British uneasy.

40

Peter

The Crash

Peter loved flying. His heart soared each time he guided his aeroplane through the cumulus clouds, flying past their silvery edges and kissing their soft underbellies, the throb of the machine keeping time with his heartbeat.

Once he started flying aeroplanes, his ambition soared and he yearned to become an 'ace' pilot. It was an impossible dream, of course. A pilot had to notch up five or more victories in aerial combat to qualify as an ace. That would require him to fly combat aircraft. Peter's dream was to fly the Beaufighters.

Aware that he had the requisites—calm nerves, a sharp brain and daring—to be a fighter pilot, he worked towards his goal. Destiny, however, had other plans for him.

The air force didn't need just combat pilots; it also needed transport aircraft pilots to support the ground troops, Peter's commanding officer had said. His words were of little comfort to the disillusioned man. Noticing his crestfallen look, the commanding officer had continued, 'But that doesn't mean you can never fly a combat aircraft.'

Peter was not surprised when he was transferred to Imphal. Transport aircraft would play a crucial role in the war. The World War was now on India's doorstep. Peter and his colleagues geared up to face the Japanese who were pouring into the country through the dense jungles of Burma. Once they captured Kohima and Imphal, it would be easy for the Japanese to travel through the hills into Assam.

He hummed as he prepared for a sortie that morning. Over the past two days, he had flown over enemy lines to airdrop supplies for Indian soldiers fighting on the Burma border. His mission that day was to airdrop a cargo of urgent relief material to forward troops stranded deep inside enemy territory on the Kohima Ridge. The ridge was a lifeline for British troops. It was under constant attack from the Japanese who wanted to cut off their supply routes.

Flying over the thick jungle and treacherous mountains was a nightmare for Peter. With no proper maintenance, the British aircraft were pushed to their limit and many of them were grounded with snags. The shortage of aircraft meant more flying hours for him.

The previous airdrop of supplies had not hit the dropping zone and much of the cargo containing food and medicines for the wounded was lost in the forests that covered the steep slopes of the ridge. Determined that the troops would have their supplies, Peter took off as soon as the cargo was loaded and the clearance given.

The weather was clear and Peter was confident about carrying out the mission successfully. With a crew of two, a couple of cargo handlers from the supply corps and a load of five tonnes of cargo, the aircraft rose to the sky.

A little over twenty minutes into the flight, Peter realised the aircraft was losing height. The engine had developed severe technical snags and was on an uncontrolled descent. He had two alternatives: crash-land or try to return to the base. The area below was densely forested and mountainous. His only concern was to land on the British-controlled side of the border. Scouting for a suitable place for an emergency landing, he spotted a clearing along a riverbank.

With a horrible crunching sound, the plane came to a bumpy halt after crashing into the trees. The wings severed and the plane swerved drunkenly to the right before flipping on its side. It didn't burst into flames, which was nothing short of a miracle.

For a few minutes, his mind was disoriented. Then, Peter realised the aircraft was badly damaged and they had to get away before it exploded. As he tried to unfasten the seat belt, he realised that he had fractured his left arm. His body was throbbing with pain and he could barely move. Bleeding from multiple lacerations, Peter had also suffered a minor concussion.

Struggling with the right hand, he popped the seat belt and clambered out of the aircraft, his head spinning with the effort.

How much time did he have before the plane burst into flames or the enemy arrived? He stumbled for a few yards before catching his breath and then his knees gave way and he sank to the ground.

He looked around for the others. Horrified, he saw the inert bodies of the two corporals, crushed under the heavy cargo. Where were Sergeant Pilot Sundar Singh and Corporal Ramsay? Were they trapped inside the aircraft?

'Sundar Singh!' Peter called out. A groan reached his ears after repeated calls. There was intense pain in his left arm as he dragged himself towards the surviving crew with great difficulty.

The navigator was lying supine, his leg soaked in blood. He was groaning with pain. 'Sir, I can't get up,' Sundar Singh said, his face contorted into a grimace. 'My leg is wounded.'

'Where is Ramsay? Is he trapped inside the aircraft?' Peter's voice rose in anxiety.

It was several minutes before he located the last member of the crew. Corporal Ramsay was lying not too far from the aircraft, his head bleeding. The airman was unconscious.

Damn! With a broken arm, there was no way he could move either the navigator or the corporal. They had to get away before the enemy troops arrived.

'We have to get away before the Japanese get here.' Peter removed his torn shirt and made a sling to support the arm.

'I won't be able to walk. Leave me here, Sir,' requested the navigator. Pain clouded his eyes. 'Find help, Sir. I will try to distract the Nips.'

'Don't be stupid. I can't abandon the two of you.' With his right hand, he tried to examine Sundar Singh's bleeding leg. The wounded man winced and shut his eyes tightly. 'I think your right leg needs medical attention.'

'Sir, you must leave before the Japs reach this place. Ramsay and I will remain here.'

'Nonsense! Give me a few minutes to think.'

Despite the brave words, Peter knew it was impossible to move the two men. The idea of abandoning the men was appalling. The Japanese soldiers were a brutal lot. They did not carry wounded enemy soldiers.

I have to move Sundar Singh and Ramsay away from the aircraft. The question was how.

'Sundar, can you hobble up to the trees?' Peter handed him a sturdy branch. 'You can use this for support.'

As Sundar Singh attempted to get on his feet, Peter continued, 'We can't let the Japanese get hold of the cargo. The aircraft has to be set on fire.'

'Set it on fire, Sir?' The navigator looked at him anxiously. The blast could blow them to pieces even if they were a hundred yards away.

'I will try to drag Ramsay away,' Peter replied to Sundar Singh's unspoken question.

Wincing with pain, the navigator hoisted himself up to a standing position. Leaning heavily on the stick, he took a faltering step. 'I think I can manage a few steps.'

'Good! Just keep moving towards the clump of trees while I drag Ramsay.' For a moment, he wondered if he had the time to take his pistol from the cockpit.

Peter struggled to pull the comatose man to safety with his functional hand. He was so engrossed in the task that he didn't see the enemy soldiers creeping towards him.

Soon the Japanese surrounded him. Nudging him with bayonets, they shouted at him to put his hands up in the air.

41
Indraneel

Trapped by the Japanese

The INA soldiers marched through the jungle, cutting a path through the tangled vines with their machetes. The last few weeks had been miserable. Plagued by insects and battling the heat and humidity, they had marched through dense jungles towards Imphal, led by pitiless Japanese commanders.

Neel cursed the day he had allowed himself to be persuaded to join the INA. Too late, he realised Banerjee had tricked him into joining the INA instead of the Forward Bloc. Lodging him with the keen recruits had been a clever move.

The cunning man had used psychological means to influence his decision. That morning in Calcutta, Neel had decided he would accompany the young recruits to the Burma border. Whether it was the faith of the recruits or their optimism, he didn't know. Years later, he attempted to analyse but could never be sure. Two days later, the four of them left Calcutta. Singing patriotic songs and mouthing slogans for freedom, Neel's comrades trudged through treacherous jungles and negotiated dangerous terrains. Exhaustion and hunger played their part and, by the third day, the three had stopped singing. The reality was very different from the rosy pictures painted by Banerjee.

All illusions had vanished by the time they reached the Burma border. Neel's companions were rapidly becoming unsure about their decision to join the INA. The short but tough military training took the wind out of them. The Japanese were hard taskmasters.

Within a few days, the truth came to light. Despite Netaji's declarations of taking the help of the Japanese to wage a war against the British, there was little on the ground to prove that the Japanese were not using the INA soldiers to fight their own war. Most of the INA soldiers had been British soldiers till the Japanese defeated the British. The British officers fled and the Japanese took forty-five thousand Indian soldiers as prisoners of war (POWs).

The Japanese respected no convention or law. There were spine-chilling stories of inhuman torture. When offered a choice to join the INA, most POWs opted for it. It was a choice between the devil and the deep blue sea. Those who didn't join the INA were tortured and shot. The Japanese never treated the INA soldiers as equal partners.

Indraneel and his three comrades joined the Japanese on the Indo-Burma border. With them were hundreds of INA soldiers. Once the basic training was over, Neel marched towards Kohima. He was now a part of the Subhas Brigade fighting under a Japanese general. Operation U-Go, an ambitious plan to wrest northeastern India out of British control, was in motion.

Neel now knew it had been a mistake to join the INA. He had faith in Netaji but he didn't think that joining the Japanese to fight the British was the right decision. There were many in the INA who felt the same way. By the time they started marching towards the Indian border, Neel realised the Japanese were unlikely to leave India.

We will just exchange one master for another, a more brutal one at that. Neel decided to escape at the first available opportunity.

That morning, his section of six INA and nine Japanese soldiers went on a reconnaissance mission into the thick jungles of Kohima. Their task was to find the best route to attack the British camps. The mountainous region made their progress slow and laborious. They had trudged a few miles through the jungle when one of the Japanese soldiers pointed animatedly towards the sky. Looking up, they spotted a British aircraft plummeting towards the ground.

They shouted in excitement.

'Halt!' ordered the Japanese corporal.

The radio operator got busy with the wireless. Neel, along with a couple of Indian soldiers, sat down to catch his breath. The corporal started shouting obscenities in Japanese and ordered them to march towards the crashed aircraft.

'Bloody Japanese,' muttered one of the Indian soldiers under his breath. 'They never rest.'

Driven by *seishin*, or willpower, the Japanese soldiers had an inhuman capacity to march long distances at great speed through the hostile landscape, with minimal logistic support. They could also carry double the load of a normal soldier.

The Japanese expected their Indian counterparts to have the same level of endurance but the undernourished INA soldiers could not match up to them.

'Let's get moving before they kick us,' Neel said, pushing a fellow soldier forward.

It was a long and arduous trudge as they marched through the jungle to reach the crash site.

'The bastard thinks he has an inbuilt radar that will lead us to the aircraft,' Neel muttered as they followed the Japanese corporal.

After a few false starts, the corporal decided to march along the river bed. It was almost afternoon by the time they found the aircraft. Both its wings wrenched away, it lay on its side. Ready to shoot the survivors, the Japanese advanced cautiously ahead.

As they walked around the aircraft, Neel saw the pilot. He was trying to drag the inert airman. A makeshift sling supported his left arm and sweat ran down his blackened face. The Japanese moved stealthily towards the pilot and prodded him with their bayonets. 'Move!' they ordered.

The Japanese corporal strutted over to the inert airman lying on the ground and poked him with the bayonet.

'Leave him alone!' shouted the pilot.

In response, the Japanese corporal stuck his bayonet into the airman's ribs. A single shudder and then it was all over for the poor man. A few Japanese fanned out and started searching the area for the rest of the crew. They returned with an injured airman.

Some of the Japanese soldiers gathered around the prisoners, threatening and mocking them, while a couple of INA and Japanese soldiers climbed into the aircraft to search for useful items and survivors. Inside the aircraft, they discovered two more bodies and the cargo.

The Japanese ripped the packages open and discovered tinned food, cigarettes and drinks, medicines, ammunition and other supplies. Rushing out, they reported the discovery to the corporal who relayed the exciting news to the commander. Instructions came from the headquarters swiftly. The cargo had to be carried back to the headquarters. One section of soldiers was to remain at the crash site until reinforcements reached them.

Hauling the cargo from the mangled interior of the aircraft was a tough job. They had to open the cargo inside the cramped space of the aircraft before carrying it out. There was also the danger of the aircraft exploding. Sweat pouring down their back, harried and hurried by the Japanese, the Indian soldiers toiled. Some soldiers were put on the job of opening up the cargo and breaking it up into smaller packages that could be carried easily.

Darkness fell sooner than expected. The meagre light from the candles was insufficient for the task. They had brought out about two-thirds of the cargo but a third still remained in the aircraft. The corporal decided to continue the task in the morning.

A small area was cleared and the Japanese began opening the food tins. Excited at the sight of ham, cheese, sausages, tinned meat and fish, they fell upon the food with enthusiasm. Alcohol flowed freely and a feast began.

Grudgingly, they handed over a few tins to the INA soldiers, instructing them to guard the prisoners. The corporal brushed aside Neel's request to give food to the prisoners. He laughed and made a rude gesture.

'They are prisoners of war,' insisted Neel. 'We must feed them.'

The corporal looked balefully at the adamant Bengali. Then he agreed to give them some cheese and bread.

'They need medical attention,' Neel pressed.

'No medicine.' The Jap's voice hardened. 'You make too much trouble already. Go!' he shouted.

Neel knew pressing further could make the corporal change his mind about the food. Resolving to deal with the matter discreetly, he walked over to the supplies which were being guarded by a few soldiers. 'The corporal has ordered food to be given to the prisoners,' he told a Japanese soldier.

The corporal and other Japanese soldiers were enjoying a feast a little distance away. For a few seconds, the Japanese guard was undecided. Should he confirm with the corporal? He looked at the corporal who was enjoying a swig of brandy straight from the bottle. Then he hesitated. Everyone knew that the *gochō* had a violent temper and he was just a *nitōhei*, a lowly private. The worst of the duties came to him. He was stuck with guarding the supplies while the others were feasting. He licked his lips and shrugged.

Emboldened, Neel made his way towards the pile of food tins. Once there, he grabbed as many as possible and tossed them into the dark area beyond the dim light of the candles. The tins landed on the soft soil under the trees. Then, he picked up a first-aid box and other essentials and lobbed those too. He shoved some medicines into his pockets and picked up a loaf of bread, slices of cheese and a jam tin.

Unsure of the gochō's instructions, the Japanese guard abused Neel for tarrying. The Bengali threw him a mock salute and walked away with his bounty.

The night was perfect for his plan. The thick foliage and darkness, the inebriated Japanese and the isolated spot were ideal for his escape plan. He had planned for many weeks. The cache of food, medicines and other essentials would come in handy.

The first thing he did was to make an elaborate show of going into the jungle to relieve himself. In a loud voice, he complained about an upset stomach and disappeared into the thickets. It took him a few minutes to locate the tins and supplies he had tossed. Swiftly, he packed them in a folded bag hidden in his jacket and placed it near the bushes. Then, gathering the bread and cheese, he walked over to the prisoners.

'I have brought you some food.' Neel stopped near the pilot and whispered. 'Eat quickly before the Japanese change their minds.'

The pilot raised his grimy, blood-stained face and Neel gasped.

42

Peter

The Daring Escape

'Peter,' Neel hissed in his ears. 'It's me, Neel.'

'Neel?' Peter's swollen eyes stared back at him. Was he hallucinating? Squinting in the dim light, he looked at the man. The face, with a beard and moustache, was somewhat familiar. Running into the chameleon was the last thing Peter had expected.

'Don't speak. Just listen. But first, drink the water,' Neel held a canteen of water to his friend's mouth. 'Not too fast,' he warned as Peter gulped down the water.

Next, he held a slice of bread and cheese to Peter's mouth. 'Do you want to get away?' Neel whispered.

His mouth full of bread, Peter shook his head.

'I am planning to escape tonight. You can accompany me. It will be dangerous and we might die but that's a chance we have to take. We have just one opportunity and a very fleeting one at that.'

'I can't leave Sundar Singh here to die,' Peter objected.

'You have to make that choice. The corporal has been instructed to interrogate you before killing both of you tomorrow.'

Neel pushed the canteen of water near Peter's mouth. 'I will come as soon as the guards are lax. In the meantime, move your legs and arms to improve blood circulation and warm up the muscles.'

He loosened the rope binding Peter's hands. 'I have untied the rope but don't let anyone know your hands are free.'

Peter noticed a Japanese soldier walking towards them. He was gesturing for Neel to leave the area. Handing over the bread and water to an Indian soldier who was also on guard, Neel instructed him to feed the prisoners.

'Why bother?' countered the soldier. 'The poor sods are going to be shot in the morning. The Japanese don't march with POWs. Not with wounded ones.'

'We are not Japanese. Let's try to ease their suffering until they die.'

A tiny sliver of moon struggled with the clouds, casting more shadows than light. It was the perfect night to get away.

Patiently, Neel and Peter waited for the inebriated soldiers to fall asleep. The long march and the excitement of discovering the cargo had taken their toll. The feasting did the rest. Most of them were drowsing. Disturbed by the constant drone of mosquitoes and other insects, the corporal and a couple of Japanese soldiers had clambered into the aircraft to sleep. As soon as the corporal left, the other soldiers relaxed. This was the opportunity they had been waiting for. Neel marched up to the INA soldier guarding the prisoners and offered to take up the duty.

'You look exhausted,' he told the fellow soldier. 'Why don't you snatch a nap while the Japanese are sleeping? I have eaten, so I can relieve you for a couple of hours.'

The grateful soldier cast one look at the drowsing Japanese guard and whispered, 'Thank you, bhai. I will take over from you after two hours.'

Neel had taken his military training seriously. He knew the essentials required for a trek. In his bag were chocolates, tinned food, a torch, a first-aid kit and some ammunition. He ensured the kit was not heavy enough to hinder their escape. Patiently, he waited for the right opportunity.

A little after midnight, the INA soldier guarding the prisoners whispered, 'Will you hold the fort for a few minutes while I find something to eat?'

'Don't worry, I am here,' Neel assured the soldier. He laughed and pointed at the prisoners. 'Do you think they are fit enough to escape?'

'In that case, I will grab a tiny nap,' the hefty Pathan said with a wink. 'Just whistle if you see the Japanese.'

As per the plan, Peter called out to Neel as soon as the soldier left. 'Guard, I want to go behind the bushes,' he said.

Neel escorted him towards the bushes where the bag was hidden. The moment they were behind the bushes, he picked up the bag and pulled Peter towards the beaten track he had marked on the map. They walked without a word for about a hundred metres and then Neel whispered, 'Let's run as fast as we can. We have just a few minutes before someone spots our absence.'

It was a matter of life and death.

Steeling himself, Peter began running. Neel had given him a couple of painkillers and a swig of brandy before starting. The intense pain in his arm had reduced to a throb and the brandy had made him light-headed. The tough air force training came to his aid and he began sprinting.

They raced through dense foliage, the carpet of dead and dry leaves crunching under their feet. Hacking away at the vines and the undergrowth, they willed themselves to keep moving. The darkness was disorienting. They stumbled through the narrow path overlaid with knotted roots and shrubs.

Since they were moving downhill, they covered a substantial distance in an hour. Then, out of breath, Peter halted, leaning against a tree. His arm was throbbing and he felt thirsty. 'I need to rest,' he said, panting heavily. Sweat dripped down his back.

'Take a sip,' Neel extended a canteen of cool water. 'I studied the map and marked our route on it. There is a rivulet close to this area. Let's head in that direction.'

Peter was reluctant to move. 'Can't we rest here for a while?' he asked. 'My arm is getting worse by the minute.'

Neel warned him of the dangers of halting. They had to cover as much ground as they could before dawn. The Japanese would not pursue them in the darkness. Not with the stockpile of food and ammunition to guard. He knew the Japanese were sticklers for discipline. The first thing the corporal was likely to do on learning of their escape was to inform the headquarters, which would alert the other sections and platoons in the area. It was a vast jungle and it would take time for them to work out the direction in which the two had escaped.

'Let's make it to the rivulet. It's not too far. Come, let's go.' Neel helped Peter get up. 'You are in much better form than you think.'

From the kit bag, he extracted a bar of chocolate and, breaking it in half, he gave one piece to the pilot. Neel was being stingy. His kit bag held several tins of sardines, peas, pears, biscuits and jam but the food had to last for a while. 'Here, that will give you energy,' he said with a grin. 'Come on, Peter, we have survived the Andamans. We can do this!'

'True! This is nothing compared to the Andamans.' Peter grinned back at Neel and started running.

In half an hour they reached the rivulet. Energised by the cool, gurgling water, they filled up the canteen and took deep swigs. After washing their faces, they took off their boots and dipped their feet in the stream.

'Just ten minutes,' warned Neel. 'We can't linger longer. It is easy to lose track of time when one is exhausted.' Soaking his shirt in the water, he used it to sponge himself.

He spread his shirt on a boulder and rested against it, while Peter removed his jacket and lay flat on his back, the rolled-up jacket functioning as a pillow.

'Are you sure we are on the right path?' Peter sat up and looked at Neel. He had followed the Bengali this far without knowing where they were heading.

'Yes, we are. I have been planning this for long,' Neel replied. 'There wasn't a day when I didn't think of escaping.' Taking out a well-worn map from the bag, he held the torch with his mouth and focused the beam of light on the route. The map showed the northeastern parts of India and some parts of Burma. The map was labelled in Japanese but the topography was clear. 'Can you see this body of water?' Neel pointed at the stream flowing before them. 'It is this rivulet.'

'We are a good hundred miles north of Imphal,' said Peter, studying the map. Having flown several times over the Imphal region, Peter was familiar with its topography.

'The Kohima–Imphal Road is about twenty miles from here.' Neel ran his finger down the map. 'If we can hit the road, we may find some vehicle . . .'

'And run into either the Japanese or the Brits,' Peter finished the sentence for him. 'This is the war zone, Neel. It is crawling with soldiers. If it is the Japanese, we are both in danger and if it is the Brits, you are at risk. Either way, we are doomed.'

'I have a plan.' Neel's eyes shone in the dark. 'If we come across British soldiers, you will act as my captor and if it is the Japanese, I will tell them you are my prisoner.'

'It won't work.'

'Let's hope it won't come to that. Our best bet is to reach that road. Once there, we can decide how we will travel.'

'Where do we go from there?' Peter swatted blindly at a droning insect.

'You will go back to your squadron in Imphal and I will sneak away. My destination is Calcutta.'

'Calcutta is a long way from here, my friend.'

'Not as far away as the Andamans.' Neel laughed bitterly. 'It's going to be the journey of a lifetime.'

The two of them gazed at the sliver of moon that appeared occasionally through the canopy of trees above them. 'I thought you joined the INA to fight the Brits,' Peter remarked. 'So why do you want to escape?'

'It's true that I joined the INA to fight the British but I didn't sign up to becoming a slave to the Japanese bastards. Netaji allied with them for a common cause but his calculations seem to have gone awry somewhere down the line.'

'You were a die-hard follower of Subhas Bose, weren't you?' There was scorn in Peter's voice.

'I am still a follower of Netaji but wise men can also make mistakes.'

'You mean it was a mistake to ally with the Japanese?'

'Netaji is looking at the alliance from a different perspective. The Japanese generals must have painted a picture where the yellow and brown skins fight together to defeat the white bastards. I am a foot soldier, the lowest denomination in the set-up. The situation at the ground level, as seen by the INA soldiers, differs from what the higher-ups see. There is intense hatred and discrimination at our level. We get the worst of rations, clothes and ammunition. The food is insufficient and inedible, medicines unobtainable and the treatment is insufferable.'

Neel stopped and lit a matchstick. He touched the burning matchstick to a leech that was clinging to his leg. 'I am horrified by some of the things I have seen in the last few months. The Japanese have no intention of leaving the country once they defeat the British. We will just exchange one ruler for another. That's all.'

'How can you be so sure?' Peter slapped at the mosquitoes buzzing around them.

'I have learned a lot and the learning didn't happen overnight. Whether it is the British or the Japanese, I have seen them at their worst. They didn't come all the way to do us a favour. India is a part of their Asian strategy. They are here to stay. Many of the INA soldiers have already deserted. More will desert by the time the Japanese attack Imphal.' Neel's dejected voice conveyed his disillusionment more effectively than his words.

He got up briskly and picked up the bag. 'We should be going. We have to walk many miles to reach the road to Imphal.'

Reluctantly, Peter got to his feet and they began walking along the rivulet.

'You are one lucky bastard,' said Neel, slapping the Anglo-Indian's back. 'Had your aircraft landed on the eastern side of Kohima, we could never have escaped. The jungles on that side are teeming with the Japanese.'

'Well, I have been lucky throughout my life. Whether it was in the Andamans or now. When the aircraft was losing height, I turned west and headed towards Indian territory. Anyway, the crash was a blessing. Else the two of us would not have met.'

For a while, they walked in silence.

'What will you do in Calcutta?' Peter asked after some time.

'I don't know, my friend. For the first time in my life, I do not know which way to go. A disillusioned man is a dangerous man.'

'Just don't join another radical group. The country will soon be free. Don't stick your neck out and get it chopped off before that day arrives.'

Neel halted in his tracks and turned to face his friend. 'How can you be so sure?'

'Every British officer knows that the days of the Raj will soon be over. No one will openly admit the truth, though. It's just a matter of time. Be patient till then.'

'Sometimes I wonder if I will live to see that day.' Neel began walking again.

They had been walking for several hours when the sky brightened. The Japanese had taken away Peter's watch while tying his hands, so there was no means of knowing the time.

'Let's rest for a while,' Neel suggested as they neared the spot where the river looped in another direction. It had acted as their compass till then.

Neel took out a loaf of bread and a tin of jam. They ate in silence and lay down for a while. *The jungle appears so different in the daytime*, Peter thought. At night, a deathly silence had gripped the forest. But now, it was alive with sounds. There were birds and squirrels and an occasional deer darting across their path.

Saving their breath for the trek, they continued to walk. At noon, they took another break. Resting against tree trunks, they devoured the remaining bread, finishing the meal with tinned sardines and a bar of chocolate. Peter wished the bag had some cigarettes.

'Why don't you come with me to the air force base?' he asked the Bengali, who was studying the map. The journey to Calcutta was a long and dangerous one and he was concerned about Neel.

Neel's head jerked up in surprise and he began laughing. 'Are you aiming for a Victoria Cross?'

'I can tell them you have deserted the INA and want to join the Brits.'

'Don't be naïve, Peter. The British will hang me.'

'In that case, hide somewhere near the base. I will bring you food and supplies.'

'Then they will hang you.'

'Do you ever regret the path your life has taken?' Peter asked. Neel was an educated man. He could have landed a good job with the British.

'Yes, I have. I have regretted it three times, actually. The first time was when my family was wiped out, the second was when I lost the only woman I ever loved and the third was when I travelled to Rangoon to join the INA.'

Neel in love! 'Who was the lucky woman?' Peter wanted to know.

'That's a long story. I will tell you some other time.' Neel's voice was gruff with emotion. He would not reveal the name of the woman he loved. The two of them had shared the same ideals and dreams. They had dreamt of a future in independent India and put their self-interest on the back burner as they fought for freedom. It had been a brief but torrid romance. Both of them had been acutely aware of the tragic fate of their love, yet their feelings for each other couldn't be denied. She was dead and he had escaped death by a whisker. Her name would remain buried in his heart forever. 'Let's walk towards the road,' he said shortly.

Dusk brought the welcome sight of the road, along with fears of detection. They were still a long way from Imphal. How would they make the journey?

They halted on the edge of the jungle and rested for a while, trying to decide on the next step. After a quick bite, Neel removed a few things and discarded the bag. He tied a torch, the map, some chocolate bars and medicine into his shirt. Naked to the waist, he looked like a local. The scruffy shoes and unkempt hair and beard added to the look.

'There won't be many vehicles on this road after dark. Let's hope we can get a ride,' said Neel.

They dragged their tired feet down the road. After what seemed like hours, a bullock cart trundled up. The cart driver, a young man, shouted out a greeting to them in an alien language.

'Where are you going, Bhai?' Neel asked in Assamese but the chap didn't understand. He gave them a broad smile and told them his name. 'Yaangba.'

'Can you give us a ride in your cart?' Neel tried in Bengali.

His question brought a bigger grin and the man nodded. 'Where do you want to go?'

'We have to go to Imphal. How far are you going?'

'Imphal is very far from here. I am going up to Kangpokpi.'

Kangpokpi, they learned, was about eight miles from where they were standing. Grateful for small mercies, the two of them climbed into the cart loaded with vegetables and poultry. Yaangba was taking his farm's produce for the weekly haat to Kangpokpi.

43
Indraneel

Time to Part

Neel noticed large dumps of ammunition and ration, and ordnance stores in army camps on both sides of the road. The British were stockpiling for the war.

'The war is here,' remarked Yaangba, noticing Neel's interest. 'The Japanese are coming and everyone is fleeing towards Imphal.'

'Do they support the British or the Japanese?'

'Most people don't support either of them. No one wants war. There has been a deluge of Burmese refugees lately. They come with horrendous tales of barbarism. There is no food, no medicine, no supplies.' Yaangba stole a look at Peter and whispered, 'He is a British officer, isn't he?' There was bitterness in his voice.

Clearly, the locals hated the English and the Japs.

'He is a Royal Air Force pilot. He was imprisoned by the Japanese.'

That silenced the young man for a while.

'Bhai, you are a Bengali but you don't look like a soldier or a pilot. Why are you with him?' Yaangba probed. Leaning towards Neel, he whispered, 'Are you a deserter?'

The conversation was taking a dangerous turn. If he admitted to being a deserter, the man could take him to the nearest army camp and ask for a reward. These were dangerous times. Trust came at a high price. Neel hesitated.

'Have no fear in telling me the truth. We have helped many deserters,' the Manipuri whispered conspiratorially.

The reassurance didn't help. Neel didn't trust him. Not yet. 'No, Bhai, I am not a soldier. Just a refugee trying to make my way to Imphal,' he said.

The young man shrugged. 'The gora can find a more comfortable means of transport at any of the army camps lining the road,' he suggested.

'Peter!' Neel shook the Anglo-Indian who had nodded off. 'Yaangba will drop you near an army dump from where you can find transport to Imphal.'

'Come with me,' Peter appealed. He took Neel's hands in his own. 'I promise to get you to Imphal. I will tell them you are my batman, or a servant.'

'No, Peter. I do not want to put our lives in danger. We will drop you at the army camp. This young man will drop me at the next village and I will find my way from there. Didn't you hear what he said? There are hundreds of refugees walking towards Imphal.'

It was an emotional moment for both. Destiny had brought them together three times and each time Neel had saved Peter's life. They travelled in silence up to the army camp by the side of the road and Peter climbed out of the cart. Neel got down and hugged his friend.

It was dark. The only light came from the army camp.

'The hour of departure has arrived, and we go our separate ways, I to die, and you to live. Which is better God only knows,' Neel quoted Socrates. 'You will be rewarded for your efforts and I for mine. What those rewards will be is not for us to surmise.'

His words wrenched Peter's heart. 'Come with me,' he said one last time.

'God willing, we will meet again,' replied Neel, his eyes misting over. He climbed into the cart and they trundled away.

'You are not a refugee,' declared Yaangba. He had witnessed the emotional parting. 'You are his friend.'

'Yes, Yaangba, we are friends because we travelled a long way together. We are from different backgrounds, beliefs and calling but we are friends.'

'I will spend the night at Kangpokpi and return home after selling my goods. Most of us sleep under our carts. It is not very comfortable but you can join me,' offered the young man. He knew Neel was neither a refugee nor a soldier. He had seen enough of them to know the difference. 'I will try to find some transport to take you a part of the way.'

'That is very kind of you.'

At Kangpokpi, after sharing the food Yaangba had brought from home, they walked to the small hooch shop where a few young men had gathered. The Manipuri knew everyone. He introduced Neel as a refugee from Burma and asked if anyone was likely to travel towards Imphal. No one was going that far but they found a cart going halfway there.

That night, lying under the cart, the bullocks tethered at a distance, Neel thought about the turn his life had taken. It had run along unplanned tracks for too long. It was time to direct it towards a goal.

'At one point I had thought of joining the INA to fight the British.' Yaangba broke the silence. Propping his head on an elbow, he continued, 'Many young Manipuri boys and girls joined the INA but I couldn't because my father died soon after. He had made me promise to look after my mother and sisters.'

Shocked, Neel sat up, banging his head against the undercarriage of the cart. 'You are an INA sympathiser?' he asked.

'That is what I have been trying to tell you. I couldn't join as a soldier but I have been supporting the deserters. I am sure you are an INA soldier but your friendship with a British pilot has confused me.'

'It's a long story, Yaangba. Peter was a friend much before he joined the air force. We have spent time together in the Andamans.'

'You were in the Cellular Jail?' Yaangba's eyes widened in surprise and his respect for the unkempt and bearded man went up several notches. 'You are a hero!'

'I am no hero, Yaangba. I am merely a victim of circumstances.'

'There is no question of your taking a ride with anyone else. Tomorrow, after selling my produce at the bazaar, I will take you as close to Imphal as possible.'

'No, Yaangba, you must return home. You have been of great help.'

Nothing Neel said could alter the young man's decision. 'You are a hero. I can't let you travel with anyone else.' With those words, he crawled out, leaving Neel flummoxed. Yaangba returned after a few minutes, carrying a plate of steamed fish and rice. 'Eat,' he commanded.

The next afternoon, the vegetables and poultry sold, they embarked on their journey. Imphal was more than twenty-five miles away.

'I have decided that I will take you up to Motbung, where I have a cousin. He has a bicycle which you can ride up to Imphal. Can you do that?' Yaangba looked anxiously at Neel. 'Imphal is about fifteen miles from Motbung.'

'I can ride that distance, don't worry.'

The Manipuri relaxed. 'I will give you an address in Imphal. You can drop the bicycle there.'

It was late evening by the time they reached Motbung. Yaangba's cousin turned out to be a rabid British hater. A year ago, he had suffered a shrapnel injury while protesting against the high-handedness of the British soldiers.

'Those bastards threw people out of their homes and turned them into battlefields. They set the local people's stocks of rice on fire so that the Japanese could not lay their hands on them.' Agitated, the cousin limped around the room.

When he heard of Neel's imprisonment in the Cellular Jail, he was more than happy to offer his bicycle. Together, Yaangba and his cousin cleaned and oiled the bicycle and checked its tyres before declaring it ready for the trip.

The next morning, they handed him a packet of food and he set off for the journey. 'Keep off the main road,' Yaangba cautioned.

The Imphal contact's address was safe in his pocket and his spirits high as Neel pedalled down a dirt road towards the town. 'The gods must be keeping a watch on me,' he said as he smiled to himself. 'Meeting Yaangba was a stroke of luck.'

PART FOUR: 1947 AND BEYOND

While people around the world were attempting to emerge from the ashes of the World War, India was witnessing violence and bloodshed. The Muslim League, under the leadership of Mohammad Ali Jinnah, was determined to carve out a chunk of the country for Indian Muslims. Nothing less than a partition would satisfy them. The national fabric was getting ruptured slowly and surely.

Realising that their days were numbered, the British hastened their departure. A Boundary Commission, led by British lawyer Cyril Radcliffe, laid out the redrawn borders of the two new countries. The commission divided Bengal and Punjab, and India was torn into two.

The following years were a hectic time as people savoured their independence and worked tirelessly to create the country of their dreams.

44
Peter

The war had ended but India was aflame. Freedom was within reach at long last. It was the midnight of 14 August 1947 and everyone sat around the radio in the air force mess, listening to Nehru's speech: 'Long years ago we made a tryst with destiny, and now the time comes when we shall redeem our pledge, not wholly or in full measure, but substantially. At the stroke of the midnight hour, when the world sleeps, India will awake to life and freedom.'

Peter joined the Indian officers as they celebrated the moment they had been waiting for. It had been a long struggle. Tears of joy ran down their cheeks as they whooped and danced and hugged and congratulated each other. There was a burst of fireworks and an officer brought out a bottle of rum he had been saving for the special occasion. Everyone toasted to a new dawn in the country's history.

With Independence came the Partition and the splitting of the air force. Men, machines, territories—everything was split into two. Once the bubbles of celebration had settled, Peter found himself attending an advanced course in flying.

Peter loved his job. He volunteered to fly where others hesitated, beyond hours considered possible. Flying on frosty nights over misted land when visibility was poor, he flew without a care in the world. By the time the word 'Royal' had been dropped from the Royal Indian Air Force, Peter had achieved remarkable recognition for his feats. Life had never been better. He had achieved his dream of becoming a fighter pilot. All he needed was a companion to share his life.

He was a great believer in destiny and knew that the right girl would cross his path at the right time. One Sunday, during the service in church, his eyes fell on a young girl seated across the aisle.

Her profile, with its upturned nose and brown curls, presented an enchanting picture. Throughout the service, he did not hear a word of what the pastor said, fascinated as he was by the girl. Intuitively, she turned and looked at him. Peter smiled and bowed his head in her direction. A blush spread across the girl's face.

She was there the next Sunday and the next. It took her a month to return Peter's smile and his heart skipped a beat. After the service, he walked up to the girl's parents and introduced himself. Charmed by the young man's manners, the girl's mother issued an invitation to tea and that was the beginning of Peter's romance with Grace Clarke. Six months later, on a beautiful spring morning in 1950, the two got married in the very church where they had met. It was an idyllic union. Grace was someone who looked at life as a gift from god, accepting life's highs and lows with enviable optimism.

Peter nursed no bitter memories of his past. He often spoke of his days on Ross Island, recalling the tiny nuggets of joy in the otherwise hopeless situation. Grace was aware of his fondness for Neel, whom she had met twice on their visits to Calcutta.

Peter told Grace all about Devyani and his fascination with her. 'I loved her but she didn't want me,' he confessed, sparing no detail of his pursuit of the widow.

The fireworks he expected didn't occur. Instead, Peter's confession drew the couple closer to each other. His choppy past left no mark on him, for he had reached calm shores.

Peter's postings saw them moving from one place to the other, making new friends and building new homes. They lived like gypsies but that didn't dampen their zest for life. The days on Ross Island had changed his outlook on life. 'I look forward to life. Each day is a blessing and must be lived as the last day of one's life, for who knows if there will be a tomorrow,' he told his wife.

Their nest was soon filled with three children. Peter's happiness knew no bounds.

45

Indraneel

1972

Twilight is that magical hour of the day when everything is swathed in an ethereal glow. Indraneel lay in an armchair, watching the colours of dusk set the sky ablaze. Dusk turned into darkness, yet he continued to sit on the veranda of the state guest room, lost in memories. He was back in Imphal, a place that had played a crucial role in his life. Manipur had just been granted statehood and he was there to attend the celebrations.

Twenty-eight years ago, he had trudged from Burma, a tired and skeletal man, the thought of escaping the clutches of the Japanese army paramount on his mind. It had been the most daring and dangerous mission of his life. Indraneel shuddered as he recalled those days.

After parting from Yaangba, he had pedalled to Imphal. Once there, things got difficult. He had dropped the bicycle at the address provided by the helpful Meitei man and exchanged his dirty clothes for a Burmese *longyi* and *leh gadone*. Dressed in those, he merged into a sea of exhausted and starving refugees trudging endlessly to unknown destinations. They climbed mountains, waded through streams on blistered feet, hunted, stole and begged for food. Their numbers diminished as they went along—death, disease and hunger taking their toll. There were no tears left to shed for the dead, nor resources to bury them. Like automatons, the ragtag group of survivors continued their journey.

Indraneel survived. Travelling sometimes with refugees, sometimes alone, occasionally finding a ride, he continued his journey. It took him two weeks to reach Silchar. Once there, he could not resist the temptation to visit his hometown. Monsoon had set in when he reached Brahmanbaria. It was just as he remembered. Many things had changed; people he once knew were dead or gone . . .. yet so many things remained the same. The Titas River was in spate, its waves just as furious and unrelenting as they had always been. His school was still the same. Its playground echoed with the joyous shouts of children.

Indraneel wandered around, asking for his friends and the Bose family that lived across from the pond. He was told that the Bose family had left a long time ago. Bats and owls inhabited the house, now a crumbling structure. The pond at the back was just the way he remembered it, its stone steps uneven and collapsing, the water cool and mossy green. He rambled through the house, touching its mouldy walls, looking through the sooty kitchen, remembering the happy days of the past. He looked at the bright sky through the gaping hole in the roof. There, in one corner, was the grinding stone where his mother used to grind turmeric, ginger and chillies.

Slumped on the dirty floor, he cried. Loud, wracking sobs shook his body. So much lost, so little gained. What had he achieved? Where had his rebellion taken him? India was still where it had been. The British hadn't left. He tossed around sleeplessly through the night, coming to terms with the truth. The next morning, he left the village.

By the time he arrived in Calcutta, Indraneel had made up his mind. He would no longer be hungry or poor. He would not be imprisoned. Never again, he vowed. While in the Cellular Jail, he had heard of the Communist Consolidation, a party founded by thirty-nine inmates in the jail. Neel joined it.

The journey from the grassroots to the upper echelons took him twelve long years. Like a skilled chess player, he strategised to reach his goal. One of his strategies was to marry Latika, the widowed daughter of the top leader of the party. The act brought him a hero's halo and a speedy rise in the party hierarchy. It was a marriage of convenience.

Neel was a generous and easy-going husband. Not one to harbour unrealistic expectations from his marriage, he adopted the role of an ideal husband. But he didn't love his wife the way he had loved Devyani. He had loved her madly and passionately. But Devyani had died a long time ago. Bonded by a common ideology, the two of them had spent many nights together. Neither Neel nor she wanted to marry before India was a free country. They had loved each other intensely and unconditionally. Then Peter had barged into their lives. He pursued Devyani and vowed to love her forever. Nothing she said could deter the young fellow.

Neel was devastated when he learned of her death. He never fell in love again. His love for Devyani remained a secret, to be shared with no one. Not even Peter.

The hectic events that swept the newly independent country into a frenzy had taken most of his time in the following years. Neel's unerring plans vaulted him to a ministerial berth in the late 1960s, and his dream finally came true.

In the meantime, he had fathered two sons and bought vast tracts of land. He was a successful and satisfied man. Gone was the firebrand of yesteryear. The chameleon had turned into a suave and scheming politician. Sometimes he looked back on his life and wondered about the transformation. It was difficult to pinpoint the exact moment that had altered his outlook on life. Did it happen when he was yoked like an animal to the grinding mill in the Cell? Or was it when they put him in crossbar fetters and neck-ring shackles for a whole week? Perhaps it happened when he was trussed up on a frame and flogged. Indraneel was never sure. All he knew was that he vowed to live a comfortable life. He wanted no more pain, humiliation and frustration.

The past, however, could not be forgotten. Often, he woke up sweating in the night's stillness. He hadn't forgotten the Cell or the constant hunger that gnawed at their bellies. The cruel Japanese and their insults, Neel had forgotten nothing. The scars on his body and mind did not allow him to forget anything.

He often wondered about the turn his life would have taken had he not been a revolutionary or joined the INA. What if he had married his love and lived a secure life? What if he had never met Peter? Whatever happened to Olivia? Perhaps she had married a nice Englishman. Perhaps she had a brood of children. He hoped she was happy and secure wherever she was.

46

Peter

A Newspaper Advertisement

The modest cottage Peter bought in Whitefield after retirement turned into his haven.

Life was perfect, till one Sunday morning, sitting in the garden with a cup of coffee, Peter came across an advertisement in the newspaper. Grace was busy in the kitchen, humming as she baked a cake.

A tiny advertisement on page five caught his attention. Putting his cup down, Peter adjusted his glasses and read it once more. The photograph in the advertisement was faded but the people in it were unmistakable.

His breath quickened at the sight of the black-and-white picture of Olivia and Neel. It was the one they had taken in Colonel Bradley's bungalow on the day they had celebrated her birthday, only to learn that she had made it up.

There was another picture of Neel with a few lines below it, announcing a handsome reward for any information on Indraneel Bose.

'I'll be damned!' he swore, reading the advertisement again. A ghost from the past had reappeared.

'Grace!' he called out, hurrying towards the kitchen, newspaper in hand. 'Come and see this.'

The urgency in his voice brought her out of the kitchen.

Spreading the newspaper on the dining table, Peter pointed a shaky finger at it. 'Read this.' His voice trembled with emotion.

'Let me get my glasses,' she said, laying a reassuring hand on his shoulder. A couple of minutes later, the couple was bending over the newspaper, reading the words that had the potential to shake up their lives. Dazed, he sank into a chair.

'You must speak to the advertiser.' His wife's words seemed to come from a distance. She handed him the phone.

'Yes, yes, of course,' he mumbled.

Fingers hesitating over the phone, Peter looked at Grace for help. She nodded encouragingly and read out the number in the advertisement.

'Hello!' It was a woman's voice.

'Dr Daphne Bradley?' Peter's voice quivered with emotion.

'That's right,' came the response.

The phone threatened to slip from his sweating hand. Switching on the speaker, he transferred it to the other hand. 'Speak to her,' Grace prodded.

Clearing his throat, he continued, 'This is in connection with the advertisement in the newspaper.'

'I hope you are not wasting my time.' The voice was cool and authoritative. 'Do you have some information?'

'Are you Olivia Bradley's daughter?' Peter asked, darting a quick look at Grace.

'Yes.' Her voice was cool and distant.

'My name is Peter. I was on Ross Island.'

'Peter?' They heard a sharp intake of breath on the other end.

'Peter Flynn. Your mother knows me.' He spoke quickly, afraid she would disconnect the call.

Her voice, shaky and disbelieving, floated down the line. 'Peter?' She paused for a fraction of a second, and then the words tumbled out in a torrent. 'Is it really you? Where are you? Can we meet?'

The next day, Peter and Grace were on their way to Delhi. His mind rolled back over the years as he strapped himself to the seat on the aircraft. Memories flitted in an endless procession through his mind as he stared out of the window. Images of a wan and scarred face with a tentative smile filled his brain. Grace squeezed his icy hand.

Peter paced the hotel lobby impatiently, waiting for Daphne. It had barely been three minutes since the receptionist had informed the girl of their arrival. In those three minutes, he had looked at his watch a dozen times.

'Patience, Peter!' Grace got up and led him to the couch. 'Why don't you sit down and relax?' She saw him consulting his watch again. 'She will be here any moment.'

'She should have been here by now.' He ran an anxious hand over his thinning hair.

And then they saw a tall, slender girl with auburn hair emerging from the elevator. Her eyes swept the hall and she walked towards them with quick and eager steps.

'She's beautiful,' Grace whispered.

Her elfin face, with its freckled, upturned nose, was a replica of her mother's, but the full lips and the dark, dancing eyes reminded Peter of someone else. They reflected the intensity and joy of someone he knew well. They were Indraneel's eyes.

'Oh my God!' he muttered under his breath.

'Peter Flynn?' she stretched out her hand and smiled.

'That's me.' He shook her hand, overwhelmed by a sense of déjà vu.

'Peter! Such a pleasure to meet you!' She looked searchingly at him. 'You look just the way Mom described you. I could have recognised you anywhere.'

'You look so much like your mother.' He couldn't get over the shock of meeting Olivia's daughter.

'Let's sit somewhere. It's going to be a long conversation.' She led them to the restaurant and ordered coffee.

Peter could not stop staring at the girl. He couldn't believe Olivia's daughter was sitting before him.

'Your coffee is getting cold,' Grace said, nudging him. Turning to Daphne, she said, 'Peter is very excited to meet you.'

'So am I,' replied Daphne, smiling at the bemused man sitting across the table.

'How is Olivia?' Peter wanted to know.

A shadow passed over Daphne's face. 'She died a couple of years ago.'

Something snapped in Peter's heart. Olivia was dead. 'I am sorry.' He put down the cup with a clatter and placed his shaking hands on his knees. 'Tell me everything.'

'Where do I begin?' Her eyes distant, Daphne toyed with a spoon.

'Start from the stormy night on Ross Island.'

'Well, there is not so much to tell. Soon after the storm, my grandfather was posted to Poona and my mother was sent back to England. My grandfather was killed in an accident a couple of months later. There were all kinds of rumours. Some said his car had been sabotaged. We later learned that he had tried to swerve the car to save a dog and lost control. He was drunk. My mother didn't want him to know about her pregnancy, so he never found out about me. I grew up without knowing him. Mother had a weak heart. She kept that a secret too.'

'But she must have been very young.'

'I guess she died of heartbreak rather than a heart attack.'

'Olivia had a very unhappy life.'

'Mother often spoke about you and Indraneel. She considered the two of you as her best friends. The only other friend was a woman named Roma Chatterjee, but that was a long time ago and they lost touch.'

'Your mother was a very shy person. It took a lot to draw her out. Perhaps it was the isolation of Ross Island that brought her close to us.' Peter knew Olivia had been in love with Neel but he had always suspected that it was one-sided. He was reluctant to share the truth with the daughter.

'Have you tried to get in touch with Neel?' he asked.

'I don't know how to get in touch with him. He is my father. Did you know that?' Daphne's eyes studied him.

'I . . .' he hesitated. 'Well, I was not aware of that till I saw you. You have his eyes. Does Neel know about you?' Peter wondered why, when and how Neel had fathered the girl. *Neel had made no bones about his disinterest in Olivia, so why had he slept with her? Had Colonel Bradley stumbled upon the truth? Was that the reason for Neel's disappearance from Ross Island?*

'I don't think he does. Mother had no way of contacting either of you. She did not tell me the truth either. I was told that my father passed away during the war. I think my mother had a premonition of her death because she began talking about her past a couple of months before she died.'

'Don't misjudge your mother. I have not known a more compassionate person. Were it not for the food she gave us, neither Neel nor I would have survived.'

'Who am I to judge her? She went through hell and I salute her for her fortitude. I never held the truth against her.' Daphne sighed. Looking around for a waiter, she asked for another round of coffee. 'Did you know she maintained a diary? I found it after her death and read it. She had a miserable life.'

'I am not surprised.' Peter recollected running into Olivia while she was writing her diary. 'She had no one to share her thoughts with, so she poured them into her diary.'

'I have come all the way to India with a purpose. First, I want you to introduce me to my father. Then, I will make a trip to Benares.' Daphne came to the point.

Peter raised his eyebrows in surprise. 'Why Benares?' he asked.

'My mother wanted her ashes to be immersed in the Ganges. She told me so.'

'Weren't you surprised by her wish?' asked Grace, who had been silent all this while.

'Frankly, I am not surprised. Mother was enchanted with the idea of rebirth and *moksha*. She was a very well-read woman who took a keen interest in India and its culture.'

'I will take you to Calcutta. That's the easier part but meeting Neel could prove challenging. He is a politician and a busy man.'

'I will wait,' she said calmly. 'You are his friend, Peter. It shouldn't be difficult for you to get an appointment with him.'

It was not the meeting with Neel that worried Peter. It was breaking the news of his daughter that would be difficult.

'You are worried, aren't you, Peter?' asked Daphne. 'You are wondering about Indraneel's reaction. He doesn't even know I exist. Let me put your mind at rest. I am curious about the man but I have no wish to impose myself on him. Nor do I intend to stay in India.'

'To be fair, Indraneel doesn't know of your existence. I don't know how he will handle the sudden arrival of a daughter. It will come as a shock to him. You shouldn't forget that he is a public figure and . . .'

'And his career could suffer if people learned that he has a daughter with a British woman. And that it happened during his imprisonment in the Andaman Islands.' Daphne completed his sentence. 'I understand everything, Peter. Believe me, I have no wish to upset his life.'

'Let's cross the bridge when we come to it.' As usual, it was Grace who put his mind at ease.

It was late morning when they reached Calcutta. Peter called his friend after they had checked into their rooms.

'Hello, Anglo boy! How are you?' Neel spoke warmly. 'It's been a long time.'

Six years had passed since the two had last met.

'You are a busy man.' Although Peter had made quite a few visits in the past, there was a barrier between the two of them. It was not the same any more. Over the years, he had noticed the gradual change in his friend's attitude. Neel was no longer the man he had known. Somewhere, at some point, the two of them had exchanged their mantles. Neel had become an opportunist while Peter had become a patriot. Their last visit had ended on an acrimonious note, with the two arguing about unscrupulous political leaders.

'You insult me, Peter. I am never too busy for you, my friend. Where are you?' Neel asked.

'We are in Calcutta.'

'What are you waiting for? Walk right into my office.'

'I have something important to tell you.'

'And I am keen to hear that important something. From the sound of your voice, I assume it to be a serious matter.'

'It is, Neel.'

'Ah! You remain the same old mysterious man, keeping your cards close to your chest.'

'There is a mystery, indeed. Will you see me at eleven tomorrow?'

Neel responded with amusement at his formal tone. 'Since when did you request an appointment?' he asked. 'Just walk into my office or the house any time. Be my guest.'

'Neel,' Peter hesitated. 'I will come with Grace.'

'Why the hesitation, Peter? Grace is family. I'll be annoyed if you don't bring her.'

'I will bring another guest. She has travelled a long distance to meet you.'

'You don't have to ask for permission, Peter. Where are you staying?'

'We have checked into a hotel in south Calcutta.'

'Why are you staying in a hotel? Have I offended you in any way?' Neel asked. During his earlier visits to Calcutta, Peter had always stayed in his house.

'Of course not,' Peter hastened to reassure him. 'Grace and I have many happy memories of our stay with you. My guest might not be comfortable staying there.'

'Well, then let's meet tomorrow and we will decide. Latika will be offended to know you prefer staying in a hotel.'

'We will meet her tomorrow,' Peter promised.

'I am sure Latika will bully you into staying with us.'

The next morning, they were picked up by Neel's secretary and taken to the politician's plush bungalow in an affluent neighbourhood. Latika rushed out as soon as they stepped out of the car and embraced them. 'It has taken so many years for you to remember me,' she complained. 'In fact, I have been pestering Neel to take me to Bangalore.'

'All you have to do is book two tickets and drag him to Bangalore. If he is too busy, come alone,' said Grace. 'He will come running behind you.'

'Neel is a workaholic. He has no time for me,' complained his wife. Turning to Peter, she said, 'I hope you will stay with us for a while.'

'I wish we could,' he replied.

'What do you mean? I won't listen to your excuses.'

'Next time, Latika, I promise.' He patted her hand.

'Life is too short for next times,' she retorted. 'And you should know it better than anyone.'

'You are forgetting something,' Grace reminded her husband. She pulled Daphne forward and introduced her to Latika. 'This is Daphne. This is her first visit to India, so we are taking her around.'

'Hello, Daphne.' Latika shook Daphne's hand. 'I am sorry. I was too excited to see Peter and Grace. You are welcome to stay with us.'

'Daphne has come here all the way from London to meet Neel.'

'He will be delighted, I am sure.'

'Is he closeted with his cohorts in the office?' Peter joked.

'Not today. Neel has cancelled all appointments in your honour but the phone has been ringing all morning. Last seen, our man was speaking on the phone. I will send for him.'

'Your husband is an important man, my dear,' said Peter. 'Daphne and I will wait for him in the study.'

Latika instructed a servant to lead them to the study. 'Come to the dining room after you finish scolding him,' she said with a laugh. 'In the meantime, Grace and I will gossip about you.'

Daphne chewed her lip and cracked her knuckles. The confident young woman was now an anxious one.

'It will be all right.' Peter squeezed her arm comfortingly. 'He's a nice person.'

'I am sure he is.' She smiled wanly. 'I am just curious about my father. His reactions won't bother me.'

Peter knew it was a lie.

Minutes later, Neel strode into the room, confident and smiling. The man had an impressive personality. The lens on his glasses had thickened and the lines on his forehead had deepened, but his smile remained unsullied by the vagaries of time. His eyes sparkled with joy at the sight of his old friend.

He came forward and hugged Peter. 'It's nice to see you, Anglo boy,' he remarked.

Holding him at an arm's distance, Neel studied his friend. 'You look good. What kept you away so long?'

Peter grinned sheepishly. 'Other than the hint of prosperity around your midriff, you look the same,' he responded.

On a closer look, Peter could spot the subtle changes in his friend. The shock of hair was more grey than black. There was a perceptible droop in his shoulders and the limp earned at the Cell was more pronounced.

'And who is the pretty lady with you?' Neel turned towards Daphne.

The moment he laid eyes on her, Neel paled as if he had seen a ghost.

Neel stared at Daphne, nonplussed. His frown deepened as he studied the girl and Peter could see the wheels turning, the fragments of memory struggling to break free from where Neel had buried them. And then it seemed to strike him with the intensity of a sledgehammer. His eyes lit up in recognition and a beatific smile transformed his face.

Silence hung heavy like a blanket while father and daughter stood frozen, battling their overwhelming emotions.

Acknowledgements

This book would not have been possible without the help of several people, some of whom are no longer alive. The information about the past that they uncovered through their conversations and experiences was priceless. It would be unfair of me not to emphasise the substantial contribution of those who were kind enough to open their libraries and share their books for my research. I am thankful to the friends in Port Blair who enabled my visits to the Andaman Islands and made sure my stay was pleasant.

Several people were involved in the realisation of this book. They cleared away the barriers and pushed me to develop the initial idea. From providing inspiration, suggestions, nuggets of information and resources, they did everything to keep me going.

I owe a debt of gratitude to my parents, Bharati Choudhury and Manindra Choudhury, for instilling a love of literature in me. They taught me the importance of hard work and humility, while also giving me the freedom to dream.

I will forever be grateful to my family and friends for giving me their support during my spells of self-doubt. Thanks to Ajoy, my steadfast cheerleader and partner for life, for providing lucidity to my thoughts. A big round of thanks to Anupriya and Ankita for their faith and support. I am grateful to my sisters, Jayashree, Sharbari and Sujata, for being with me through thick and thin.

I thank Prerna Vohra and Mekhala Moorthy, the editors who transformed the manuscript into an enthralling book. I am thankful to Mugdha Sadhwani for the excellent cover design. A big round of thanks to the entire marketing team of Bloomsbury for taking the book to the readers.

About the Author

Born in New Delhi, Tanushree Podder worked in the corporate sector for eight long years before she quit the rat race to write.

A well-known novelist, Tanushree is passionate about travelling and writing. Climate change and the environment are of special interest to her. She enjoys writing in various genres. This has led to her writing in the historical, military, crime and paranormal genres for adults and children.

She has written many fiction and non-fiction books including *Nur Jahan's Daughter, Boots Belts Berets, On the Double, Escape from Harem, Solo in Singapore, A Closetful of Skeletons, Before You Breathe, No Margin for Error, Decoding the Feronia Files, The Teenage Diary of Rani Laxmibai, The Girls in Green, An Invitation to Die, Spooky Stories, More Spooky Stories* and *Ambapali.*

Thorns in the Crown is her eighteenth book.

Three of her books—*Boots Belts Berets, A Closetful of Skeletons* and *The Girls in Green*—are being adapted into web series.